CONNECTING
THE DOTS

Also by Dick Puckett

The Twelfth Angel

Yellow Ribbons

CONNECTING THE DOTS

DICK
PUCKETT

Lulu Press

This book is a work of fiction. Names, characters, and incident are the product of the author's imagination or are used fictitiously.

CONNNNECTING THE DOTS

2nd Edition

CONNECTING
THE DOTS

DICK PUCKETT

Chapter 1

JOHN SMART

NORTHERN VIRGINIA 1978

At seven o'clock John Smart's alarm went off and triggered a routine that had developed over the years that he had been working first as salesman and later as Head of New Car Sales at Langley Mercedes. He shut off the alarm, rose, showered and shaved, put on one of the five dark-blue, pin-striped suits that were neatly hung in his closet, and went downstairs to join his wife and daughter for breakfast. Normally breakfast was a time to discuss family matters, but this morning he was unusually quiet as he hurriedly finished his bowl of cereal topped by bananas and strawberries. Saying that he had a meeting scheduled with a customer who was almost a sure buyer of a top-of-the-line Mercedes in half an hour, he asked his wife if she could drop their daughter off at school. He kissed his wife good-bye, hugged his daughter, climbed into his sleek black Mercedes and drove a short distance to the dealership.

As soon as he entered the dealership, his receptionist handed him a steaming cup of coffee. With a warm "Thanks," he walked to the far corner of the show room and entered a large glass enclosure that served as the Office of Manager, New Car Sales. This was his space and it reflected his success – numerous company awards on the wall next to photographs of him standing in the middle of a group Washington Redskin football players who were satisfied clients. A copy of a Washington Post article announcing him as D.C.-area salesman of the year was placed as the center of attention. John Smart's life was well-organized and ran as smoothly as the Mercedes that he sold. He was good at selling cars and he was making a lot of money.

John Smart sat down at his desk and waited. After about ten minutes a short, heavy-set man wearing an ill-fitting black suit with a poorly-tied, red necktie entered the show room. Smart knew that it was time to be patient. He sat down at his desk, picked up the half-filled cup of coffee, and waited for the receptionist to page him. Not wanting to show his interest in the man, Smart turned to the wall and stared at the numerous plaques that had been presented to him over the years of working for the Cooper family, both father and son. The younger man was Allan Cooper and he owned a string of Mercedes dealerships. John Smart had applied for a job at the dealership in 1965, about the same time that the CIA Headquarters Building at nearby Langley was being expanded.

John Smart watched as the short man walked to the receptionist, a petite young woman named Margie. Margie represented the first line of screening at the dealership, meaning that she was tasked to size up the customer as he or she walked in the door. John Smart had instructed her on how to assess whether the arrivers were real customers or people who wanted to get their jollies off by test-driving a Mercedes. Margie had her own assessment to make: were they rich eligible bachelors. Assessment number two, was much more important to her than assessment number one. She quickly recognized that this rather seedy looking character who spoke with an accent was not marriage material. He also failed assessment number one. He did not look like Mercedes material. Marge had instructions to send such characters directly to Mr. Smart. Mr. Smart knew how to handle the joy riders.

John Smart did not have to make an assessment. He knew why the man was there and he knew that his own life was about to change. Finally, the page came over the intercom, "Mr. Smart," Marge said, "There is a gentleman here to look at our wonderful new sedan. Shall I send him in?"

"Yes, please do."

John rose to meet the customer at his door. "My name is John Smart. How may I help you?" They entered the office and John closed the door.

"Igor, how the hell are you? Are you back here in D.C.?"

"Yes, Ivan. It was either here or Kabul. I really had to pull some strings to get assigned here in America."

"No *gavno*, you almost got assigned to Kabul. That's an awful place.

Boy, are you lucky."

"Tell me about it! So anyway, we saw your signal that you wanted a meeting. What can I do for you, my friend?"

"Well, I've got an idea about how we can finally penetrate CIA's buildings."

Igor interjected, "I hope that it is a good one, my friend. I shouldn't be telling you this, but you are about to be recalled back to Moscow. When you go back, the best you can hope for is reassignment to Kabul. The worst, well, you know what they do downstairs in Lubyanka."

"Are things really that bad?"

"*Da*, my friend."

"Well, help me here. I've got and idea. And I think that it is a good one. This tunnel," he said, pointing to the Washington Post newspaper article, "Why can't we build our own tunnel under the CIA?"

Chapter 2

THE CIA TUNNEL

LANGEEY 1966

Only a few people at KGB Headquarters in Moscow knew that John Smart's real name was Ivan Oomney, and that he had been sent to the U.S. as a deep undercover agent. In Soviet parlance, Smart was an illegal. That meant that the KGB had sent him in without diplomatic cover. His job was to find a way to penetrate the new CIA addition as it was being built. If he was caught, he was in deep *gavno*.

John spent most of his time living his overt cover which was enhanced by his using skills of manipulation and practicing the art of closing a deal that he learned in KGB's training courses, John was a very successful car salesman

Unfortunately, the best of plans of moles and men often go astray. Smart organized several ill-fated attempts to penetrate the CIA construction site. KGB technicians provided him with a variety of electronic devices. Some were clever. Microphones, transmitters, and batteries were placed inside steel rebar, which was sent by ship to Baltimore where it was slipped into supplies destined for the construction site at Langley. These devices were very sophisticated. Properly placed, they could pick up people's pulses (clues that an operation is being planned), conversations, and even whispered comments (where the good often was revealed.) The plan was to use these listening devices to intercept conversations about great world events. The rebar, which cost KGB over 60 million rubles, was inserted into the construction site too late to be used in the actual building structure and ended up reinforcing the concrete in the West Parking Lot. The KGB found itself listening to the squealing of tires and slamming of car doors.

The listeners did focus on one pattern of activity that took over a two-month period in the farthest most reaches of the parking lot. Every Tuesday and Thursday, at 2 o'clock in the afternoon, 1400 hours military time, they heard a couple climb in the back of a van and indulge in extremely complicated sex.

The listeners were able to pick up a first name; Joseph, became Joey, then my Italian Stallion, then just simply "Oh, Baby, Oh Baby, O Babyyyyyy." Back at Lubyanka, KGB Headquarters in Moscow, Russian analysts poured over the audiotapes, gleaning every bit of intelligence out of these intercepts. The final report indicated several factors: The male was Caucasian, first name Joseph, LNU (meaning "last name unknown"), of Italian descent, probably well endowed. The female was of an unknown race, but apparently a credit to that race whatever it was. This judgment was based on content analysis of the squeals and moans that were picked up. Cause of termination of the relationship was revealed when she said, quoted verbatim in English text in the report, "Look Joseph, it's over. My husband is on to us. I can't see you any more." Based on the heart rates, and inflections in his voice, Joseph LNU, seemed relieved. The Russian medical team supporting the analysis of the tapes reported that Joey seemed physically exhausted by the experience and was glad to for the chance to get out of the passionate relationship.

In John Smart's mind, other attempts at installing listing devices which were imposed by Moscow were foolish. In fact, one that involved planting dummy shrubs containing TV cameras and transmitters was just plain stupid. Surely someone would notice that the shrubs didn't grow and didn't need trimming. The KGB used its sister service – some say the retarded sister service – the GRU to infiltrate Langley Gardens, the company that had landscaping services for the CIA compound. The shrubs were planted with some to the left side of the building's main entrance and some surrounding the Nathan Hale memorial near the right side. The effort looked promising until Langley Garden's landscape designer arrived for a final inspection.

When he saw the shrubs, he squealed, "Oh, no, no, no, darling. That just doesn't do. I wanted flowering plants, you know: red, white and blue. Take them out! Take them out! Take them out!"

The shrubs now grace the front yard of a ½ acre lot occupied by a fine doublewide trailer. The trailer owner, whose name was Charlie Dribble, worked for Langley Gardens for minimum wage and augmented his income by grabbing up plants as they were discarded. He kept some of them and sold the rest at a handsome profit.

Pointing to some rare orchids, Charlie would tell his beer-drinking friends, "These plants came from a rich bitch who decided that she wants pink flowers instead of blue ones to influence the sex of her unborn baby. Just last year she paid us $1,200 to put the blue ones in. Last week she gave us $1,500 to replace them with the pink ones."

Pointing to the KGB shrubs he said, "Now these shrubs never seem to need no watering or pruning."

His friends are amazed, "No bull, never?"

So the shrubs were removed, the building went up and the Soviets didn't get in under the ground floor after all. John sensed that he was about to be recalled.

Chapter 3

THE GEEKS

NORTHERN VIRGINIA

SUMMER 2009

John Smart, the car sales manager, thought back to the brainstorm that he had some twelve years ago - the tunnel under the CIA. His face flushed when he thought about how screwed up the tunneling operation had been. It was difficult to drive the negative thoughts from his head. In an attempt to divert his mind, he concentrated on watching an oddly matched couple argue. The wife, a young woman with hard facial features but a great body, was sitting behind the wheel of a cream colored 500SL with a window sticker of $104,000. "But I really, really like this little Mercedes,"

They had been to three other showrooms in the Washington D.C. area and had found that there was little variance in price of the car.

"That's a piece of crap," answered the short, skinny man who was wearing a black t-shirt with *Windows VISTA* emblazoned on the sleeve. He was, in fact, very proud of that t-shirt. He won it at a software show in Las Vegas two years ago. The contest, which was run by the local Microsoft rep, was called "Last Programmer Standing." He had deftly pulled the rug out from the last competitor he faced with the answer, "It runs on both a thirty-two bit and a sixty-four bit processor, of course."

The skinny guy, whose name was Louis Applebee but who had been known as Louie the Loser through most of his high school days, rebutted his wife. "Lexus rules. Let's go over to Alexandria and I'll show you a real car."

"But I want a Mercedes," she pouted. If Louie had listened with his heart he would have understood. But Louie had spent most of his free hours during high school and college in front of a computer and had become a master of the keyboard. He was now able to *rip off tunes*, as he called his computer coding efforts, in Java, C++, Visual Basic, just about any computer language that you could throw at him. But Louie had paid the price of not honing social skills during groping sessions in the back seats of cars with the opposite sex. He was a total, abject failure at reading people.

What Clarisse, his bride of six months, was saying was that she didn't want just any car. She wanted a Mercedes - a new, shiny, expensive Mercedes. What she was feeling down deep, down in the core of her heart, down to the bottom of her toes, was that this was the chariot that would take her in grand style to the ball at her fourth high school reunion, and it was coming up just next month. Every time she thought of it she tingled. *I'll show those bitches,* referring those girls who showed up every day in class wearing a new dress, who dated the jocks, and who hung out in the cafeteria together, smirking at Clarisse and her friends who were from what was called in the old days "the other side of the tracks."

"Come on, you'll love the Lexus. And they have got a really nice little convertible." Louie thought otherwise, *I'll convince her that we need the big SUV, not the little one, not the midsize one, but the big one. I'll dazzle her with the numbers and the specs. She'll come around.*

"Ok, but you gotta promise to come back here if I want to." Clarisse thought, *Looks like it's an Aviance night tonight. Let's see, the pink mighty, the Liz Taylor perfume. I just hope he doesn't squirt before he gets it out of his pants."* Clarisse smiled to herself, *"Louie doesn't need Viagra, he needs slow-down agra. Let's see, do I want a white Mercedes or a red one. Maybe that oyster colored one.*

Clarisse flashed back to when they first met in the Borders bookstore. She and her friend Suzie come to the store to find a copy of *The Idiot's Guide to Make-Up and Nails.* They were setting in the retro coffee house section of the store looking through a copy of the *Guide.*

Suzie finally got up the courage to ask Clarisse the question that was waiting at the tip of her tongue, "Clarisse, when did you get the boob job?" This was a fair question. Clarisse had always been the skinny one, almost anorexic. Now she was sprouting some major breasts.

"No boob job. They have been growing in leaps and bounds since I got out of beauty school."

"Oh come on, you can tell me. You got a boob job. How much was it? Who did it? Can you hook me up?"

"No seriously. They just grew there."

"Ok, sure, just like Jack and the Beanstalk. Just plant the seed and they will grow over night."

Suzie looked over at a young, disheveled looking man sitting in the corner typing on a laptop that was linked to a wireless net that Borders had just installed. "See that guy over there."

Clarisse turned her head and looked. "You mean, the geek."

"That geek is worth 3 million dollars."

"No way!"

"Yes way! My Aunt Lori is his mortgage loan officer. She's refinancing his house. It's right on the Potomac River. He even has his own boat. It's called *Bits and Bytes*. She says that he was worth over six million before the dot com crash. Lost half of his wealth in just three months."

"Only three million left. Too bad, so sad. Somehow I can't cry for him."

Suzie said, "Why don't you go over and talk to him?"

"Me, hit on him. I don't think so!" Down deep Clarisse was really thinking, *I don't want to be used again.* Last three romances were "wham, bam, thank you ma'am" and she wasn't ready for another one.

Suzie sensed Clarisse's hesitation. "Come on, just flash those hooters at him. He'll swoon."

Clarisse had only just begun to realize the power of her new possessions. It was getting common for her to catch guys staring not at her face but down lower at her chest. Unaccustomed to such attention, she as yet didn't know how to wield the new weapons. *Nothing will come of my talking to him,* she thought, *but I'll give it a try just for practice.*

Clarisse stood up, straightened her blouse, and walked over to the magazine racks. She picked up a copy of *Glamour*, which carried the feature article "Your G-spot, how to find it with or without a man." She looked at the geek. He was steadfastly staring at his laptop's screen.

Clarisse took a deep breath, walked over to him, and sweetly said, "That's a nice laptop computer you have there. Is it an Apple?"

Louie was exasperated. Without even looking up, he said, "Apple. I wouldn't be caught dead with an Apple. Whatta you think? I'm some kind of graphics fag or something. Turning his head, he started to say, "This is a fully loaded Pentium... ." He stopped talking when he found himself looking straight at a pair of the most beautiful breasts that he had ever seen. They were straining to get out of the tight blouse. The buttons seemed about to pop.

Clarisse smiled. Louie was smitten.

That night Louie had his first "non-virtual" sex. He also switched allegiances. He had become entranced by the actress Angelina Jolie from the day he first watched the movie *Hackers* (the first of 32 viewings to date). But from the first moment of his close encounter with Clarisse's charms, his memory banks had been reformatted and all remembrances of *Laura and the Temple of Doom* were wiped out. Virtual sex was out; real sex was in.

Within six months they were married. They made a well-matched couple; he made the money, she spent it. He catered to her every wish. She didn't like the boat's name. To her, *Bits and Bytes* sounded like some kind of puppy chow. He surprised her by renaming the boat *Clarisse*. Naval traditions claim that renaming a ship is bad luck. Naval traditions are right. The next time Louie took the boat out, one of the engines seized. After forking over $10,230, the couple went out again. The other engine seized. The dealer was kind. This time the bill was only $8,760. Paid, delivered, again they went out. This time the generator seized. Without the generator the boat had no air conditioning or TV out on the water.

Louie told his new bride, "Maybe we don't need the generator."

She answered, "No air conditioning and no TV means no Clarisse on the boat. Besides, the battery life on your laptop is less than 24 hours. How are you going to do without your Pentium?"

Louie paid another $5,254, not in cash but in electronic funds transfer. Almost all of his transactions were via the Internet. Louie hardly ever used cash. Since they got married, Clarisse, on the other hand, always had at least $500 in tens and twenties stashed in the inner pocket of her Louis Vuitton Backpack. She never was without some kind of backup cash.

Spending almost $24,000 put only a tiny dent in Louie's electronic account, but he still smarted from the fact that the boat had cost him almost a quarter of a million dollars. He thought that at that price everything on the boat ought to run ok.

John Smart, the Mercedes salesman, was disappointed as he watched Clarisse and Louie climb into their Acura Legend. "Looks like another deal lost to Lexus. How can anyone want that Jap piece of junk?" But he knew in his heart that Lexus was in and Mercedes was out with the newly found millionaires of the technological revolution.

The same weekend Louie paid the bill to replace the generator on *Clarisse*, fondly remembered as *Bits and Bytes*, he received a call from one of his three friends, Charlie Stromfeld.

"Hello. Louie. This is the Ayatollah Assa-Hola." Louie knew immediately that it was Charlie and that he was using his online name, reserved for game playing on the Internet. In their earlier days, Louie and Charlie had fought each other in an on-line *Desert Storm* game for two and a half days without a break. When Charlie counted the empty cans of Jolt Cola that surrounded him, he was amazed. They added up, 12 ounces at a pop, to 32 gallons of that caffeine rich fluid. No wonder he didn't need any sleep.

"Hello Charlie."

The Ayatollah began with some small talk, "How's married life?" After a spell, he broached the reason why he had called. Charlie told Louie that he was working for the Central Intelligence Agency and that they were looking for someone who knew something about encryption techniques.

Charlie said, "I told them that in the past when ever I needed to break into an encrypted file to find out the keys to *Master of Doom* or some other game that I immediately called you. I said, 'Louie Applebee always knew how to bust open the encryption. They asked does Louie want a job? Do you?"

"I don't think so. My new bride takes up a lot of my time."

"Look, I know you don't need the money. We really need you and it doesn't have to be full time. You can be a contractor and just be called in now and then."

Louie asked, "Contractor maybe, full time, no way. What about Dimitriy Nabakova?" Both Charlie and Louie had meet Dimitriy playing *Master of Doom* on line and found him to be the only other person in the entire universe to reach the supreme high plateau of play that they were on. Dimitriy's on-line name was Ivan the Terrible.

Louie continued, "Dimitriy needs a job."

Charlie responded, "I wish that I could help Dimitriy. But he is Russian, you know, and this is the CIA we are talking about. When I mentioned his name, I thought that they were gonna immediately drag me down for a polygraph. They're really paranoid over here at Langley."

Louie was saddened by Charlie's response. Both Louie and Charlie had followed Dimitriy's fall with the rest of the dot com'ers. After honing his skills in programming he was hired by the Russian Nuclear Energy Group and wrote the programs for the nuclear power plant at a place called Chernobyl. After things did not go well there, he obtained a H-1 Visa and moved to Silicon Valley where he was, in fact but not in name, cofounder of a company called Encryption Inc. All the necessary factors were there: a great name for the company, three PhDs on the payroll, a great PR brochure. Investors raced to buy stock in the company. The fact that there were no assets, no customers, and lots of cutthroat competition in Encryption, Inc.'s area of specialty didn't slow the investors downs one bit.

In fact, Encryption, Inc. could have done well based on Dimitriy's skills alone. He was the master of encryption. The trouble was that his cofounder, Jesse Jameson unfortunately discovered cocaine. Cocaine costs money, lots of money. Jesse tapped the till one too many times and the auditors caught on to it. Unfortunately, Jesse had not chosen Arthur Anderson as Encryption, Inc's trusted accountants and therefore there were no ways to hide the shortfalls with creative accounting. On a Monday morning, CNN reported that Encryption, Inc., known as EINC on the big board, had failed a big audit. Had investors been alert they would have noticed that Martha Stewart had divested her portfolio of all EINC stock the previous Friday. By noon on Monday selling activity on EINC was down from a last week's high of 72.2 to 12.7. By the next morning it was considered to be a penny stock.

Although he had never smoked dope or tried cocaine and was unaware of the financial shenanigans that Jesse had pulled off, Dimitriy was smeared by the scandal. With no job, no money, and about to lose his house and car, Dimitriy sought employment. The trouble was that everyone west of the Rockies knew of the scandal that happened at EINC and no one would make him an offer.

What neither Louie nor Charlie knew was the rest of the story. As if to prove that even God will kick a man when he is down, Dimitriy's beloved daughter was stricken with a dangerous strain of pneumonia. She needed special treatment and she needed it now. Dimitiry's health insurance had followed EINC right down the toilet. The California welfare system would not respond in a way the Dimitriy and his wife trusted. Had Louie known of the problem, he could have stepped in and helped. But the Narabokov's were too proud to ask for help. So they approached the only source of money they knew - the Russian Mafia.

Chapter 4

SUPERSPY

THE FARM

When the CIA first hired Mark Steel, his instructors at the Training Facility were sure that he would be one of the best field agents in the history of the Agency. Both women and men were attracted by his charismatic personality. He was able to develop instant rapport with almost anyone that he turned his energy towards. He was very intuitive at assessing weaknesses and desires, and he seemed to know how to treat them as vulnerabilities and exploit them. His early training reports were glowing. He was a good risk-taker. He quickly learned the spy tradecraft. There was some concern that although he seemed very capable at recruiting someone, he possessed neither the desire nor capability to take advantage of the recruitment. Once he closed the deal, Mark was no longer interested in handling his target.

His trainers thought that he could learn how to "stick with it." Even if Mark had no follow-up, a savvy Chief of Station in the field could use him to recruit a target and then turn that target over to one of the many drab officers in the station who couldn't recruit a hooker with a Gold MasterCard.

About half way through Mark's training program, his trainers found *the fatal flaw*. Mark loved to seduce women – short ones, tall ones, fat ones, small ones, Hispanic, Caucasian, Black, Oriental – he was an equal opportunity seducer. It's not that Mark just desired sex, it was the chase and the conquest that drove him. Once the consummation took place, Mark was ready to move on. He would have thrived in the French high society of the 18th century.

By the second week in the training program, Mark made his first conquest at the Training Facility. He bagged one of his fellow students, Susan Quick, in the pool in the gymnasium. She was an easy target. She was hot for his body. By the middle of his program, he had bedded - if that's the right term for activity in the back seat of a car, in the bushes, on the rifle range and in actual beds – all but one of the female students in his training course. In addition he had scored with one of the instructors, a female Army Lt. Col. on assignment to the training program.

A storm that threatened to destroy his budding spy career first brewed when he bagged the wife of one of his trainers.

Her name was Ally McBride. She was young. She was beautiful. And she was lonely. He husband Jack McBride, was a martial arts trainer and was constantly on temporary duty, or TDY as it is known to the trainers. It was as if she lived alone in her house. He was never there. And he said that it was difficult to call from all the strange places that the Agency sent him to, the various "Democratic Republics of …" in Africa, the countries whose names ended in "…stan" in the old Soviet Union, and other places with long names and poor telephone services.

Mark quickly picked up on all the signs: sadness in her eyes, evidence of crying, fleeting glances towards him. He made his move. She succumbed. He conquered. He left her.

Ally had to confide in someone. Her friend and next-door neighbor, Barbara, might help her. Barbara was older and seemed worldlier than Ally about such problems. Ally looked out the window and saw Barbara's car in her driveway. Ally wiped the tears from her eyes, turned off the TV, and went next door.

Barbara Stansfield was interrupted from watching CNN by a knock at the door. She went to the door and saw Ally standing on her porch, looking very unhappy. She opened the door and said, "Ally, what happened? Did something happen to Jack?"

Ally wanted to broach the subject of her infidelity carefully, but when she saw Barbara looking concerned, she blurted out, "No, it's worse than that, I've been unfaithful to Jack."

Barbara was relieved. Jack was ok. She thought, *What the hell, everyone's unfaithful. What's the problem with Ally?* Then she remembered that Ally was a devout Mormon. And unless it was a legal multiple wife marriage in the Mormon view, then multiple hanky panky was strictly verboten.

Barbara hugged Ally and said, "Come on in. I'll break out the B&B." Benedictine and Brandy was Barbara's beverage of choice for getting through a crisis.

"We'll talk."

Barbara herded Ally into the living room and onto the couch. She sat down next to the distraught young woman. Barbara was a part time reports officer for the Agency and was trained to get to the *who, what, why, when, and where's* of the situation.

"So tell me all about it."

"Oh, it's awful. I was so lonely. He was so charming."

"He? Who he?" Barbara impatiently asked. She wanted to get down and dirty.

Ally said, "It was one of the students."

"One of the students?" Even worldly Barbara knew that was a "No-No." You don't fraternize with the students.

But a reports officer just has to know. "Which one?" she asked.

"Oh, it's that handsome one, you know, Mark."

Barbara blurted out, "Mark. You mean Mark Steel? That hunk. How was he? Man oh man, put me in coach!"

In spite of her grief, Ally found that she couldn't suppress a smile. "Yes, he was pretty good. No, I mean, yes he was really good."

"Is he hung?"

"What do you mean, hung? They wouldn't hang him if they found out, would they?"

"No, no, of course not. I mean is he well endowed? You know. Does he have a big -- you know what?"

"Oh, you mean, is he… well … yes he is I guess. I'm not experienced in these matters. It's only been me and Jack. And they're about the … ." She stopped. This wasn't the direction that she wanted this conversation to go.

"Barbara, I really need your help. What I did was wrong?"

"Look, Ally. What you did is not all that bad. Jack is away all the time." In the back of her mind, Barbara thought, *I wish George would go away so much.*

Barbara continued, "It's lonely without your husband being around." Barbara was thinking, *If she thinks she is lonely here, wait until she gets out in the field. This is nothing. What if she is living in a country where hardly anyone speaks a word of English? And no TV. Boy, she is gonna have a tough time unless she grows up.*

Barbara decided to forgo the why, when and where questions. She already knew the answers to the "who" and "what" ones.

Barbara said, "Infidelity is not uncommon in the Agency, just as it is not in the military services and in the State Department overseas. There are some differences. Agency guys are trained to manipulate and to dominate. Sex is just another way of dominating. Being hit on will be a common occurrence during your and your husband's career. On the other hand, Military guys go for the hookers. And the gentlemen of the State Department go for each other."

They talked late into the afternoon. By the time that Barbara had completed her informal counseling session, she and Ally had consumed the entire bottle of B&B. Barbara had to help Ally across the yard and into her bed.

As she left Ally lying on the bed, Barbara thought, *I wonder if they did it here. Mark Steel. Oh My God, what a young stud.*

When her husband, George, came home, Barbara outlined her afternoon conversation, leaving out Ally's name. Mark was one of George's charges and she knew that he would handle the situation delicately.

The next morning, George Stansfield called the young student into his office for a counseling session. He bluntly told Mark, "I've got several reports that you've been screwing around. You know the rules. "All work, no play" while you are down here. If you want to graduate from this course you will stop it now. Else you're headed for a long and boring career in the Office of Finance."

If Mark Steel had a tail it would have been between his legs. He looked dejected. "Yes sir, I understand. I'll stop the liaisons." In his heart he hoped that he could live up to this promise.

Mark held out for two weeks. Then he saw Marlene Maypole, a female who worked on the guard force that protected the Training Facility. Marlene was riding a Harley Davidson motorcycle, not the smaller Sportster, but a full-blown hog. She looked hot in her tube top and leather shorts. Mark waited until she was on duty and then visited the guard shack at the front of the facility wearing a t-shirt from his college days when he rode his cousin's Harley. They got into a deep discussion of how to put a Harley down when you are in an emergency situation and ended up at her quarters indulging in intense non-verbal behavior.

Word travels fast around the CIA. After all, it is an intelligence organization full of spies. For example, within a week of Ally's misdeeds, her husband heard of them. His first reaction was to immediately fly home. George saw the message that stated his itinerary and was able to intercept him at the arrival gate at the airport. Jack had blood in his eyes.

George said, "Slow down, Jack. I see that you're upset. Take a deep breath."

"Don't use that counseling crap on me. I'm gonna kill the bastard!"

"No, you're not. You are going to calm down. The course is over in a week. Steel will be out of here. I've arranged it for him to be assigned to a remote post in sub-Saharan Africa. Meanwhile, you are to stay away from him. Do you understand? Stay away from him!"

After graduation ceremonies, the students gathered in the facility's bar to celebrate. As was tradition, a velvet painting of a nude woman was taken out of its hiding place and hung on the wall above the bar's fireplace. As course director, George was given the task of explaining the history of the picture. He began:

Back in the late '60s, Marty Saunders was COS (that means Chief of Station – the big CIA boss at the particular station) in a country in the Far East. A well-respected local artist whose media was acrylic on velvet lived in the capital of the country. Admiring his work, Marty commissioned him to paint a picture. Marty handed the artist a photograph of his wife. A deal was struck. Hands were shaken.

The artist worked long and hard and produced what he believed to be a true work of art. He met with Marty and showed him the results. Marty, for some reason, was not pleased with the finished product and refused to pay the artist.

The artist was offended. He had put his heart into the work and felt cheated. But Marty was adamant and refused to pay. He left the artist standing in the street.

About a week later, Marty was driving down the main drag of the capital. As he passed by the local market, he noticed something out of the corner of his eye. He stopped the car. He looked. There was a picture painted on velvet of a voluptuous nude. His wife's head was on the magnificent body. He knew that the body wasn't his wife's. She's kind of skinny. But there was no doubt that the face and hair was hers. He quickly bought the picture, intending to destroy it. As he was leaving, he looked at the other stands, there were about twenty copies of the velvet picture scattered around them. He couldn't buy them all, so he just got in the car and drove off.

This, my friends, is one of the pictures. Marty's underlings bought several of them.

Raising his glass of beer, George said, "To the velvet lady."

The students and trainers all raised their glasses to join in on the toast. "To the velvet lady!"

Sitting on a barstool, Mark looked down the bar and saw Alexandra Pack. She was the only student that didn't give in to his advances. This evening was his last chance. He rose to meet the challenge.

Alexandra was a mystery to most of the students. Although she was ranked top in the class at graduation, she was not overly sociable and didn't reveal much of her inner self. Rumor was that her great grandfather had been of Russian nobility and that her great grandmother was an important spy, but no one knew the details. Alexandra was a jock. She had a brain. She had looks. She had it all. And Mark wanted to own her for just one night.

For the first time that he could remember, Mark felt ill at ease when he approached his fellow student. His mind didn't function in the usual mode and he couldn't come up with a great line for setting up a winning move. So he started the conversation simply.

"Hi, Alex," he said.

"Well, good evening, Mark. How are you this evening?" Alex was wary of Mark. Mark said, "Congratulations on being top of the class."

"Thanks, but it didn't do me any good."

"What do you mean?"

"I'm not being assigned to the field. I'm going up to Headquarters in DC."

"What are you going to do there?"

"I'm assigned to the Counter Terrorism Center. I asked for a field assignment. They wouldn't give me one. Something about 'there is no place suitable for a woman right now.'"

Sensing her anger, Mark saw an opening. He moved closer to her and established eye contact. He put his hand on her shoulder and said, "I understand how you feel."

Alexandra immediately knew what he was up to. "No you don't, you jerk. That stuff isn't going to work with me." She turned around and walked away, leaving a stunned Mark behind.

After graduation, Mark was assigned to a small station in the heart of Africa. At first, he tried to contain his desires, but Mark's *fatal flaw* soon emerged. But the embassy was not what the military calls a "target rich environment." There were no young attractive women working at the local embassy. Rampant AIDS inhibited his desires for the local femme fatales. There was a female Marine guard at the embassy, but she seemed more interested in other women than in male companionship.

Then, the US ambassador's daughter, a sweet young thing from Georgia, arrived for a two-week visit with her daddy. It took two days for her to come up on Mark's screen. It took one more day for him to bed her. Things would have been all right, she was hardly a virgin, but Mark wasn't savvy enough to continue to court her for the rest of her stay. After all, there was only a week and a half left before she returned to the states. So he dumped her.

Well, Georgia girls don't get mad, they get even. The sweet young thing had a heart to heart talk with daddy, telling him how that evil young man, Mark Steel, had seduced her. "Yes daddy, it was the first time for me, and it was horrible. He is such a monster!"

The ambassador immediately called the chief of station and invoked *persona non gratis* status for Mr. Steel. The COS explained to the ambassador, who had no international experience but had given substantial amounts to the Committee to Reelect the President, that *persona non gratis* is used by a country to force a foreigner to leave that country. He went on to say, "And I don't think that you can use it on your own people."

The ambassador angrily responded, "I don't give a damn what you call it. I want him out of the country on the next plane."

Mark flew out of the Heart of Darkness on the same aircraft that the Georgia Peach was on. She smirked when she saw him get on the airplane. He smiled when he saw the stewardess. She was a babe. *Time for action*, he thought.

Mark reported to headquarters to get his butt chewed out. He received medical leave and was ordered to report to the office of a Dr. Mackey, a renowned sex therapist. He thought, *I don't have any problem with sex*, but he knew that he had to follow orders.

When Mark entered the doctor's office, an attractive woman, probably in her late thirties, greeted him. "Hi," he said, smiling. "Is the doctor in?"

"Hello," she responded, "I am Dr. Mackey. And you are...?"

Mark was pleasantly taken back. "I'm Mark Steel."

During the third session, Mark bagged the doctor. This time, he was savvy enough to stick it out for all six of the required sessions. The doctor wrote on a report that she sent to the Agency that he had "performed well during the sessions and tests" and that "he is qualified for return to duty."

Mark wandered around the headquarters looking for another assignment. He ran into Alexandra in the headquarters cafeteria. He begged her to go out with him. At first she said no, but later relented and invited him to join her at a party at the home of Dr. Gotlieb, the head of the Office of Technical Services – the Agency's spy gadget shop. Mark agreed. Alex reaffirmed that their relationship would be at the maximum just friends. Mark agreed.

That evening Mark met one of the prettiest young women he had ever seen, Elizabeth Gotlieb, the granddaughter of Dr. Sydney Gotlieb. She was so young, so sweet, so naïve, so vulnerable. Mark threw caution to the winds. He moved quickly, striking with deadly accuracy. Within two hours, he convinced Elizabeth that the two of them should go out on the back porch. The stars were out. The moon was full. Music was playing softly in the background.

Within another half hour, Mark had lifted Elizabeth's sweater, removed her bra, and was softly fondling her small breasts. She moaned. He sighed. The door opened. Dr. Gotlieb came out, lighting a cigar.

Gotlieb popped a cork. He grabbed Mark by the shirt and threw him off the porch. Then he turned to his granddaughter and said, "Did he hurt you, darling?"

"No, Papa," she answered quietly.

Mark quickly walked to his car, climbed in and drove away.

Dr. Gotlieb didn't say anything more about the encounter. He knew who Mark was. He knew that Mark was supposed to be a superspy. He knew that the DO would protect Mark. So Gotlieb just settled in for a long wait. Gotlieb didn't get mad; he got even. It may take a while, but he would get even.

Chapter 5

THE SCIENTISTS

NORTHERN VIRGINIA

Carl St. John had only been with the Agency for one year. From the first day when he entered on duty, he knew that he was starting down a separate and unique path than chosen by the three friends that he shared a pad with in Georgetown. Of the four occupants of the place, he was the only graduate of the Massachusetts Institute of Technology. His roommates were all Harvard men and were also all lawyers. His Ph.D. allowed him to make good science. Their J.D.s allowed them to make good money. They all owned brand new Mercedes and Lexus automobiles. He owned a beat up old BMW. Two of his roommates worked in one of DC's most prestigious law offices, Hemp, Hemp, and Coke. The third joined the White House staff, providing advice on sexually transmitted diseases. Carl worked as a lowly GS-11 reviewing scientific proposals.

Totaled together, the combined annual income of the four roommates was $790,000. Carl's part of the amount was $72,000. It didn't seem fair; his mates were keeping drug dealers out of jail and developing ads to get horny teenage boys to wear condoms. They made the big bucks. Here he was, serving God and Country, making peanuts for a salary, and driving a jalopy.

After over a year at the Agency, Carl found himself still living the rich life vicariously through his roomies who were always ready to pick up the tab for his bar bill. Working for the CIA did have its advantages. He could get the chicks. But he wanted more. And Carl had entrepreneurial skills. He just needed to watch for the door to open leading him to riches. When he saw it, he would be ready to walk through it.

At the Agency, Carl worked for the Office of Technical Services. This is the gadget office for the CIA. The office can provide small guns, large guns, little bombs, big bombs, listening devices that fit in every crevice of a wall or every orifice of the body, TV cameras, disappearing ink, fake passports, fake stamps, inflatable dolls (some with fully functioning parts), just about anything an agent in the field might need. Many of these items are commercial, off the shelf items, known as COTS in the acronym-laden government, that are bought locally at the local Radio Shack or Spies R Us. Others are manufactured either in-house or in mom-and-pop operations conducted in garages across the country.

In government babble there is a term "unknown – unknown." What it means is that there are things out there in the universe that you don't know about and haven't even thought about. CIA employees are obsessive-compulsive about knowing everything. So they let the marketplace tell them about things that they don't think up. If you have a good invention, CIA will pay you for it, and you even get to keep the patent. What a deal!

One of Carl's jobs is to examine proposals that have been sent in to the Agency. If it seems like a good idea, Carl will write up a quick evaluation and forward it to his boss, Dr. Sydney Gotlieb, Chief of OTS. If it's a marginal idea, Carl will index it and file it away. If it's just plain stupid, he will throw it in one of the burn bags that are scattered around the office.

At about three o'clock in the afternoon, Carl began to go through a series of proposals that had arrived over the weekend in the mail when the door he was looking for opened. He had just finished reading a proposal for tinfoil condoms. The idea was that when CIA agents were searching for weapons of mass destruction they were sure to come across high levels of radiation. The idea of the proposal was that the tinfoil condoms would protect the agent's private parts from the radiation. Carl wadded the proposal up and threw it in the wastebasket.

Carl opened up the next envelope. It came from Sedona, Arizona.

There was something about that location in the back of Carl's mind, but he couldn't bring it into focus. As Carl read through the proposal, his interest grew. The proposal was a page-turner. By the time Carl reached the last page, he knew that this one was a winner. He picked up the gray telephone and was about to call his boss when he paused and hung the handset up. He thought, *Forget this problem tonight. I'll do something on it tomorrow. It's late anyway.*

That evening, Carl examined his options. He knew that promotions would be slow in the Agency. Technicians just didn't get the grade that people in important jobs like those in the Equal Employment, Publications Review, and Inspector General offices. He had tried some schemes to make money to augment his income. One was working fairly well. Using a combination of his MIT technical skills and craftsman talents, Carl was constructing fake Louis Vuitton purses and wallets and selling them on e-Bay as authentic items. He had all the features covered: brass not too shiny, serial numbers in the right place, leather edging feathered but not covered, and so forth. He had enormous patience and provided excellent attention to detail. He had not received a single negative feedback on his items on e-Bay. But such subterfuge seemed unseemly for an MIT graduate. Also, he had to hide this operation from his roomies and from the office. This was becoming a difficult thing to do. He needed something else. Discouraged, he went to bed.

At exactly 3:30 AM, Carl had a dream. He saw a door opening in front of him. He saw himself walking through the door and standing among piles and piles of money. Carl woke up with a start and was unable to go back to sleep. By 5:00 he was dressed and headed for the officer. He entered the OTS facility at 5:25 and went directly to the safe where he had stored the proposal. He opened the safe, then the proposal document and read it through again. He was right. All of the evidence was there.

The idea came from a quiet, graceful woman, Martha Woodward, who had been studying the effects of what she called pyramid power. For a long time, psychics have contended that you can get reenergized by lying under a pyramid. The concept lacked evidence. Ms. Woodward, a mathematics teacher at Sedona High School, had experimented with various sound and light waves and how they interact in the geometry of the pyramid. She began developing mathematical models and soon, unbeknown to her, she reinvented the mathematics of chaos theory, a field that Carl had minored in at MIT.

Ms. Woodward's concept was to examine the natural frequencies that exist in nature. She began to examine and manipulate harmonic frequencies. She advanced her testing to include higher-level harmonics and their interactions. The vibrations became chaotic, seemingly without patterns. She continued manipulating the interactions. All at once, she saw things flow into order, like a river shoreline or a snowflake, or a leaf on a tree. Examined from the right perspective, the apparent chaos associated with the sizes and shapes of such items emerged into patterns.

But Ms. Woodward carried her experiments further into the area of practical application. She modeled the way quartz crystals were able to transfer and conduct apparently chaotic energies into patterns. She extended her modeling activities to allow her to use pyramids to focus and amplify energy. She found that the more effective energy conductors were found in dodecahedrons. It was, actually, these twelve-sided shapes that gave her the first practical success.

Simply put, Ms. Woodward found a way to create and amplify energy to stimulate objects without touching them. All the sudden, Carl remembered something about Sedona, Arizona. Sedona is the center of New Age philosophy in the North America. Ms. Woodward was naively focusing on New Age applications. Carl St. John had other ideas on how to use this discovery.

Carl began planning in his head. First, he needed to bury the Ms. Woodward's application somewhere. That would be easy, just misfile it. Then he needed to construct an apparatus using the detailed designs that she provided in her application. That would also be easy. He had most of the tools and materials he needed at home. The rest he could borrow from the office. Next, he needed to test the apparatus. And finally he needed to find a way to use it to "maximize his profits" without getting caught. He already had an idea or two of how to do this.

Carl took leave from work for the next three days. By the Friday afternoon, he had a working model that was ready to test. He knew that the office would be empty on Sunday. That would be the day he tested the model.

Saturday night, Carl and two of his roomies hit the Georgetown bars. Carl was feeling frisky. He felt that success was just over the horizon. He just knew that everything would come together. Mid-evening, he saw a striking blond standing by the door looking bored. He just moseyed on over and began his subtle routine, "Are you my contact?"

She looked at him skeptically: "What do you mean, your contact?"

"If I said, 'a wet bird never flies at night,' would that mean anything to you?"

"What, 'a wet bird never flies at night,' what the heck is that?"

"I'm sorry, I thought that you were someone I was supposed to meet."

"What are you, some kind of spy?"

"Damn, I'm going to fail the field exercise."

"What field exercise?"

"Don't look around, don't react. I am on a field exercise. I'm in training for a government agency, I can't tell you its name."

"Oh, your CIA!" she exclaimed.

"Shhh," he cautioned, "I am supposed meet a beautiful blond here in this bar. Well, you are that most beautiful blond in the room. I thought it was you."

"Please help me," Carl begged, "Play along for a while."

"Oh," she giggled, "This sounds fun."

Carl knew he was well on the road to recruiting her.

Sunday morning, Carl awoke with a hangover. Rolling over, he noticed that the blond had already dressed and was about to leave. He asked, "Where you going?"

She smiled and said, "I'm late for church. Why don't you hurry up and get dressed and go with me?"

"Nah, I'm already doing enough for God and Country."

"I left my phone number on the bed table. Call me next week. I want to hear about how your exercise came out. You certainly passed your orals last night. By the way, what is a dodecahedron? You kept muttering that in your sleep."

"Oh, it's nothing. See you." He answered.

"Some spy," he muttered to himself after she left, "I give everything away in my sleep!"

Carl got dressed, picked up a cardboard box from the bedroom closet, and left for the office. Traffic was light, so it only took him twenty minutes get to the office. He entered the office, checked to be sure that no one else was there, and opened the box. He carefully took out an apparatus that looked like a paintball gun, except it had a dodecahedron-shaped object on the end of it.

He carefully sat the apparatus down on the end of a long workbench. He placed a cue ball he had lifted from one of last night's bars on the other end of the workbench. Then he returned to the apparatus and plugged it in. He could hear the frequency generator that he had picked up at Radio Shack on last Thursday warming up. He turned the generator dial through a range of frequencies. The dodecahedron began to heat up. Sighting down the top of the apparatus, he aimed it at the cue ball. Nothing happened. He continued to move the frequency setting up, trying to find another harmonic. The dodecahedron cooled down and then, as he upped the settings, began to warm up again. Nothing happened at the end of the table where the cue ball was laying. As he moved the settings to the next harmonic, the dodecahedron cooled down and then began to brightly glow. All of the sudden, the cue ball went flying across the room, crashing into the side of a metal desk, seriously denting it.

"Jesus Christ," he said, jumping back, "It works."

For the rest of Sunday Carl played with his new toy. He found that by changing the level and duration of the harmonics, he could control the energy that was transmitted to the cue ball. By midnight, he found that he could suspend the cue ball in the air for 30 seconds. This achievement required careful manipulation of the settings. By 2:00 AM, Carl had packed all of the apparatus up in the cardboard box and carried it out to his car.

On the way home, Carl thought, *Ok, it works. Now what do I do with it?* He decided to sleep on the issue.

Over the next week, Carl played with the apparatus, moving pencils, balancing balls, and even bending metal clips. By feeding three cameras onto a computer screen, he found that by looking at an object in three dimensions, he could make it do about anything.

It was during the third week that Carl had the inspiration. On Tuesday evening, while he was driving home, Carl saw the sign. It was as if it were a sign from the god of money. Red and blue lettering read, "The Virginia Lottery. $140,000,000." As Carl stared at the sign, his car drifted over, forcing a gray-haired lady in a blue Lincoln Continental to honk her horn. He swerved back into his lane. Accelerating her car to pass him, she gave him the finger.

Carl ignored the old bitty. He thought, *The lottery, that's it. How do I pull it off?*

As soon as he got home, Carl logged on to the Internet and searched for anything that he could find on lotteries in general and the Virginia Lottery in particular. He found several things about the lottery. There were three versions of the lottery: Pick3, involving three numbers; Pick4, involving four numbers; and Mega Millions, involving five numbers. He zeroed in on Mega Millions. It was up to the $140 million listed on the billboard. He thought, *Why screw around with the little stuff!*

Carl learned that players choose their numbers on a play slip that looks kind of like an old IBM card. They can choose any number they want. Some pick a day that was lucky for them such as their birthday, or the date of their divorce or the day they first got laid. Others let the computer pick the numbers. They select five different numbers ranging form 1 through 52. Then they select one Mega Ball number from 1 to 52. Carl ran the statistics and figured that the chances of winning a fair draw were 1 in "all the grains of sand on the beach at Nags Head, North Carolina." But he was ready to make sure that it wasn't a fair draw. A drawing was scheduled for that night. It would be seen on Channel 7 at 11:00 p.m. Another drawing was scheduled for Friday at 11:00 p.m.

At 10:55, Carl turned on the TV. He was anxious to see how the draw worked. At 11:00 an announcer came on stage. He made a few comments about how the lottery was helping Virginia, and then the lottery machine was turned on. It was what Carl had hoped for, a machine that selected balls as they bounced around inside a glass case. It wouldn't be easy, but he could handle it.

No one won Mega Millions that evening. That meant that it would be worth even more next Friday. That is when he would make his move.

By Wednesday evening, Carl had all the details on the security that surrounded the lottery. Several sets of balls and machines were made available for each drawing. Two hours before the drawing three draw officials would show up and randomly select a ball set and a machine. This way no one could bugger up the machines and balls.

Then the officials would pretest the machines by drawing numbers. At 11:00 p.m. the drawing would take place and the numbers recorded. At this time thousands of people across the great Commonwealth of Virginia would be angry, ripping up their tickets and throwing them in the trash. Once in a blue moon, a lucky winner, if he survives his heart attack, will be a multimillionaire. The officials would then post test the machines by drawing numbers again. All of the results would be recorded.

Carl carefully reviewed these procedures and was sure that none of them would be deterrence to what he had in mind.

Carl needed to get cameras in place to allow him to have a three-dimensional view of the ball machine. OTS had the right cameras, small ones about the size of a dime with an ability to transmit an electronic signal representing an image over 200 feet. As long as he could get access to the draw room, he could place the cameras were he wanted to. They had sticky backs and he had lots of practice clandestinely sticking them on walls and under counters.

The next obstacle would be to get him in a position where he could view the three-dimensional image and manipulate the apparatus to direct the balls. This was a major problem. He remembered that OTS had some eyeglasses that from the front looked normal but on the backside allowed the wearer to view images. If he could get the cameras in place, then he could stand in the back of the room and track the balls with the three-dimensional image that he was receiving.

Then he remembered the fake movie camera housing that OTS had developed in anticipation of a hit on Fidel Castro back in the 1970's. It was an empty shell that looked on the outside like a movie camera. It had adequate room inside to hold a small machine pistol as long as the stock was removed. The case was in the OTS historical display, located in the director's office. With some modification, Carl's apparatus should fit inside the case. With luck, this would solve the apparatus problem.

On Friday morning, Carl called the Virginia Lottery and asked to speak to the director. He was routed to the director's assistant, Charlotte Carson.

She picked up the phone: "Ms. Carson speaking."

Using one of his OTS aliases, Carl said, "Hi, I'm Elmer Gloschester. I'm a student at the American University."

"Yes, Mr. Gloschester, how may I help you?"

"I'm about to graduate from AU and am in my last course. It's *Film Directing*. To graduate, I need to produce, direct, and film a project. I've chosen the Virginia State Lottery as my project."

"Oh, that sounds exciting." With visions of stardom dancing in her head, she asked, "Do you want me to be in the film?"

Carl wanted to say, *No, dummy, I want to use you to get my cameras and apparatus in place to rip off the lottery.* Instead he said, "Well that would be beyond my wildest expectations. Could you, would you let me film you talking about the lottery?"

Charlotte's voice had a thither in it: "Of course, I'd love to be in your video."

"Can we do this tomorrow night at the drawing?"

"Well, normally we don't allow filming at the drawing site."

"But it would just make my film. You showing everyone how the lottery works. Getting close-ups of the balls. You holding the balls in your hands. Sensing the rhythmic up and down motion of the balls as they fly in the air. Watching them thrust themselves down the receptacle chambers."

Charlotte succumbed. "I'll get permission from the director."

"Great, I'll meet you at the drawing. Say at about 10:30, so we can get set up and go through the preliminaries?"

"Ok."

Carl added, "I'm really looking forward to meeting you."

Friday afternoon, Carl began to gather up all the devices. He got three dime-cameras out of the Surveillance Devices room and checked them to be sure that the batteries were fully charged. Since Friday afternoon was the office chief's day to play golf, Carl knew that his boss's office would be empty. Carl went in to it and removed the fake camera housing from the historical display case. He loaded all the items into two cardboard boxes and took them home.

At home, he found that the apparatus was just a little too large for the hollow camera case. He took an Exacto knife out and cut out a ¼ inch square from the back of the camera case. He then wedged the apparatus into the case, with the front sticking through the pseudo camera lens. He tested the dime-cameras and the eyeglasses. Everything seemed to be working.

Chapter 6

THE LOTTERY

At 9:00 p.m. Carl put the three dime-cameras in his pocket, picked up the camera case, and went out to his car.

Looking at his old BMW, he thought, *Goodbye Beemer, Hello Lexus!*

He drove over to the Virginia Lottery facility where the drawing would be held. At 9:45, he approached the guard at the door. The guard asked for his id and checked his name against a list of people authorized to enter the facility. Charlotte had come through. His name was on the list.

Entering the room, he looked around. Three people stood over by the machines and balls examining them. *That's going to be the officials who run this show,* he thought. He looked around and couldn't see anyone who seemed to be Charlotte Carson. He walked around the room, being careful not to draw the attention of the officials. He sat down in one of the spectators' chairs that lined the front of the room facing an empty area.

That has got to be where they roll out the machines, he thought.

Carefully scanning the walls and curtains, he spotted the places where he wanted to position the dime-cameras.

At 10:20 p.m. a young woman entered the room.

This must be Charlotte, he thought, *Hum, not bad looking, maybe a little chunky, but not bad.*

That must be Elmer Gloschester, she thought, *Hum, not bad looking, maybe a little geeky with those large glasses on, but not bad.*

They exchanged greetings and Carl, also known as (called AKA in the trade) Elmer, got down to business: "I'd like to put you before the camera and have you say a few words about the lottery, you know, about its purpose, how it benefits the people of Virginia, and so on."

"Ok, where do you want me to stand?"

"Over there please. In front of the stage."

Charlotte moved over to the place Carl had indicated, pulled a mirror from her purse, straightened out her dress, and put on some lipstick.

Jez, I should have brought a makeup artist, for God's sake, Carl thought.

He said, "Ok, are you ready?"

"How do I look?"

"Dynamite, let's roll." Carl picked up the pseudo camera and pretended to be filming.

"What do I say?"

"Just say your name and what you do. Then start talking about the lottery. This is what's called *cinema verite*. We're catching things with no script. Just be natural."

"Ok here I go. My name is Charlotte Carson. I work for the Virginia Lottery."

She paused.

Carl said, "Go on."

She started again: "Hi. My name is Charlotte Carson. I work for the Virginia Lottery. The lottery has provided a lot of good things for the Commonwealth of Virginia. Funds for schools, highways, and the like."

Carl thought, *What about all those pitiful kids who go without milk when their moms spend their alimony on lottery tickets, hoping for the big one? What about the dads who spend half their welfare checks on booze and the other half on lottery tickets?*

He thought, *When I win, maybe I'll pass a little on to those kids.*

Charlotte continued, "Help your state and maybe you will win the big one." She paused.

Charlotte said, "Is that enough Elmer? Elmer, do you hear me? Is that enough?"

Carl, aka Elmer, came back to attention and said, "Yes, Charlotte. That was perfect."

"Can I see a replay?" she asked.

"No. I'm afraid that this old camera doesn't have playback capabilities."

The officials had moved the selected draw machine into place. Carl thought, *Now's my chance.*

"Charlotte, can we get a close-up of the machine?"

"Normally, they don't let anyone near it once it's in place, but they know me. Come on, let's go look at it."

As Charlotte took Carl AKA Elmer over to the draw machine, he reached into his pocket and palmed the three dime-cameras.

"What is it made of, glass or plastic?" he said, touching the side of the machine. As he removed his hand, he left behind a dime-camera stuck to the surface.

"Oh, that's glass, she answered, "Safety glass."

"And is the back the same thing?" he asked, touching it and leaving another dime-camera in place.

"Yes, it's all glass."

"Can we look at the balls," he asked.

"Yes, they're over there," she said, pointing at a table at the side of the room.

As he started over, Carl AKA Elmer, stumbled and caught himself by grabbing the side of the draw machine. When he pulled his hand away, it left behind the third dime-camera.

Because the cameras became activated on contact with the glass, they were already transmitting images to the inside of Carl's glasses. It became a challenge for him to walk. He hoped that he wouldn't trip again.

Finally, the head official, who was Charlotte's grandfather, said, "Charlotte, you and your little friend need to take your seats now."

The TV studio cameras were turned on. The lights dimmed. The action started. Carl raised the pseudo camera up and pretended to be filming.

As the balls went up into the air, the microcomputer in Carl's jacket pocket began to seek out and identify the numbers that Carl had selected on the ten pay slips that he had purchased. As each was identified, it showed in color in the display on the back of Carl's glasses.

The first number came up. Carl manipulated the apparatus, focused the energy, and the ball dropped into the receptacle. One down.

The second number came up and Carl deftly dropped it into the receptacle. That's two. Carl's pulse speeded up.

The computer took a little while to find the third number and Carl was just barely able to nudge it into the receptacle.

Capturing the third, fourth and fifth numbers was pretty easy. One more to go; the Mega Ball.

Carl's hands were now sweating. This was the big one. The prize had risen to $162 million.

The balls were in the air. The microcomputer connected to his dime-cameras quickly identified the number 17, which was Carl's number.

Carl manipulated the apparatus to nudge his ball towards the receptacle. First it moved near the opening and then it flew back over to the other side of the case. Another ball was about to enter the receptacle. Carl quickly pushed it away. He moved number 17 back towards the opening. It stalled in the air but wouldn't drop. Carl turned the apparatus's power up. The ball bounced back towards the back wall. Carl turned the power down. The ball moved forward. All this action took place in just seconds, but it was just taking too long. Carl decided to take a chance. He aligned the apparatus on a path that went directly through the center of the ball towards the opening. He was going to take a pool shot. He turned the power up to max and released the energy.

The ball disappeared.

Carl looked shocked.

Charlotte looked confused.

The official looked upset. Not remembering that he was on camera, he said, "Holy crap, where did the ball go?"

Charlotte said under her breath, "Gramps, remember, you're live on camera."

The official looked at her, looked at the camera, looked at the draw machine, looked back at the camera and, reverting back to the time where he ran bingo at St. Judes Catholic Church, said, "Ladies and gentlemen. Hold on to your cards until we check if there is a valid winner."

The three officials stood in front of the machine with their backs to the camera.

"What happened?"

"I don't know."

"Where's the ball?

"I don't know?"

"Did it fly out?"

"I don't think so."

"What do we do?"

"I don't know."

The Channel 7 reporter covering the lottery was busy relating his own version of what had happened over the live feed to the station. Three other TV stations already had dispatched mobile units to cover this mystery.

Carl knew that the disappearance meant big trouble. He picked up his pseudo camera and began to pretend to film the chaos. This allowed him to cover his face from the TV cameras. A reporter from Channel 9 came in, saw him filming, and said, "Hey kid, I'm from Channel 9. We'll give you $500 for your tape."

Carl shook his head indicating, "No." He didn't say anything because he didn't want anyone to be able to identify his voice from the tapes later on.

The Channel 9 guy was persistent. He upped the offer for the film several times until he reached $5,000, his upper limit for in-the-field expenses. Each time Carl shook his head, indicating "No."

Carl just wanted to get the dime-cameras and get out of there.

The lottery officials wouldn't let anyone near the draw machine. Within five minutes, four police officers and three state troopers were in the room. Carl knew that he wouldn't be getting the dime-cameras back today and that he better leave before they were discovered.

Carl said to Charlotte, "I've got to go out and get some film from my car. I'll be right back."

Charlotte had been ditched by first time dates a number of times and, even through all the confusion going on around her, she recognized the tone and inflection in Elmer's voice. It was a ditcher's voice.

"Goodbye, Elmer, call the office if you want to see me again."

"No, Charlotte, I'll be right back."

"Ok, Elmer. I hope so."

Carl, AKA Elmer, rushed out, climbed in his car, and sped away.

The next morning, Carl switched on the TV. The local news channel was carrying the story *Mystery at Virginia Lottery Drawing*. The reporter, a black woman, outlined the known facts: drawing started, five numbers captured, Mega Ball number about to drop, ball disappears. She emphasized the last phrase, "The ball, number 17, just disappeared."

The reporter continued, "At least three people called in, stating that they held tickets with the first five numbers and were waiting for the Mega Ball number to be called."

Finally, she concluded, "The FBI has been called in to investigate."

Carl switched the channel to CNN where a short blond, mouthy lawyer/newscaster was ranting, "The Virginia Lottery has defrauded innocent people. I stand ready to represent people who have purchased tickets in a class action suit."

Carl changed the channel to Court TV where two lawyers were debating whether or not a class action suit or a series of single suits would bring a larger settlement to the "informed investors" of Virginia lottery tickets. Both lawyers stood ready to represent clients.

On MSNBC, a lawyer and an ex-senator were debating the Virginia lottery situation. The lawyer called it a plot by the Democratic Party to hold republicans up to ridicule by creating an embarrassing situation. The ex-senator countered that it was just another attempt by the Republican Party to circumvent restrictions to campaign financing. When challenged, the ex-senator provided no defense for his position; he just began to shout. The lawyer shouted back at him. For about three minutes they shouted back and forth, interrupting, cajoling, trying to score points by bullying each other. The lawyer raised his hand, the discussion, if you can call it that, stopped. He concluded with the statement that he was ready to represent the three people who called in to the Virginia Lottery claiming to have matches to the first five numbers drawn.

Carl though, "What happened to unbiased news? This is all advocacy crap. I hope that the FBI is this inefficient."

Chapter 7

BUSTED

When Carl arrived at work, he unfortunately found that the FBI wasn't as inefficient as he had hoped. As he entered the office and went toward his cubicle, he saw his boss, Sydney Gotlieb, in a deep discussion with two men in dark suits. He thought, *Oh, no! Did they find the cameras already?*

Carl hastily walked to his office space, avoiding eye contact with Gotlieb, who glanced his way.

After about ten minutes of discussion, one of the men in dark suits left. After about two minutes of discussion, Gotlieb picked up the gray phone and dialed a number. The gray phone on Carl's desk rang. Carl paused to compose himself before he answered, then he picked the phone up.

"Hello."

Carl, you know who this is. Come into my office. Now."

Carl hung up the phone, picked up a pad of paper and a pen, and went into Gotlieb's office.

"Yes, sir," he said, innocently.

Then he saw the three dime-cameras that lay on Gotlieb's desk."

Oh, oh, he thought, *Busted.*

Gotlieb looked Carl in the eye and ask, "Do you recognize these?"

Carl looked at the man in the dark suit and hesitated to answer: "Can I talk about classified things?"

Gotlieb turned red in the face: "Look, young man, just answer my questions. Now, do you recognize these?"

"Yes sir, their miniature cameras. Look like ours."

"Damn right they're ours. No body else makes these. They're my personal design. How did they get into the Virginia Lottery room?"

"I don't no."

"Goddamit, St. John, I looked over the automated badging system. You were here last Sunday all night. And according to Tracker, you went into the surveillance vault yesterday." Tracker is a system that monitors personnel movement in sensitive areas of the office.

Gotlieb continued, "This man is Irving Wallace. He is with the FBI. Lucky for us, he recognized that this is OTS equipment. He has come directly to me to find out what the story is. The only way you can save your ass is to cooperate, and to cooperate now."

Carl St. John thought for a moment: *Should I go on the defense and deny every thing? What about going on the offense and attacking the whole issue? Rant and rave like those lawyers on TV. Or should I just come clean?* Then he realized the obvious. *CIA couldn't let this all get out into the public eye. If I come clean, maybe I'll just get fired and it will be over with. No jail, no publicity.*

Carl started the story with a spin. "Sydney, I was just testing a new concept. I didn't want to tell you about it until I found out if it worked."

Both Gotlieb and Wallace knew that this opening was bull, but they let Carl run with the story.

Carl told them about the woman from Sedona and how she had rediscovered the laws of chaos theory. He went on to tell how she developed mathematical modeling techniques based on her theories. Then he told them how he built an apparatus that put her modeling techniques to practical use. He described how the cue ball flew into the desk, pointing toward the dent that was clearly visible through the open door of Gotlieb's office. Finally, he outlined how he played around with the apparatus, manipulating balls.

The FBI agent spoke for the first time since Carl entered the room: "So what were you doing with the cameras at the Virginia Lottery."

Carl thought for a moment, then tried his bluff: "I was conducting a field test. The cameras were positioned so I could keep track on the balls in a three-dimensional space. They sent images to a screen where I could view the images and manipulate the balls with my apparatus. It seemed to work. At least for a while."

Gotlieb interrupted, "Carl, we all know that you weren't conducting any field test. You were after the lottery millions."

Carl just stood there without answering.

Gotleib said, "Show us your apparatus. Show us how it works."

"It's in the car. Should I bring it in?"

"Yes, get it now."

Wallace said, "I'll walk out with you."

After retrieving the cardboard boxes, Carl set the equipment up on the long table where he first experimented with the apparatus. He began by replicating the experiment with the cue ball, showing how he could hold it up in the air. He then reproduced the other tests that he had run on the first day.

Gotlieb then asked him the critical question: "What happened to the Mega Ball?"

Carl looked Gotlieb square in the eye and said, "I don't know. I honestly don't know. It just … disappeared."

"What were you doing when it disappeared?"

"Just trying to manipulate the balls. I got all of them to respond except the Mega Ball."

"Did you do anything different with it?"

"No, well..., yes I did. I turned the power up."

Carl then exclaimed, "That's what made it disappear! I turned the power up to max!"

Wallace asked, "How did that make it disappear?"

"I don't know," Carl answered.

Gotlieb was already thinking about the issue. "You say that the apparatus amplifies energy levels. That you are manipulating frequencies and harmonics. I think that you have found a way to tinker with basic particles, maybe molecular structures or even quarks."

Pointing to the cue ball, Gotlieb said, "Try to make this disappear."

Carl said, "Ok, but stand back. You saw what I did to the metal desk."

Both Gotlieb and Wallace stood directly behind St. John, out of the line of fire and looking over his left and right shoulders respectively.

Carl fired up the apparatus. After a few seconds, he had the cue ball hovering in the air. Then he said, "Ok, here I go."

He cranked the apparatus up to max. The ball began to radiate, became translucent for about three seconds, and then disappeared. Carl turned the apparatus off. They heard a clunk, clunk, clunk, as if the cue ball had dropped and was bouncing on the hard floor. But they couldn't see anything on the ground.

Gotlieb became even more excited. "Maybe the apparatus alters visible wavelengths, changing them to be in the non-visible spectrum. Maybe the ball isn't destroyed. Maybe it just is invisible. Let's try to find it."

The three men got down on their hands and knees, searching for the cue ball with their hands. Carl felt something. He moved his fingers to feel it out and encompass it. "Holy cow, here it is," he said, holding up an empty hand with his fingers curved inward.

"This is cool," Carl said. "Hold out your hand, Sydney. I'll hand it to you."

Gotlieb held out his hand, palm up, and Carl handed him the invisible cue ball.

"Now that is cool," Gotlieb said. "It's an invisible ray."

Wallace had an inspiration: "I wonder if this would work on humans."

"Maybe we should test it on Carl," Gotlieb suggested. "Better than sending him to jail,"

"I don't think so," Carl exclaimed.

Gotlieb said, "Let's test it on some living thing. Any ideas?"

Carl had a brain fart, "How about Geraldine?"

Gotlieb smiled, "Good idea, the Director is away in Afghanistan. We can get her down here and try the apparatus out on her."

Geraldine was a member of Herman Goodwalk's staff. Goodwalk was the director of the Agency's Directorate of Science and Technology. He was Gotlieb's boss. Geraldine provided Goodwalk's answer to many of the difficult problems that his underlings brought to him. When, for example, Gotlieb came in to complain about how his office had been severely cut back in the last program budget call, Goodwalk responded, "Do what Geraldine does."

As soon as Goodwalk spoke the name Geraldine, over in the corner, in a cage, the gerbil named Geraldine climbed inside a Ferris wheel like apparatus and began running. The wheel went round and round, and Geraldine ran faster and faster.

"See," Goodwalk said, "Look at what Geraldine does. Just work harder and faster." Goodwalk had attended the Harvard Business School and studied under the author of *Do More with Less*. He had been taught that rule as the answer to most business problems.

Goodwalk's underlings hated Geraldine. She was more than just a gerbil; she was a symbol of everything bad about Goodwalk's philosophy of management. They thought more of the gerbil's activities as "spinning your wheels" and "the harder I run, the farther back I get" than as "do more with less."

Sydney and Carl both agreed; Geraldine would be a perfect test animal.

Sydney went up to Goodwalk's office. Jennifer, the secretary and guardian of the gate to Goodwalk's office, said, "Good morning Dr. Gotlieb. And how are you today?"

Sydney answered, "Fine, Jennifer. I got a call from Dr. Goodwalk. He wanted me to repair Geraldine's cage."

The secretary looked skeptical. She knew how the troops hated Geraldine. "Dr. Goodwalk didn't say anything to me about her cage."

"I know," he said, "He said that he forgot to mention it to you. I need to take the cage for a while."

"What do we do with Geraldine?" she asked, hoping that she wouldn't be stuck with the hairy little bastard.

"I'll just leave her in the cage. She'll be all right."

Jennifer breathed a sigh of relief. "Ok, Dr. Gotlieb. Just get her back in one piece."

Sydney took the cage with Geraldine in it down to the OTS lab.

"Why don't you put the cage on this stool? That way I can get a good alignment of the apparatus and the cage."

Sydney placed the cage on the stool.

The gerbil seemed to suspect that something was up. *Where was Dr. Goodwalk? Why was her cage brought down to this brightly lit room? The lights hurt her eyes. Dr. Goodwalk would never allow the light to hurt her eyes. Why are these men staring at her?*

The gerbil jumped on the wheel and began to run as fast as she could.

Carl made an adjustment to the alignment of the apparatus on the gerbil.

He looked at the Geraldine. Geraldine looked back. Carl felt a moment of guilt. " What if Geraldine dies?" He asked, "Do we really want to do this?"

Both Gotlieb and Wallace looked at him. "It's either Geraldine or you. Take your pick."

Carl activated the apparatus.

First he tried low levels of activation. Then he turned it up. Geraldine uttered a squeak.

Gotlieb said, "Don't pussy around. Go to the max, like you did with the cue ball." Upon saying that, both Gotlieb and Wallace assumed the "behind the boy" position and peered over Carl's left and right shoulders respectively.

"Ok, here goes." Carl cranked the apparatus up to maximum.

Geraldine stopped squeaking and just kept running.

After about three seconds, she became translucent. Although she was still there and they could see her outline, the men could actually see though her. She kept running on the wheel.

Then she just disappeared.

The wheel kept turning.

The two scientists and the gumshoe were amazed.

Gotlieb said, "Is she still there?"

Carl answered, "Looks like it. The wheel is still turning."

Wallace said, "Carl, why don't you see if you can pick her up?"

Gotlieb said, "Yes, Carl. Open the cage. But be careful. Don't let her get out."

Carl carefully opened the cage door just enough to slide his hand in. He cautiously reached inside the wheel. He moved his fingers in a curved fashion.

"I got her!" he exclaimed, "I can feel her warmth. I can feel her pulse."

Carl seized the initiative. "Hey guys. We have really got something here."

"Don't even think about another scam to make money," Wallace said.

"No, I wasn't thinking about that, I was thinking about how we can use invisible animals as intell...."

Gotlieb interrupted him, "As intelligence collectors. Think of the possibilities. Irv, let's forget any investigation. Find a way to bury the Virginia Lottery problem. Talk to your bosses; I'll talk to mine. Play down Carl's stupid attempts to rob the Commonwealth."

Wallace said, "I'm with you. Do you think that this would work on humans?"

Gotlieb answered, "I don't know." But he was way ahead of Wallace. He already had a plan and even a man in mind.

Gotlieb turned to Carl and said, "Keep your mouth shut and we'll try to keep you out of jail."

"Yes sir, boss. But I want to be part of the project."

Gotlieb turned to Wallace and said, "We gotta keep him on. He understands the apparatus and how to use it."

"Ok, as long as he stays in line."

Gotlieb thought, *My God, we could make H. G. Wells' Invisible Man*.

Chapter 8

SECOND CHANCE

Everything was not going so well for Ahmad Dursak. For the last several years, every morning, when he awoke, Ahmad felt the sting of failure. He had missed the big one. All because of a mechanical problem. He could still remember how he had been chastised by the Ayatollah. "Allah akbar. Ours is a life of sacrifice. We shun the western music. We help our women resist temptation. We follow the holy one. And in our fight against the infidel to eradicate him from the face of the earth, we suffer depravation and eschew pleasure. You had the great honor to be called to play a role in the battle. You had a chance to sacrifice your life to be able to sit with the Great One with virgin handmaidens providing your every wish for eternity. And you failed because ... because ... your alarm didn't go off?"

"But, your holiness, it wasn't my fault! Allah akbar."

"Allah akbar! Allah akbar! You blame this on Allah? Did Allah fail to check the alarm? Did Allah force you to stay up all night?

"No, your holiness, I cannot blame Allah. Allah is great! But it's not that I was partying all night. I was writing my will and praying. After all, it was to be my last night on this physical earth."

"The others were prepared. Atta didn't sleep through the morning. All of the others woke to the glorious dawn and carried out their missions. The twin towers fell, the Pentagon burned. But for a godless infidel and his "let's roll," the White House would have burned. All of our martyrs sit at the foot of Allah. And you stand here making excuses."

"I cannot make an excuse. I have none. I can only hope that you grant me another chance."

"In his great glory, Allah, not I, will grant you your wish."

You will go to Taif. You will meet with Mohammed. He will give you the details of a plan. We will, Allah akbar, show the infidel that Allah is all-powerful and that he can reach all the way out from Iran to the capital of the infidel. Washington will feel pain! Allah akbar."

Mohammed Kia was the chief of the Iran's Intelligence Service. At tall man with a flowing beard, he looked much like the biblical sketches of Moses. Ahmad had met with him on two other occasions and had quickly learned to be cautious in his presence. Stick to the issue. Don't fail to answer questions, but don't reveal too much.

Ahmad was glad that the meeting was set in Taif, Saudi Arabia. Taif was historically the summer home of the Saudi king. Because it was up in the mountains, it was cooler than Jedda. He wouldn't have been able to take the temperature of the lowlands, which, according to the TV, would be in the 100's during his stay.

Ahmad was bored on the flight into Jeddah. He picked up a book that someone had left in the pocket on the rear of the seat in front of him. It was called *Scientology* and was by someone named L. Ron Hubbard. Ahmad began to read the book. It seemed kind of trashy, but something caught his eye. Hubbard said that when something was bugging you and kept reoccurring to bug you that you should think back to earlier periods in your life to identify the seeds of your discontent. Hubbard said that you shouldn't stop at the most recent event you remember, but keep on working back farther and farther until you get to the prime occurrence that caused this reoccurring bugging. Sometimes, Hubbard claimed, the person might go all the way back to before his birth, in the womb of his mother, before he found the root cause of his discontent. Hubbard called this activity "regression."

Ahmad thought that he would give it a try. First he picked out something that bothered him recently. It was the meeting with the Ayatollah. He felt stupid in the meeting.

Then he took the next step and looked for a predecessor event that may have led to him feeling stupid.

It was the alarm clock that didn't go off. He remembered waking up and seeing that it was well pass 9:00 a.m. His operation was in disarray.

Ahmad remembered the next step in the *Scientology* approach. Regress back to the next level.

Ahmad regressed back to when he went on his first pilgrimage to Mecca thirty years ago. He thought long and hard about this period in his life. He was seventeen years old. He, his father, and his grandfather were making the trip to the holy site. Ahmad was upset because he had just had an argument with his girlfriend. She was just sure that she would lose out to another in an arranged marriage. Ahmad promised her there would be no other, but deep in his heart he wanted to go to America and meet a blond from California. You know, one who drove a Cadillac convertible, wore a bikini and had a wonderful body.

He remembered how they arrived at the Hajj airport in Jeddah where the temperature was 105 degrees. The Saudis were efficient at processing pilgrims through customs but there were thousands of them. Lines were long. People were impatient. Ahmad couldn't see if there were any chicks in the crowd. Everyone was dressed the same: boring white gowns and nothing else. This was Islam's way of saying that everyone is equal on hajj. Ahmad thought, *Yeah, sure, and the Saudi king is a Christian!*

The trickiest time on hajj is during the Erd al-Adha. This is the most accident –prone time to be on the trip. Everyone wanted to at Mecca at that time. It's kind of like being in Cannes, France during the film festival.

The trickiest place to be during this time is at the bridge at Jamraat. This is the holy site where pilgrims throw stones at three pillars that symbolize the devil. When Ahmad approached the site, he made a game out of seeing how many times he could skip the rock he threw before it his one of the pillars. Because he slowed down the line, pilgrims began to bunch up. Panic began. Ahmad was hit on the head by one of the rocks that a pilgrim threw before fleeing the crowd. Ahmad blacked out.

When he awoke, he had his epiphany. There, standing over him was Allah, or at least he thought it was Allah. Something came to him, an unspoken message, *Ahmad, I want you to follow the path. Forgo the earthly pleasures. Forget the forbidden fruit. Come and serve me.* Ahmad was recruited into Allah's army.

Things moved fast for Ahmad in this new role. He participated in the takeover of the American embassy in Tehran in 1969. Next he went to Afghanistan to fight and help defeat the Russians. It was thrilling to see the infidel run with its tail between its legs.

Finally he was recruited into a hard-core terrorist group and, through dedication to Allah, hard work, and sucking up, he worked his way up the ranks to lead his own group.

Then came the failed alarm episode.

According to *Scientology,* the next step is to feel what you were feeling at the time that you had regressed to.

Ahmad closed his eyes. He thought back. The trip to Jeddah, the crowded airport, the search for chicks, the … That was it. He was conflicted. During his teens his heart was full of lust and his desires were many. None of them had been fulfilled. He was still a virgin. Then he had his epiphany at the bridge. After being hit by the rock and encountering Allah; Ahmad, his father and his grandfather had gone to the Grand Mosque to follow the rite of encircling the cube-shaped Kabbah. As he went around, it wasn't enough to pray, he wanted to run, to sing, to feel glorious. He had found the way. On the spot, he abandoned the old ways of lust and greed. Now he would fight for Islam. He would fight against the Infidel.

Ahmad didn't realize it, but down deep in his brain, somewhere near the limbic stem, little cells were singing, *Ha, ha, ha, ha, ha. Your still a virgin.* Of course, his superego had tuned out of that channel. But the tune was still playing.

Ahmad's thoughts returned to the present. He fell asleep and was awoken as the aircraft became wheels down.

The meeting with Mohammed went well. Ahmad was, in deed, getting a second chance.

Mohammed was direct and to the point: "Look, Ahmad, we both know that you are in deep camel dung. For crying out loud, you missed the airplane because your alarm didn't go off? How lame!"

"Allah akbar, I was up late preparing …"

Mohammed interrupted Ahmad: "You don't need to make excuses. Dung happens. And let's skip the 'Allah' stuff. Save that for the Ayatollah. We've got work to do."

Ahmad was relieved but remained guarded. He knew that Mohammed was a dangerous man who, with the crook of a finger could have anyone tortured with a thousand cuts.

Mohammed continued, "Look, Ahmad, you've got the contacts and I've got the money. Together we can make beautiful music."

Ahmad said, "I stand ready to serve."

Mohammed began a string of questions.

"How many people are in your cell?"

"Three of us. All three are faithful."

"Are you all willing to give your lives?"

"I said that they are faithful. I stand ready. The others can be tricked into making the sacrifice."

"Do you have good cover in the US?"

"Yes, I have an H-1 visa as a systems analyst. The other two are on student visas."

"Are they attending school?"

"One is and one isn't. The universities have a very poor tracking system. One of my team penetrated the University of Miami computer system and changed his immigration status from 'out of date' to 'current.'"

What Ahmad didn't know is that the young terrorist, Ebriaham, also changed all his grades from C's and D's to A's while he was in the university's system. He also captured the phone numbers of a couple of coeds who were, according to the computer records, on probation for flashing the football team when it ran onto the field during opening ceremonies of the Orange Bowl.

"Do you have any reason to believe that you have been penetrated by the FBI or the CIA?"

"I have seen no evidence of such a penetration. We were not visited after 9/11. We follow good counter-surveillance techniques. We have detected nothing."

"Good. How do you handle money exchanges?"

"We have friends in the US who have relatives in Pakistan, Sudan, and Saudi Arabia. They are our conduits for getting money. We call it the 'mom and pop' network."

"Do you trust your people?"

"Yes. One has been on hajj to Mecca six times already, and he is only 24 years old. He's a religious freak. The other is too dumb to question me. Last month I caught him reading Playboy, a filthy capitalistic piece of propaganda. He cried when I accosted him. Said, 'Please don't tell Allah.' I told him, 'Allah already knows.' He hasn't stepped out of line again."

Mohammed thought, *Oh yes, it's about time to renew my subscription to Playboy.*" He said, "Keep an eye on him. Anyone reading such decadent literature needs extra watching."

Mohammed continued, "I've got about $25 million for an operation. Can we transfer that much money though the 'mom and pop' network?"

"Holy moly! We've never handled over $500 thou before."

"Holy moly? What does holy moly mean?

"It's a term I picked up in Florida when I was staying with Atta. The old folks from places like North Carolina who moved to Florida for retirement use it. Dale Earnhart used it all the time."

"Who is Dale Earnhart?"

"He was a race car driver until he got killed in a crash. Anyway holy moly' means ... well it says ... well, I don't know what it means. I guess it's just an expression of surprise or something."

Mohammed was impatient: "So can you handle the $25 mill?"

"I don't think so."

"Tell you what. This operation has two parts. One involves people in Russia. The other - people in the states. I'll take care of Russia. You handle the stateside work. I'll keep $20 mill and will send you the other five. Can you handle $5 million?"

"I think so. What are you gonna do with the $20 mill?"

Mohammed snapped back, "You know the rules. Keep the list of people who know about the details of ops to a minimum. Since I gotta handle the Russian end, you don't need to know what I'm up to. If you are captured, you cannot tell about the operation."

Ahmad thought, *Yeah, sure. Take the $20 mill, pay the Russians $10 mill, keep the rest. This guy is a capitalist at heart.*

Mohammed thought, *Hey, this is great. Take the $20 mill, pay the Russians $10 mill, keep the rest. I guess that I'm a capitalist at heart.*

Ahmad asked, "So what am I supposed to do on my end?"

"I'll let you know this much. I'm gonna get you a bomb, a big bomb. You gotta find a place to put it. I'll leave it up to you as to where to put it, but the Ayatollah wants this operation to be even more spectacular than the twin towers, Allah akbar."

"An ideas as to where to put it?"

"No, it's up to you. Just make it be glorious."

That evening, Ahmad bought tickets to Miami. The flight was scheduled to leave at 9:00 the next morning.

The Saudi's found out that Mohammed and Ahmad had met in Taif, but they did not know what transpired. Saudi Intelligence put both their names and known aliases in the system. In real time as the airline reservationist typed in the request for his ticket, a record was printed out on a printer in the communications basement of Saudi Intelligence. Fortunately for the CIA, this was an odd-numbered week and the Saudis were on the side of the US. A telephone call was made to the CIA Chief of Station located in Riyadh.

That evening, one of the station's officers bought a ticket on the same flight as Ahmad had scheduled. CIA Headquarters was informed of what was going on and a call was made to the CIA liaison at the FBI. Agents from the Miami field office were assigned to set up a surveillance operation covering Ahmad as soon as he left the aircraft. Something was up, but no one knew what it was. Concerned people wanted to know.

On the flight from Jiddah to Miami, Ahmad continued to read *Synetics*. Following the guidance provided by Hubbard, he tried to regress past the time in Mecca, but found that whenever he remembered his earlier life, he grew red in the face. All he could recall is looking at the pictures of females in the medical books and feeling his blood pressure rise.. It was as if he had a fixation on female breasts. But he was comfortable around women. After all, he had five sisters. Finally, Ahmad gave up his pursuit into his mother's womb. The closest he could get was to remember the pleasure that he got from breast-feeding. He laid the book down and slept until the aircraft entered Miami air space.

Chapter 9

THE CHASE

As Ahmad walked through the exit gate at Miami International, he was relieved to see that Ebrahimi hadn't forgotten to show up to pick him up. The young terrorist walked up to him and said, "How are they hanging, big guy?"

Ahmad didn't say a single word to Ebrahimi. At the baggage carousel he just pointed at his bag, indicating that he wanted Ebrahimi to get it. The young terrorist said, "So you want me to schlep the bags? Ok. The car is just across the drive. Come on, I'll show you the way."

As soon as they got in the car and closed the doors, Ahmad unloaded a world of hurt on Ebrahimi. "What do you mean, 'how are they hanging?'" Why do you use words of the infidel?"

"Hey boss, I thought that you wanted me to live my cover. Remember me, I'm a student at the University of Miami. Somehow I think that if I threw around too many 'Allah akbar's' someone might take note of it. Hey, man, I'm just getting into role."

Ebrahimi had always thought that in his next life he would be a movie star or a TV star, like that David Hassleeverybody, or whatever his name is on "Babe Watch." Ebrahimi loved that show. After all, it is the most popular show on earth.

Ahmad realized that he had overreacted. He did instruct Ebrahimi to act just like his peers at the university, right down to what they wore, where they went, and how they spoke. Ebrahimi was even given permission by the Ayatollah himself to eat the infidel's food and drink the infidel's drink. Wanting to understand how best to fill his assigned role, Ebrahimi had checked out Lee Strasburg's book on acting and found that the actor must throw himself thoroughly into the role. So Ebrahimi did so. Sex, booze, and rock and roll. He loved being a terrorist spy in the U.S. because of the wavers on the rules that came with it.

Ahmad was so busy being mad at Ebrahimi that he failed to notice the dark blue Ford Expedition that pulled out of the parking garage and was following a few car lengths behind.

FBI agent Fred Sandstone was in charge of the surveillance effort. Using radios that operated on special bands used only by the bureau and monitored only by every foreign intelligence agency in the Western Hemisphere, Sandstone controlled the cars as they switched off coverage. Six cars were used the surveillance operation against Ahmad. Sandstone, who was riding in a dark blue Ford Expedition, code number 1, had his driver take the lead.

After traveling 1.6 miles, Sandstone ordered his driver to pass the target car and take the next turnoff. A second car, a dark blue Ford Expedition, code number 6, fell in several car lengths behind the target vehicle. Sandstone's car did a 360-degree loop off and then back on the exit and then entrance ramps and continued following the target vehicle, but from about a mile behind. As the target vehicle turned off the freeway, Sandstone ordered car code number 6 to not take the turn off but to continue straight on down the freeway, with orders to execute a 360 degree maneuver, return to the exit that the target vehicle had taken and fall in on the chase, some 2.3 miles behind the target vehicle. Meanwhile, a third car, a dark blue Ford Expedition, code number 2, took over a position several car lengths behind the target vehicle. Two other cars, a dark blue Ford Expedition, code number 3 and a dark blue Ford Navigator, code number 6, were moving on roads that ran parallel to the route that the target vehicle was taking.

Sandstone was comfortable that the target would not recognize that he was being tailed.

The passenger of car 2, a petite brunette named Agent Silverstein, spilled the remnants of a cup of coffee on her skirt. As she lifted it up to pat it with a napkin, the car's driver, Agent Sommers, caught a glimpse of her underwear. He recognized it as Victoria Secret, Sweetheart Red. He took a long peek.

Ebrahimi saw the low fuel light glowing on the Chevelle's dashboard. He wondered how long it had been on. He noticed that he was passing a Chevron gas station. At the last minute, he swerved into the station, passed around a recreational vehicle, and entered the pump area. The RV had Virginia license plates bordered by a silver frame that indicated "Williamsburg is for Old Farts." The RV was about the size of a Boeing 747, without wings. The RV owner, an old man named Gary was living with a sweet young woman named Diane who just loved the size of his RV, cursed. "Goddam punk kids. They drive like maniacs."

The driver of car 2 looked up. He was bewildered. He turned to his companion and said, "Where did they go?"

Agent Silverstein answered, "Jez, I don't know. It's like they just vanished. You better let Agent Sandstone know."

"He'll blow his stack if we lost the target. Let's go a few more miles before I call. I know that we didn't pass him on the road. I'll speed up."

After about three minutes, Agent Silverstein said, "If I were you, I'd make the call."

"Hunter One, this is Hunter Two."

"Go ahead Hunter Two."

"The deer is lost. I say again, the deer is lost."

"What do you mean, you lost the target? Goddamit where are you?"

"GPS has us at the 34.6 mile mark."

"I'm just approaching the Chevron gas station at the 32 mile mark. All cars, meet at the gas station. We'll decide what to do there. "

All six of the bureau cars headed for the Chevron gas station. As they drove in, one-by-one, Gary said to his longtime girlfriend, Diane, "Look, that must be one of those car clubs, like a Harley motorcycle club, 'cept it's the big goddam SUV's. Look at all the damn dark blue Expeditions. No, that one is a Navigator. Now that's like seeing a Honda in a Harley rally."

As soon as car 2 pulled up, Agent Sandstone jumped out of Car 1, quickly moved to Car 2, and began to berate Agents Sommers and Silverstein who remained in their vehicle, hoping that it would provide some shelter from Hunter One's wrath. "What the hell is the matter with the two of you? Can't you even handle the simplest of tasks? The rest of the 12-man team joined in the fray. "I'll have your asses …"

Just then, Agent Sandstone saw a Chevalier emerge from the side of the gas station where the door to the men's room stood open, lights shining on the asphalt. He said, "Don't look, but there they are."

Eleven heads jerked around to see where Sandstone was looking. Twelve pairs of eyes watched as the target vehicle with two passengers drove by the six dark blue vehicles, out of the station, and continued on down the highway.

Ten agents jumped into their vehicles. Six drivers gunned their engines and started out following the Chevalier. Agent Sandstone got on the radio. "This is Hunter One. Activate plan 32. I'll take the lead."

At a listening post located about 240 miles southeast of Bogotá, Arturo Mendez called his boss, Juan Perez, and asked, "Hey boss, we got any drug drops going on in Miami?"

"No, Juan. Why do you ask?"

"Well, Senor Perez, the troposphere bouncing is great tonight. I'm picking up radio traffic on the Fibee frequency. They got some kind of op going on in near the Miami airport. Sounds like it's turning into a goat grope."

"No, amigo, none of our guys are up to anything tonight. But good work anyway. Why don't you record the intercept? The drug cartel bosses meets tomorrow. They might get a chuckle out of it."

"Roger, boss. I'm on it. I'll send tapes over within the early morning."

"Thanks amigo. And I'll send you over some of my richest blend in coffee."

Some distance to the north of Colombia, in Fort Huachuca, Arizona, an intercept operator wrote a Flash Precedence message to the headquarters of the National Security Agency, commonly known as NSA.

"INTERCEPTED TRAFFIC, Ref Op Drug Cartel. Preliminary translation. Major Meeting of Cartel Bosses scheduled for tomorrow. Details to follow on verification of translation."

Both Ahmad and Ebrahimi were oblivious of the fact that they were targets of one of the largest surveillance operations to be conducted by the FBI, since the John Walker case. Although the outcome of the Walker case provided a mark in the "win" column for the FBI, it was a close call. FBI surveillance temporarily lost Walker when he left his home via the back door and bicycled over to the local McDonalds. The Agent in Charge of the surveillance freaked out when he walked into Mickey D's and saw Walker woofing down on two all-beef-patties, special sauce, lettuce, cheese, pickles, onions on a sesame seed bun.

The FBI lost Walker a second time. They were convoying up the East Coast on I-95, from Richmond to Washington, tailing Walker, who was alone in his car. About Fredericksburg, the lead Bureau vehicle lost contact with Walker's car. In addition, the pursuit vehicle's radio went dead. It took the FBI a couple of hours to find Walker.

Agent Sanderstone had been a part of the Walker debacle. Although he was the junior man on the surveillance team and wasn't even in the lead vehicle, somehow or other all the crap associated with the screw up flowed down on him. Thus Newton's theory of gravity was reaffirmed. Sanderstone's career was seriously slowed down. He vowed that he would never allow a surveillance exercise go bad again.

And now, the surveillance of the century, one that would be used as a case study at the Academy, was now under way. And already it was off to a bad start.

Ebrahimi parked the Chevalier in front of a townhouse at 3235 Bayless Lane. He got out, unloaded Ahmad's bags and went into the townhouse. Ahmad was already sitting on the couch, watching TV. Outside, five dark blue vehicles surrounded the townhouse, out of sight, but covering all avenues of egress. The sixth vehicle was dispatched to the nearest

McDonalds with a mission of surveilling the Golden Arches looking for signs of Ahmad or Ebrahimi. Agent Sanderstone was adamant that there would not be a repeat of the Walker case.

Inside the townhouse, Ahmad and Ebrahimi were having an argument.

"No," said Ahmad, "I will not fund a trip to Cancun over this holy period of the Infidel, Spring Break! How could you think that I would ever pay for such a thing?"

"But, Ahmad, if I stay here in Miami, my friends at the university will be suspicious. The campus will be deserted. Everyone will wonder what's the matter with me. My cover will be blown!"

"There is no way that I am going to pay for a trip to Cancun."

"Look, Ahmad, some of the students are heading west to someplace called the Colorado River in Arizona. Would you pay for that trip?"

"No, that's going to be even more expensive."

"Then let me go to Cancun. It's cheap. One of my friends, Sam Irwin, said that I could bunk with him. His dad is rich and money don't mean anything to him."

"Then let him pay for the trip."

"Then I can go if it doesn't cost you anything."

"It's not my money. It's the Ayatollah's money. If I don't have to account for any funds, you can go. But just for five days."

Ebrahimi had generated a neat little profit by contracting out his computer skills to other students. The university president had reported in his weekly staff meeting that he was pleased. The university's average grade point average had improved dramatically over this semester. He instructed the department heads to instruct the professors to instruct the students to keep up the good work.

Ebrahimi said, "I've got a little money saved up. But I need seven days. It's just one more weekend."

"Oh, ok. One more weekend." Ahmad couldn't help but feel that he had been had.

Outside the townhouse, a short woman had aimed a digital Nikon video camera with a long lens, through the window of a dark blue Ford Expedition that was parked down the street towards the townhouse. She watched as the young man, name unknown, seemed to be in deep discussion with Target One, known to be Ahmad. Although she didn't know what they were saying, she was able to discern from the nonverbal behavior that they were probably arguing. She saw the older man give a nonverbal gesture of "giving up" in the argument. When he turned his back to the other man, she could clearly see the young man mouth the word "yes!"

The older man moved out of her line of sight. She clicked the microphone and said, "Hunter One, I've lost Target Number One. I'll track Target Number Two."

"Roger," came the reply. "Photo Two, can you pick up Target Number One?"

"Negative," came the reply.

"Keep watching," answered Hunter One.

The plump woman, identified as Photo One on the radio net, followed the young man as he entered a bedroom. She zoomed in on his face to get close-ups. Holding the camera steady with one hand, she pushed a button on a laptop. The image of his face was instantaneously sent from the camera through a wire to the computer. Within ½ a second, it was processed and sent by a satellite data link to FBI headquarters. Within another 72 seconds, the computer was undergoing matching operations in the FBI's mainframe computer. After 2 minutes of processing against federal files, gathered from State, CIA, and INS, and joined with the FBI's own images, a match was made. According to a photo on a passport, the young man was Ebrahimi Hassan, a Saudi citizen.

Photo One was pleased. She would get at least 10 brownie points for capturing the initial image. She continued to observe and record.

The young man took off his shirt. Photo One thought, *Nice body. Lean. Not muscular. No hair on his shoulders or back.*

The young man loosened his belt and dropped his jeans. Photo One purred to herself, *"Nice legs. Nice butt. Good taste. He's wearing Polo underwear.* Actually, they were Polo rip-offs that Ebrahimi had bought at an outdoor flea market. Photo One later realized this as she was playing the video back the fifteenth time.

Photo One saw the red record light glowing on the camera. She quickly zoomed the camera lens out and continued to record. At 11:32, the bedroom lights went out. She could see the light from a small TV reflecting on the window frame. Photo One deployed a high-resolution, image enhancing, multifrequency imaging camera. After several minutes of adjusting and processing, she was able to determine the nature of the TV program. It was *Snoop Doog's Girls Gone Wild – Las Vegas.* She watched the young coeds lifting their tops while the boys stood around and stared at them. She thought, *That's disgusting. Why do men treat women like sex objects all the time?*

At 1:30, a.m., Hunter One released most of the surveillance team and left the four dark blue Expedition's to cover the four streets that were accessible to the townhouse. The dark blue Expedition continued to cover the local MacDonald's restaurant. Photo One took her videotape with her and went home to her warm bed and VCR.

Chapter 10

RECRUITING JOHN SMART

Ahmad assembled the two other members of his terrorist group and raised a question. Suppose we had access to a large bomb. Suppose that the Ayatollah wanted us to place it somewhere that would result in spectacular results. Where would we put the bomb?

Hosein, the third member of the team, asked Ahmad, "What kind of bomb are you talking about?"

Ahmad answered, "I don't know much about it. Just that it is going to be a big one. How big, I don't know?"

Ebrahimi interrupted, "Before we go any farther, can I suggest something?"

Ahmad was irritated but answered, "Yes, Ebrahimi, go ahead."

"I just finished a course in creativity at the university."

"Creativity, what's that?"

"It's a way to draw out ideas. The assumption is that people tend to be conservative when they are trying to solve a problem. They tend to be afraid to go 'outside the box.'"

"We don't have time for such nonsense."

"Nonsense! Now wait a minute. Disney World uses this approach in many of its group problem solving sessions."

Ahmad was impressed. Disney World did have its act together.

Ahmad said, "Ok, so tell us about this thing called creativity."

Ebrahimi responded, "The basic premise is that, at least during the first part of a problem solving session, no idea is a bad idea. Sooner or later you will be taking out useless ideas and focus on others, but at the beginning you consider everything that is thrown out on the table."

"You mean that if I said, 'you waste too much of my time, I'm gonna rip off your head and defecate down your neck,' that you wouldn't evaluate that idea."

"According to our professor, such an idea might be the seed for thought of a great idea. He said that we should take the idea, turn it around, enlarge it, shrink it, and so on until we get something workable."

"Ok, let's start. My first idea is, 'if you waste my time, I'm gonna rip off your head and defecate down your neck'."

"Ok. Let's look at rip off your head. That brings to mind the head of the government. How can we 'rip of the head of the US government?'"

Hosein said, "Let's blow up the infidel president in the White House."

Ahmad thought, *Holy moly, this might really work?*

Ebrahimi said, "Ok, let's think about how we can blow up the White House."

Hosein said, "We'll fly an airplane into it."

Ahmad said, "That's a stupid idea. They'll be ... ."

Ebrahimi interrupted Ahmad: "Wait, the professor said that we never say anything is a stupid idea. That's a no – no. Let me put it another way, what obstacles do we have to overcome to fly an airplane into the White House?"

Ahmad responded, "Well, we have to get through some of the

toughest airport security that the US has ever used, then fool an air traffic control system that is geared up to identify our actions. After that we have to avoid interception by the most powerful air force in the world. And finally, we have to overcome ground missiles that are on 24 hour alert at the White House. Just a few obstacles."

Hosein said, "Well it worked once. If it wasn't for the alarm clock we'd ..."

"Shut up, Hosein," Ahmad said sharply.

Ebrahimi tried to reinsert himself in the creativity facilitator role. "So let's turn this around. If we can't get to a target from the air, how about on the ground?"

"We could place a truck bomb next to the White House."

"Holy moly, are you stupid? We can't do that," Ahmad impatiently said.

Ebrahimi once again interrupted, "Remember, nothing is a stupid idea. Let's put it another way. What obstacles do we need to overcome to get at the White House from the ground?"

"Well, we have to get through one of the toughest cordons of security, involving the FBI, the Secret Service, the White House guard force and the Washington police. Then we need to get close enough to the building itself. That means that we need to get through an iron fence or past concrete barriers. Then we need to get through multiple sensors and past guns, rockets, and grenades. Just a few obstacles."

Hosein sulked and decided that he wasn't going to play this game any more. He fell silent.

Ebrahimi said, "Let's try turning this problem upside down. If we can't get to the White House from the air and can't get to it on the ground, is there a way to get at it from underground?"

It was Hosein's time to lash out and get back at Ahmad and Ebrahimi. "That's a stupid idea. I saw the movie Murder at 1400 Pennsylvania Avenue. Sure they got tunnels under the White House. But they're gated and alarmed. Even have TV cameras covering them. There is no way to get through those security obstacles."

About this time, Ebrahimi got fed up. "You guys just don't get the creativity process, do you? I give up. Go do whatever you want to." Ebrahimi stalked out of the room and slammed the door.

The sound of the door slamming reminded Ahmad of something. His mind regressed. He thanked *Scientology* for his new skills of regression. He went back, farther back, and finally settled on Afghanistan, 1978. He remembered how the mujahadeen had captured the Russian KGB officer. How they slammed him around. How he had pleaded for his life. How he had said that he had secrets that the CIA would want to buy. How it involved a tunnel and the CIA headquarters compound. How the CIA knew nothing about the tunnel. He even remembered how, just before he died, the KGB officer had given the mujahadeen a name, Jack Smart, or John Smart or something like that. *Darn, this Scientology stuff really works,* he thought, *I even remember the name.* Ahmad also remembered what the KGB agent said was the code name for the operation. It was Operation Groundhog. He also knew that the mujahadeén had not passed the information on to the CIA.

Ahmad smiled to himself. "I better look up this Jack Smart or John Smart, or what ever his name is."

Following good operational security practices, Ahmad kept his brain fart to himself. Over the next few hours, he searched "White Pages" on the Internet, looking for the name Smart. He found that there are 102,000 Smarts in the US. He narrowed his search down to Virginia, Maryland and DC. He found that there are 22 Smarts in the local area. He narrowed the search down further to include just the given names John and Jack. He found two Jack Smarts living in Virginia Beach, and one in Woodbridge. Then he saw the name he was looking for. John Smart, 2 Richmond Court, Langley Virginia. He ran the address through Google Earth and found an image of a large house at 2 Richmond Court. It was located adjacent to the southeast edge of the CIA headquarters compound. He smiled, thinking. "This has got to be the man."

Early the next morning, Ahmad parked on Richmond Court, just up from Smart's home. The house was huge, with a brick façade on the front and three story pillars on the corners of the front steps. It had an overwhelming rock garden in the back yard. Ahmad waited, watching for activity. At 8:32 a.m. the garage door opened. A black Mercedes convertible backed out, driven by a male driver.

Ahmad thought, *That must be Smart.* He started the Chevalier and began to follow the Mercedes. In less than five minutes, the Mercedes pulled into Langley Mercedes and the driver parked it in a space marked Director of New Car Sales. The man, dressed in a dark suit, a white shirt, a yellow and blue tie, and wearing alligator skinned shoes, got out and went inside the dealership.

Ahmad waited a few minutes, then got out of the Chevalier and went inside the showroom. An attractive young woman who was wearing a nametag with the name "Marge" printed on it greeted him. She seemed to be scrutinizing him for some reason or other. She asked him, "Good morning sir, are you interested in looking at our new models?"

Ahmad answered, "I'm just looking around, if you don't mind."

She answered, "Please, be our guest. There is coffee over there in the corner. Help yourself."

"Thank you," he answered.

Ahmad walked around, peering into the different floor models. He edged close to the sales manager's office and saw a name plate that read, "John Smart, Director, New Car Sales." He carefully scrutinized the man who was sitting inside, memorizing his features. After Ahmad collected the information he wanted he turned to the receptionist, said "Thank you," and left. He drove the Chevalier down a side street that was adjacent to the dealership and parked it in a position where he could observe the exits to the Mercedes dealership. He waited.

Inside the sales manager's office, Smart was reviewing sales figures. "Those goddam Japs and their Lexus. They're ruining our sales," he muttered to himself.

Smart had even more problems. The house payments on that monster that the KGB had ordered him to move into were astronomical. And now that the great Soviet Empire that would live forever in Lenin and Stalin's glory had crumbled and the great protector of the Empire, the KGB, had followed it into the abyss, Smart was stuck with the monthly payments. The house was in his name. Not that this was necessarily a bad deal. If he got pushed to the wall, Smart could sell the monstrosity and rake in the rather large equity that was in the house, which was located in a prime location. As that capitalist once said, what ever his name was, there are three important things to look for in real estate: property, property and property.

The other thing that caused Smart pain was his wife's nagging about getting a boob, nose, eye, and lip job. It all started when his neighbor three doors down, a lawyer turned newscaster named Greta, got a nose job. This set a trend and all the wives on the block went to Greta's savior, Dr. James Van Rightman, the premier cosmetic surgeon on the East Coast. Smart had to admit some of them looked really good. Of course there was his next-door neighbor, Janice Quinn, who couldn't be improved unless she got a full body transplant. The trouble was that Dr. Jim, as he was affectionately known, was very, very expensive. Smart tired offering him a deal on a Mercedes, but Dr. Jim said that he preferred the Lexus. He owned four of them.

Smart groused, "I really don't want to sell the house, but maybe it's time."

At two minutes after noon, John Smart left Langley Mercedes for lunch at O'Toole's over in Vienna, Virginia. Ahmad spotted him as soon as he drove out of the parking lot, started up the Chevalier and followed him. Smart parked in the small lot behind O'Toole's and entered the small restaurant. Ahmad parked across the street, got out and went inside the restaurant.

Seasoned spies know that there are several ways to recruit a source. Ahmad knew them all. And he knew that Smart knew them all. First, the officer can take a long-term approach, spotting and assessing a target, finding a way to meet with him or her, developing rapport over a long period of time, and then making the pitch. This way is pretty effective, but expensive in time and money. A second way is to take a shorter route, tightening up the spotting and assessment process and entrapping the target, often through a "honey trap" operation involving drugs, sex, and rock and roll. If the target can be compromised by movies of him in a "belly-bumping operation" or playing "hide the salami," this method often works. During the Cold War, the best bet was to entrap someone in a homosexual tryst, but things had changed every since *My Tryst with the KGB* won best film at the Gay Film Festival in Rehoboth Beach. Now when the existence of movies and photos were made known, the target usually asked for copies so he could show them to his friends. A third way is to make a "cold pitch." Don't beat around the bush. Meet the target, make an offer and hope that it works. This third method is highly risky and often backfires.

Ahmad thought about how he should approach Smart. He didn't have any time to fool around. He really had no choice. Going through the restaurant's door, he committed himself.

John Smart was setting at a small table towards the rear of the restaurant, about to take a bite out of a huge hamburger with onions, tomatoes, cheese, and ketchup. With no hesitation, Ahmad walked up to Smart's table, sat down, and said, "Hello, John Smart."

At first, Smart was taken back. Then he recognized the man who just sat down at his table from the dealership. He was looking for a car. Smart went into his salesman role. "Oh, hello. You were looking at Mercedes. Are you interested in buying a new Mercedes?"

"No. I'm interested in Operation Groundhog."

Smart felt like he had just received a slap in the face and he flinched. At that moment, Ahmad, knew that he was right. This was the man that the KGB agent had revealed just before he died a thousand deaths. This was the man who knew about the tunnel.

Smart tried to recover. "Operation Groundhog. What are you talking about?"

Ahmad knew what to say next. "Let's cut through the dung. I've got two million dollars to lie on the table. I just want access to the tunnel."

Ahmad knew that this was the critical moment that everything was riding on. He waited.

Smart took five seconds to assess the implications of what this unknown man had just said, to weigh all the costs and benefits and to reach a conclusion. He said, "What do you want to know about the tunnel?"

Chapter 11

THE TUNNEL

John Smart was cautious as he opened up the conversation with Ahmad. He wanted to feel the stranger out to make sure that he wasn't an FBI plant. He asked Ahmad, "How do you know about Operation Groundhog?"

Ahmad knew exactly what to say. "Do you remember Yuri Kovsloff?"

Smart not only knew Yuri, he was his best friend and roommate at the KGB academy. He knew that Yuri had disappeared in Afghanistan.

"What about Yuri," he asked.

"I was there when he died."

"What happened to Yuri? How did he die?"

"It was not a pleasant death. You know those Afghan mujahadeen. They are not like us Iranians who respect warriors. They are barbaric."

Ahmad hoped that Smart would not press on the question of what role he played in Yuri's death.

"How did he die?" Smart asked again.

"You don't want to know the details. Sufficient to say that he told us all about you and the tunnel. He said that the CIA would pay for the information. Later, all of the other mujahadeen were killed in a battle. Although I was seriously wounded, I was the only one left alive. Only I know about the tunnel."

"How much money are we talking about?" John Smart asked.

"Two million, plus expenses if there are any."

"What do you want to do in the tunnel?"

"We want to set up a listening post. That's what you had in mind, wasn't it? Bugging the CIA?"

Ahmad didn't answer.

Smart made an assessment of Ahmad and his story. After a minute's pause, he said, "Do you want to see the tunnel?"

Ahmad's heart raced. "Yes, please." He thought, *Allah akbar*.

Smart brought out his cell phone from his jacket pocket. He dialed a number and said, "Honey, I've been thinking about that surgery that you need to have… Yes, the one like Greta's…. Yes, Dr. Jim. Get it set up as soon as you can… I love you…. Bye."

John Smart knew his wife, Allison. She would be out the door and heading for the Dr.'s office in five minutes. He also knew that she would be gone for several hours. That way, he wouldn't have to explain to her why he was bringing a stranger in to see his wine cellar. Allison not only was clueless about his earlier life as a KGB illegal, she also didn't have the foggiest notion that a large tunnel ran from her basement into the depths of the CIA compound.

The two conspirators waited ten minutes. Smart called his home phone. No one answered. He said to Ahmad, "Come on, let's go see a tunnel."

When they entered the Smart residence, Ahmad was impressed by the furniture, wall fixings, and floor coverings. Either someone who lived here had good taste or someone got paid a lot of money to decorate the home. Ahmad noticed that an almost priceless Iranian wedding carpet lay on the floor in a small room to the left of the entranceway. It made him miss his parent's home.

John led Ahmad down into the basement, passed a bar stocked with booze, including Stoly vodka, and into a back room. There was a small door on the room's back wall. He opened it and said, "Welcome to my wine cellar.

Ahmad ducked his head and entered a long but narrow room. The long walls were lined with wine racks, red wines on the left and white wines on the right. At the end of the room, which was about forty feet long, was a wine rack that was filled with German Reisling.

Ahmad waited for John to come into the room. He moved aside to let John pass him. John went over to the Riesling wine rack and twisted a bottle on the top shelf to the left. He then twisted a bottle on the bottom shelf to the right. Ahmad heard a whine as electric motors turned, separating the Riesling rack in the middle and rolling into each side. As soon as the racks were drawn completely into the sides, a string of overhead lights came on, revealing a long tunnel covered with cobwebs. About 1/3 of the lights were out. It was obvious that no one had been in the tunnel for some time.

John said, "This is the tunnel. It heads straight into the CIA compound."

Ahmad could see that it would be necessary to stoop down to walk through the tunnel. He saw a small enclave to the right of the tunnel entrance. It was a little taller, about six and one half feet from floor to ceiling. John directed Ahmad to enter the enclave. John followed him into the area. He reached up to the top of the back wall and pulled down a map. Ahmad could see outlines of buildings. John pointed out where the tunnel was depicted on the map. It went straight out from the house towards the south side of the compound. It stopped under a medium sized building that was well south of what appeared to be the main buildings of the compound.

"This is the tunnel," John said, running his finger along the two straight lines that showed the tunnel route.

"What is this building?" Ahmad asked, pointing to the place where the tunnel appeared to end.

John wondered how he should answer. Then he decided that honesty and openness were called for. But he decided to go in an around about way to get to the answer.

"We began planning the tunnel after the original building was built. We got word that the compound was undergoing major renovations. We got plans that included new areas in the headquarters building and an unknown building to be built on a remote part of the compound. Our analysts in Moscow studied the plan. We all discussed whether to build the tunnel to go under the headquarters building or under the mysterious new building. It had all the markings of a special facility, isolation from other areas, filtered water, special electrical lines, and other features that only our elite facilities in Russia would have."

John was quiet.

Ahmad asked, "Obviously, from the drawings its clear that you all decided to go for the special facility. What did you find out? Is it a torture chamber? Is it a place to house prisoners? Or a communications facility? What?"

"Well," John said, "We finished the tunnel just as the facility was finished. The Americans love to hold opening ceremonies for their buildings. We barely got our listening devices in place when that day came. We even brought senior KGB officers and special interpreters in. The tunnel was packed with bodies."

"And," Ahmad said.

"And the speeches began. The opening line tells it all. It went 'Welcome to the opening day of the Langley Day Care Center."

"Day Care Center. What do you mean, 'Day Care Center.'"

"That's the same thing that a KGB general asked me. I turned to an interpreter to let him explain that it's a place for spies to send their kids for school during the day. The general was really pissed off."

"I'll bet he was!"

"I thought that my career, and maybe my life, was over. But then the trouble started in the Soviet Union and before anyone could react to the debacle, the Union crumbled and the KGB followed. They seem to have forgotten me."

Ahmad said, "So this tunnel doesn't go under the headquarters building. It might still be useful."

"We did run the listening operation and even got a little intelligence out of it. We picked up comments like 'Ok, Johnny Ridgeway, when your daddy gets back from Moscow, you're gonna get a whipping.' We passed these intercepts to Moscow. They were able to use that intelligence to finger Matt Ridgeway as a CIA officer operating in our capital."

"No that's not what I'm thinking. How long would it take to take a turn in the tunnel and extend it to the north and under the main buildings?"

"We still have the drilling machine with a diamond-faced bit here. It's at the end of the tunnel. It works pretty fast. We could cover that distance in about two months."

"Could you do it in three weeks?"

"No way!"

"Could you do it in three weeks for a million dollars?"

"Way! But you gotta cover expenses."

"We'll split expenses down the middle."

"Done. When do we start?"

"Right now!"

"I need to get my wife and daughter out of the house."

"Your wife and child don't know about this tunnel?"

"No, it was built before we moved in. The construction of the house provided cover for earth removal. By the way, my wife also doesn't know about my KGB past."

"Can you send them somewhere."

"I've got an idea. I'll be right back. Wait here."

John left the tunnel and went back up stairs.

While Ahmad was waiting, he looked at the chart, thinking, "How could the Russians be so stupid? Day Care Center. Why if we ever did anything that foolish, the Ayatollah would have us sent on an early trip to Allah."

In about ten minutes, John returned. He said, "Problem solved."

"What did you do?"

"I made a call to a doctor, Dr. Jim is his name. I made him an offer. I told him that I would pay to put him and his staff up in a great hotel in Cancun for three weeks if he would take my wife and daughter with him and give my wife some cosmetic surgery. First he said no, and then, after I said that I would put him in the presidential suite and throw in $100,000 dollars, he agreed. He makes that much in just two weeks, but he likes the idea of a vacation."

Ahmad said, "We agreed to split expenses, but I'm not paying for half of your wife's cosmetic surgery."

"Ok, Ok, Don't worry. Just put in half the $100,000. Fair is fair. He's willing to leave on Friday. Says that his partners can take care of business."

"Done deal."

"I'll get my assistant, Margie, to set up the travel arrangements. She just loves Cancun. Goes there every year."

Ahmad thought, *Seems like everyone wants to go to Cancun. I wonder why?"*

Two days later, John packed his wife and daughter into the Mercedes and drove them to Dulles Airport. When they arrived, they met up with Dr. Jim's party. Smart handed Dr. Jim an envelope that included airline tickets, first class of course, a paid in full statement for the hotel, and $100,000. He kissed his wife and daughter good bye and waved as the traveling party entered the telescoping bus that carried them to the waiting lounge. He returned to the Mercedes and sped home. Ahmad was in the tunnel enclave looking at the map.

As soon as John went down stairs, he heard the doorbell ring. He went back up and opened the door. Three heavy set, unshaved men stood on the porch. John greeted them and said, "Come on in."

He directed them downstairs and into the tunnel.

"Ahmad, this is our work force. Let me introduce Ivan, Stanislav, and Gorky."

Ahmad noticed that John did not give their last names.

John turned towards the Iranian, "And this is Ahmad."

John went on to explain, "These three are ex-GRU. They all are tunnel experts. They worked on the original tunnel and know the equipment. They're expensive, but we need them to get the tunnel done in three weeks."

The three men smiled at Ahmad. Two were missing several teeth. All three wore old, worn out clothes. One reeked of the smell of beer. Ahmad thought, *It doesn't matter. We'll all be dirty by the time the tunnel gets built.*

Smart said, "I've been thinking this problem through. Last time, we were able to use the house construction as a cover for getting rid of all of the dirt that we excavate. At first, I thought that we would have trouble with the new excavation spoil. But then Ivan, Stan, Gorky and I conducted a "brainstorming" session and we thought of a way to cover the operation."

Ahmad thought, *Maybe this creativity stuff really works.*

He asked, "What are we gonna do?"

"Well, I've called Langley Gardens and told them that I want to redo our rock garden in the back of the house. At night we'll excavate and pile the dirt up and during the day they'll remove it."

"There'll be a lot of dirt. Won't they be suspicious?"

"They won't notice or even care if they do, as long as we pay them enough. They'll be here tomorrow morning to begin removal."

"Ok, let's get started."

"Stan, check the drill. You better change the oil. Then crank it up and see if it works. Gorky, go through and replace all the lights that are out. Check the air units and make sure that they will provide enough air for us to work at the end of the tunnel. And Ivan, check out the conveyor belts and see if they are still working. I'm a little worried about the rubber backing. Also figure out how we are gonna make that ninety-degree turn."

Ahmad was impressed. John Smart seemed to know what he was doing.

The next morning at 7:15 in the morning, two workers, Charlie Wilbran and Rocky Stonehead parked in front of the Smart residence. They were arguing.

Charlie was insistent. "Friggin DC Nats are going to the World Series this year."

Rocky countered, "No friggin way."

"Ya just don't know nothin. I heard on Howard Stern that DC was due."

"Due what, a lobotomy?" Rocky snickered out.

"F U," Rocky countered.

"Stern said that we was due. He musta meant that we was getting a new coach. Howard's my man. He knows it all."

"Bullcrap! All he knows is to chase women."

"So, what's that got to do with him sayin,' we're getting a baseball team?"

"So!"

"So!"

Rocky changed the subject. "What kinda crummy job you got for us to do now?"

"This's an easy one. We just gotta clear out the back yard so this jerk can build a new rock garden."

"What's wrong with what he's got now."

"Nothin'. You know these rich people. Don't know dollars from donuts."

"So how much they payin' us?"

"That's the cool part. We's gettin ten thousand dollars to move a few rocks."

"Ten thousand dollars! No bull!"

"Yeah, but the guy said we gotta stick with it until all the rocks and dirt is gone. How much can there be?"

"Good thing we brought the big pickup. Let's go look."

The two gentlemen walked around to the back yard. Before them lay a large mound of spoils from the night's tunneling operation.

"Holy cow! Look at all them rocks. Look at all that dirt. This is gonna take all day."

"Let's go back and get the dump truck."

"Better get the bobcat too."

Once they got organized, the two gentlemen were efficient. By the end of the day, they estimated that they were about half way done. They agreed, "Still, ten grand for two days work. Not bad at all."

As they packed up their tools, Charlie said, "Baseball, can't wait till our team goes all he way."

Rocky responded, "Ain't gonna be no friggin all the way."

"Oh yea, just watch Howard Stern tonight."

"Yeah, you watch how he never puts his hands above the table."

"So!"

"So!"

The four men watched as the two gentlemen pulled away in the dump truck. They went downstairs to restart the tunneling operation. Everything seemed to be going smoothly.

Chapter 12

NEGOTATIOJNS

Half way around the world, in Sevastopol, Russia, Mohammed was about to start the process that would lead to getting a bomb to the US. His contacts with the Arab Afghans had given him a name: General Vladimir Kutusin. This was the man who could get a bomb into his hands. Not just any bomb, but a nuclear device. Mohammed's contacts warned him, however, that Kutusin was a dangerous man. He was the Godfather of the Russian Mafia. Mohammed expressed no concerns to his contacts. He could handle any infidel.

Allah had blessed Mohammed. He arrived in Sevastopol the day before a special day in the life of the General. It was the Russian's daughter's wedding day. Mohammed had been briefed that the General had to receive him on that day if he requested an audience. Mohammed also found out that the General could not refuse any request on that day. Mohammed thought, *Allah akbar*.

Mohammed found out other things during the briefings that he received on the General. For one, the General and all of his close companions were all of pure Slavic blood. Blood was blood and nothing else was its equal. The General's adjutant, Colonel Slavinski, acted as his chief advisor or counselor. The Colonel was, of course, a full-blooded Slav.

The Russian Mafia is not a new phenomenon. It went back to the dark days of Soviet communism. The General, who was not really a general at all, also went back to those days. He started as a common street thief.

His Mafia career began when he prowled the civilian airports, hustling foreign visitors to extort exorbitant fees from them for drives to the city. He found that he couldn't act alone, but needed to pay tribute to the Mafia boss that controlled the airport area. Some gypsy cab drivers flaunted Mafia authority. When caught, they were brutally beat up or even killed. Always prompt in his payments, Kutusin was recruited into that boss's organization as a common foot soldier.

Kutusin showed initiative. He organized a scam that paid off royally. The idea was to spot some middle-class citizen, follow him home and determine if he had the hard-earned privilege of a car and a home. A lucrative target would be identified. A traffic accident was staged against him or her. The police were called. The police, on the payroll of the Mafia, would warn the citizen to quickly settle an accident claim with the Mafia. The hapless victim, typically devoid of savings, would then often be forced to sign over his or her family's apartment and move out to some God-forsaken place.

Kutusin soon became an enforcer. He was called in on special cases, where store owners resisted the Mafia's sales talks, where entrepreneurs tried to sell drugs in the Boss's turf, and where college girls were freelancing as hookers on local streets to pick up some spending cash.

Because of his special powers of persuasion, Kutusin was promoted to be head of "sales talks," responsible for ensuring that local stores only stocked items approved by the Mafia. Approval was obtained by paying tribute, of course. Like any good salesman, Kutusin came to understand the benefits of undercutting his rivals in price, barring them from distribution outlets by persuading storeowners to drop the rival brands. Like any good businessman he aimed at holding monopoly by forcing his rivals to abandon the field or by merging with his own company.

His boss failed to notice that, by the force of his own personality and his reputation, Kutusin was becoming a man of respect. One day, the two men, Kutusin and his boss, went on a long drive. Only one came back. No one asked what happened to the boss.

No one objected when Kutusin sat in the Godfather's chair at the next planning meeting. He opened with a simple request, "Call me General."

Since the collapse of the Soviet Empire, the Mafia had become the second government, far more powerful than the official one in Moscow. And the General rose to become the most powerful of the Russian Mafia chiefs. His power came from two sources. The first was his organizational skills. The second was the respect that was given him.

Between the head of the family, the General, who dictated policy, and the operating level of men who actually carried out the orders of the General, there were three layers. Nothing could be traced to the top. In his system of organization, he gave two Slavs each the title of captain, and the men who worked beneath them the rank of soldier. He named Colonel Slavinski, who had actually served in the Soviet Rocket Forces, his counselor. He put layers of insulation between himself and any operational act. When he gave an order, it was to one of the captains alone. Rarely did he have a witness to any order he gave.

He earned the respect of his troops. When a soldier of his was arrested and sent to prison by some mischance, that unfortunate man's family received a living allowance; and not a miserly pittance, but the same amount that the man earned when free. He did not hide his pleasure when the Russian Minister of Finance sent a wedding present to his daughter. He was pleased when so great a man showed him such respect. The minister was one of the great stones in the General's power structure and, with this gift, had reaffirmed his loyalty. In fact, a system of payoffs had been set up and the General's organization had a sizable list of officials entitled to a monthly sum.

As the wedding reception proceeded, a long string of people seeking favors stood outside the General's study, waiting for an audience. Inside, the Colonel kept the line moving. In fact, there was nothing much to decide. All the requests would be acted on. Of course, the Colonel was keeping a list. Debts would be called in.

One of the soldiers entered the study, went over to the Colonel, and whispered in his ear. The Colonel shook his head and waved the soldier away. As soon as the current request was fulfilled and the requester left the study, the Colonel spoke softly to the General, "There's a man outside. He says that he has traveled far. He says that he has a request. He says that with the request comes an offer. As your counselor, I think that you should turn this man away. We do not know him. We cannot trust him."

"No, it's my daughter's wedding day. I cannot deny this man an audience. Bring him in. But stay here."

The General watched as a man who looked like Moses from the Old Testament of the Bible entered the room. The man spoke, "Greetings, I am Mohammed. Thank you for receiving me on this your daughter's wedding day."

"And how may I help you?"

"I know that you help the little people, I ask for your support in helping the little people of the Muslim world."

"I care for everyone – rich and poor, powerful and humble – equally. It is my character."

"And I represent the hopes of the Middle East to throw off the yoke of imperialism."

"I care not for politics. We fought our battle with the West. We lost the Cold War. I care only for my people."

"Your people would be enriched by access to our oil fields."

"You tempt me. What do you wish?"

"I want a nuclear weap…"

The General interrupted Mohammed. "I do not get involved in such issues. However, I will grant you access to my experts. If they can find a way to help you, so be it. But do not count on using your oil fields. You do not have access to them yourself?

"Right now, I have no access. But our time will come. Meanwhile, I have other things to offer."

The General said, "Please, respect me. Do not make an offer to me on the day of my daughter's wedding."

He turned towards Colonel Slavinski and said, "Meet with this man tomorrow. Strike a deal. Keep it simple. Keep it clean."

The General stood up. Mohammed knew that action signified that the meeting was over. He said, "Thank you, General. Allah will bless you and the union of your daughter with her new husband."

Colonel Slavlinski walked out of the study with Mohammed. He said, "Where are you staying?"

Mohammed said, "At the Interpole."

The Colonel said, "I'll pick you up in the lobby at 8:00 tomorrow morning. Wear heavy boots. We'll be doing a little walking."

"I'll be ready."

That night Mohammed dreamed of the Kabbah, the ancient oblisk at Mecca. He saw himself running around and around it. He saw the Kabbah disappear in a bright light. He saw buildings being burned down. He saw terrible winds blowing trees flat. He had pleasant dreams."

The next morning, Mohammed dressed in hiking pants, a light long-sleeved shirt and hiking boots. He went down to the lobby and saw the Colonel who was dressed in combat gear with combat boots. They greeted each other and the Colonel directed Mohammed to a military vehicle that was waiting outside.

After a long drive, they entered a remote facility. It was surrounded by two fences with concertina wire on top. The gates were broken open and hanging on their hinges. Mohammed saw no guards.

They drove into an area that looked like a series of weapons bunkers, separated from one another and surrounded on three sides by mounds of earth. Several of the buildings had vaulted doors that were open. The open ones looked empty.

They drove up to one of the locked bunkers. It held a sign that warned of radiation. The Colonel got out of the car. Mohammed joined him. The Russian entered a code into the keypad that controlled access to the bunker. The lock clicked and the door opened. The Russian and the Iranian entered the bunker.

Mohammed saw twenty bombs in racks that lined both sides of the bunker. Because he had carefully studied *Jane's Weapons*, he recognized them as dial-a-yield nuclear bombs.   He thought, *Allah akbar. What I could do with these weapons. I could make them instruments of Allah.*

"Let's deal," the Colonel said, "How many do you want? How much you gonna pay?"

Because Mohammed had taken an on-line course from the University of Arizona titled *How to Negotiate*, he knew that he should let the Colonel lay down the first figure. Mohammed said, "How much do you want for just one?"

The Colonel, who had attended the Harvard School of Business, knew what Mohammed was up to. He countered, "What would you pay for one of these babies?"

Mohammed didn't yield from his strategy. The Colonel decided to go ahead and start the bidding. He said, "These are state of the art. See this dial? You can set the yield all the way from .1 kiloton to 20 kiloton. Depends on how much death and destruction you want to inflict. I think that we can let it go for ...," he paused and looked Mohammed up and down, spotting his expensive Eddy Baer shoes, and continued, "For twenty million. US dollars."

Mohammed winched. "Get real," he responded, "One of these is not worth that much on the open market."

"Then make me an offer."

"Eight mill."

"No way. Make it 18 mill."

"Ten mill, no more no less."

"Tell you what, let's not talk dollars. Let's talk opium. I'll trade for two tons of opium and 5 million dollars, US of course."

"Mohammed quickly calculated. Two tons opium would cost him 6 million dollars. Add to that 5 million. That makes 11 million. But then he thought, *What do two tons cost the Russians?* He remembered a deal from two years ago. *One ton of opium equaled 5 million dollars. So the Russian was willing to let the weapon go for 15 mill.*

Following the rules for closing a deal according to the University of Arizona course, Mohammed spoke with a tone of finality in his voice. "Two and one half tons of opium. That's my final offer. Let's shake."

The Colonel looked Mohammed in the eye. He thought for a moment, mentally calculating the offer. Finally he said, "We'll deliver the bomb to a port near Vladivostok. You are responsible for picking it up there. We'll trade the bomb for the opium at the port. Agreed?"

"Can you get the bomb there by the weekend?"

"We can get it there by tomorrow, if you want."

"No, the weekend. I got to get the opium part set up."

So we agree?"

"Yes, it's a done deal."

The two men shook hands.

When Mohammed got back to the hotel, he made a call on his cell phone to a contact in Afghanistan.

When the contact answered the phone, Mohammed said, "Cousin Hamid, this is cousin Jack." As soon as the contact heard the name Jack, he knew who was calling.

"Yes, cousin Jack, it's good to hear from you. How is Anna?"

"She is fine."

As soon as Mohammed uttered these last words, the large computers located at NSA confirmed by voiceprint the caller's identification. The recorders began to capture the conversation in bits and bytes. Unfortunately, at the same time, the two night-duty NSA analysts, who were deeply in true love, began to grope. As the young man reached up the older woman's skirt, she sat back on a keyboard. Neither had their eyes open for three minutes. The recording system went to pause. As he reached her g-spot, her gyrations caused the entire bank of screens to go black. When the young man finally saw the screens, he quickly restarted the system. The conversation, of course, was lost.

When he turned off his cell phone, Mohammed was pleased. The arrangement had been made to deliver two and one half tons of opium by air to Vladivostok. In addition, the delivery aircraft would fly the bomb to Havana, Cuba, where it would be taken by land to the Bay of Pigs, on the northern side of the island.

The operation was going smoothly.

Chapter 13

SPRING BREAK IN CANCUN

Ebrahimi met his travel companions, David Isaak and Bobo Lambrowski, at Miami International Airport. Although it was not yet noon, Bobo, already well on his way to being hammered, said, "Come on, let's find a bar."

Miami International is full of people on a twenty-four hour, seven day basis. They tend to fall into two categories: the locals, about half of which are beautiful women with hard bodies and that sexy Latina look, and the tourists, mostly heading for some Royal Caribbean cruise liner, average weight 205 pounds or returning from some Royal Caribbean cruise liner, average weight 227 pounds.

In his rush to find a bar, Bobo bumped into a prime example of the second category, a fat little lady, causing her to drop a bag that contained six bottles of booze, two Bombay Sapphire Gins, two Chivas Regals, and two Captain Morgan's Dark Rums. The lady shrieked with a New York accent, "Ya Basstad." This was an expensive accident. Factoring in the cost of the booze – $42.00, airfare - $434, cost of cruise, - $2,355, and losses at Gin Rummy - $17.00, the booze cost about $475.00 a bottle. Bobo's buddies knew how to handle the situation. They closed ranks behind Bobo and hurriedly scurried off, leaving the lady on her hands and knees, looking for the diamond ring she had purchased in St. Thomas and had hidden in the bottle of dark rum to evade the customs officials.

Ebrahimi stopped to help a sweet young Latina who was trying to stack her suitcases, seven in all, on a cart. He lifted the first one on the cart. She smiled. He lifted the second one, she spoke, "Thanks, you're a life savior. I'm in a rush to get home. It's my fifteenth birthday, and daddy coming to pick me up for a big party that's waiting."

Ebrahimi stopped lifting the suitcases, "You're fifteen years old?" he asked.

"Yes, daddy says that I look older. He also said that I shouldn't talk to strangers. But you're so nice."

Ebrahimi looked for his friends. They were about to turn left into the corridor where stores and bars lined the walls. He looked at the bags. He looked around to see if anyone who might be "daddy" was around. He saw a large Latino man, wearing at least ten pounds of gold chains around his neck, and with an "I hate Fidel Castro" tattoo emblazed on a huge bicep, rapidly approaching. With an Allah-given show of power, Ebrahimi lifted all five of the remaining bags in one move onto the cart, said "Happy Birthday," and ran off to catch up with his traveling companions.

As he turned the corner, Ebrahimi saw the Ernest Hemmingway Bar and Fishing Gear Shop. A franchise establishment, the bar was one of seventeen that sprung up from Miami all the way down to Key West. One of the boy's favorite trips was to travel south from the University of Miami campus, hitting every one of the bars. The concept was "least wasted person drives." The goal was to make it all the way down to Key West making only bar and pee stops. The farthest they ever got was to bar number seven, located at Hawk's Cay, about half way down the string of islands. It wasn't the beer that stopped them. By number seven, they invariably got hooked up with some babes and found it necessary to overnight, often six in a single room. Ebrahimi knew that the boys would be in this bar.

Walking up to the bar, Ebrahimi said, "Remember, Bobo. You promised to buy my beer for the entire trip."

"Yeah, yeah, I know. You changed my grade in the Animal Husbandry course. I wouldn'ta got an "F" if the prof never caught me with that sheep."

"Yeah, and you wouldn't be graduating if I didn't change your grade to an "A.""

Bobo didn't care; he was on a football scholarship. School didn't cost him anything. And the alumni association was giving him an extra three thou a month, to get tutor assistance, of course. Plus a bright red Mustang convertible to get to the tutor's house. He said, "Another round of beer, bartender. And include my friend here."

None of the boys noticed a man sitting at a table in the corner of the bar. They didn't notice him because he looked just like the other cruise ship customers, a white hat with the words "Captain, Royal Caribbean" in blue letters, red and white t-shirt that read "Dive, St. Thomas," and blue gym shorts with the letters "FBI" printed on the side. The man carefully aimed a small digital camera that was sitting on his table towards the boys. He looked down at a flat panel TV screen that was swung up so he could view it from a 45-degree angle, made a final adjustment and clicked the button.

Almost instantaneously, an image of all three boys was flashed back to a van that was parked in the "No Parking Zone" of the airport. Inside the van a specialist received the image, repackaged it and forwarded it via satellite to FBI headquarters in Washington, DC. Outside the van, its driver was arguing with an airport cop."

"I don't care if you're the friggin' FBI, I have orders to not let anyone park here. This comes from Homeland Defense. Don't you guys work for Homeland Defense? For all I know, you might have a bomb in that van. Now get it out of here."

"Look, dip stick, we're running an operation here. And no, we don't work for Homeland Defense. They may be here today, but come tomorrow they'll be gone. We don't need them."

"No body told me about no operation by the FBI or anyone else. If you don't move that goddamn van, I'll have it towed."

From inside the van, the specialist called out, "Come on, Agent Getty. The boys are boarding the plane. We got a match. It's Ebrahimi. And we got something else. Come and see."

The airport cop said, "You ain'ta gonna look at anything while you are parked here. Here comes the tow truck. Move it or loose it."

Agent Getty got into the van, started it up and drove into the underground parking area. He parked in a handicap slot near the elevators.

He climbed into the back of the van and asked, "What do you have?"

The specialist flashed an image on his laptop screen. "As I said, this is Ebrahimi. So we got the right guy. But look at this guy," he added, pointing to a short, blond-haired boy. This is a David Issak. He is a student at the University."

"So, big deal. I could have guessed that."

"Yes, but he also was an intern at CIA last summer."

"An intern, you mean, he worked at the Agency while he was a student?"

"Yes, they got a program where they bring in promising young students. It's like a recruitment effort to get good employees."

Agent Getty picked up his cell phone and dialed a number. After a few seconds, he spoke into the phone. "Agent Wallace, this is Agent Getty. I've got something for you. You are gonna like it."

As soon as he got off the phone, Irv Wallace dialed a number. He spoke into the phone, "Sidney, I think that we have a way to get to this guy Ebrahimi. Can you find out anything about a David Issak? He interned with the Agency last summer."

After a pause, Wallace responded, "Yes, David Issak. He's traveling with Ebrahimi.... Oh, he worked for you.... Outstanding young man.... Solid citizen.... No, I'm down n Miami. I'm leaving for Cancun now. Call me on my cell phone.... Yes, this is good news."

Agent Wallace looked out the window and saw the same airport cop writing a ticket. The cop said, "You're parking in a handicap space. Shame on you." Slapping the ticket under the windshield wipers, he walked away.

As the three young travelers entered the aircraft, the stewardess said, "Go on back with the rest of the animals. We'll be taking off in a few minutes. And yes, don't ask. I'll be bringing beer around as soon as the captain turns off the seatbelt lights. So lay off the call light."

The three young men found themselves sitting in row 25, behind three semi-babes. They put their carry-ons in the overhead rack and plopped down in the seats. Bobo said "I wanna beer," and pressed the call button. The stewardess looked back saw that no one was suffering a heart attack or throwing up, though there would be enough of that on the return trip, and ignored the signal.

The guys were silent, mostly because of incipient hangovers. Bobo and Ebrahimi almost immediately fell asleep. The three girls in the seats in row 24 were busily chatting away.

"So Sherri, 'What did you bring to wear?'" The questioner, Brandi Knowles – a junior at the University of Maryland, already knew that the answer would involve lots of expensive things. She thought of Sherri, also a junior at U of M, as a "rich bitch."   Not that she was a "bitch, she was actually Brandi's best friend, along with the girl in the third street, Nikki. But Sherri was rich.

Sherri answered true to character, "Well, I went to Nordstrom's and bought six bikini's, one for each day of our vacation."

Brandi thought, *She'll be begging me for stuff by the second day.* Brandi was mentally reflecting on the contents of her carry-on: anti-diarrhea pills, six bottles of suntan lotion, bug spray, and aspirin.

Nikki perked up, 'Oh good. You got lots of bikinis."

Sherri asked, "Why?"

"Well, … I forgot my bags."

Her two friends were of a common mind, *Should have figured that she forgot something. Typical dumb blond. Would forget her head if it wasn't attached to her neck.*

Then Brandi, the "mother-hen" of the group, asked Nikki, "Did you bring your passport?"

"No, it was in my bags."

"Do you have your birth certificate?"

"No, it was in the bags too."

"Oh shoot. You need some id to get through customs. What are we going to do?"

"Will my name bracelet work?

"No way."

David Issah was following the girls' conversation. He had an idea. He made his move. He tapped Brandi, the serious one, on the shoulder.

"I'm sorry. I couldn't help overhearing your discussion. I think that I can help you with your problem."

Brandi looked suspiciously at this intruder. "Any who are you?" she asked.

"My name is David Issah. I'm a senior at the University of Miami."

Nikki blurted out, "Miami sucks, Terps rule."

David asked, "And what, pray tell, is a Terp?"

"That's our school – University of Maryland."

"That's not my question. What is a Terp?"

Nikki confessed, "I don't know. I guess its some kind of animal or something."

David continued, "But anyway, I think that we can help you."

"What are you going to do?"

"Not me, we. You just gotta trust me."

"Trust you. Why should we trust you?"

"How could you not trust someone with a name like David Issak?"

"That's true. What do we have to do?"

"I want Nikki, that's your name isn't it, to go back with me to the lavatory."

"Oh sure, and join the mile-high club!"

"No, no. It's nothing like that. Brandi, that's what they call you, isn't it? You can stand outside the lavatory door. If I do something that Nikki doesn't like, she can scream or kick the door or kick me."

The girls turned to one another and whispered. David heard words like "…kind of cute." and "…looks harmless enough."

Niki turned towards David and said, "Ok. But no monkey business."

David opened the overhead compartment and took out a black carry-on with a University of Miami sticker on it. Nikki and David went towards the rear lavatory. Brandi followed them. Sherri looked over the back at the seat. She felt left out.

David opened the lavatory door and stood aside as Nikki walked in. He followed her, and with a less-than-graceful effort, managed to close the door.

Once inside, he said, "I'm kind of a short guy. You're kinda tall. I think that these will fit." He pulled out a pair of baggy cargo pants and a gaudy Hawaiian shirt. "Here, put these on."

"Over my clothes?"

"No, take the shorts and blouse off. I won't look."

She slipped off her shorts. She unbuttoned her shirt and took it off. He peeked. She smiled.

She put on the cargo pants. They were a little big, but she was able to cinch the belt tight enough to keep them up, although they hang low on her hips.

She put on the Hawaiian shirt.

"Don't tuck it in," he ordered. "The bras gotta go."

She reached up under the shirt, unsnapped the bra and pulled it out from underneath.

"Now, pull your hair back into a pony tail."

She made a ponytail.

"Pull it tighter," he instructed.

She followed his orders.

"Now, put these on," he said, handing her some sunglasses. Look in the mirror.

When she looked in the mirror, she saw an androgynous looking person looking back.

"Now for the final touches. Wipe off your lipstick and makeup."

As she rubbed the cosmetics away, she was amazed by the transformation.

"Let's see what Brandi thinks of the new you."

David wiggled to the side and opened the door. The stewardess watched the two young men exit the lavatory. She just shrugged her shoulders and said, "I don't think that two men having sex qualifies for joining the mile-high club, but what do I know?"

It took Brandi a few seconds to overcome the cognitive dissonance that she was experiencing. She said, "Nikki, is that you?"

"Yes, it's me."

"Why are you dressed like that?"

"I don't have the foggiest notion, but it's pretty cool, isn't it?"

As they stood in the back of the aircraft, David outlined his plan. The two girls agreed. It ought to work.

Bobo was officially hammered by the time the boys' flight arrived in Cancun at 2:42 p.m. David and Ebrahimi helped him off of the plane. They followed the three girls, no the two girls and one boy, no the three girls, whatever, towards the immigration post.

As they approached the lines, David whispered in Ebrahimi's ear, "See that guy?" pointing at Nikki in drag.

"Yeah, what about him?"

"I want you to stay behind him."

"Why?"

"Because I asked, that's why. It's a game."

David knew that Ebrahimi loved to play games.

"Ok."

"Then, just when that guy puts his birth certificate on the table for the inspector to look at, I want you to stick your finger down Bobo's throat. Make him puke."

"What? You gotta be BS'n me."

"No. Timing is important. You gotta do it just as the inspector begins to look at that guy's documentation."

"No way. I ain'ta gonna do it. You do it, if it's so important."

"I can't. I'm going through the other line. I'll be ready to raise a ruckus if things go wrong. You know, fake a heart attack or something like that."

Ebrahimi was adamant, "No way."

David was desperate. But he was also able to think quickly on his feet. I've been talking to the girls sitting in front of us while you were asleep. You see that redhead over there?"

"Yeah, what about her?"

"Word is that she gives the best sex in Maryland. Even better than Monica Lewinski."

"No kiddin, so."

"I can hook you up with her. I've got an inside track."

"You want me to make Bobo puke?"

"Yes."
"Does Bobo know about this? What if he's pissed and wants to beat me up?"

"Don't worry about Bobo. He's wasted. Will probably be happy that he made room for more beer."

The six travelers approached the immigration police. Ebrahimi pulled Bobo to the left line just behind Nikki. David and the three girls went to the right line.

Nikki was third in line.

Standing in line right behind them. Bobo leaned against Ebrahimi's shoulder. Ebrahimi was having a hard time holding up the dead weight.

Nikki was now second in line.

Bobo dropped his head to his chest and began to snore through his nose.

Nikki moved up and began to pull David's birth certificate out.

Ebrahimi reached up to insert his finger into Bobo's throat. He couldn't get Bobo to open his mouth.

Nikki placed the certificate down on the table. The Inspector looked at it. He then looked at Nikki.

David stomped his foot and pretended that he was putting his own finger down his own throat.

Ebrahimi shrugged his shoulders

The Inspector looked at the certificate and again at Nikki. He looked skeptical. "Where were you born?"

Although she had studied the certificate, Nikki forgot where David was born. After all, her memory, or lack of it, was what got her in this situation in the first place. She looked desperately at David.

David stomped his foot and pinched his own nose shut.

Ebrahimi understood. He pinched Bobo's nostrils together. Bobo gasped and opened his mouth. Ebrahimi jammed his finger down Bobo's throat. Bobo gagged, then spew out a ton of green, beer smelling vomit.

The line scattered. The inspector quickly stamped Nikki's forms and waved her on. He then closed his line and called for clean up.

David smiled as he handed his passport to the Mexican customs official. He followed the girls out to the luggage claim area.

As Ebrahimi was helping Bobo get cleaned up in the men's room, David met with the girls. They were giggling. "How did you ever think of that?"

"Oh, if I told you, I'd have to kill you," he answered.

He found out that the girls were staying out in the hotel district at the Omni Hotel, some distance from town. They exchanged hotel addresses and promised to meet the next evening at La Boom, the hottest nightclub in Cancun.

Nikki gave David a kiss and said thanks.

David waited for Ebrahimi and Bobo to return. When Bobo came out, he said, "I need a beer."

Ebrahimi said, "Let's get to the hotel first."

The three lads piled to a cab and headed for the Hotel Casa Maya.

David had been the one who picked out the Casa Maya from the list of sixty some hotels in Cancun. He chose it and the other boys agreed because it was relatively cheap, it was near town where the serious partying went on, it had a great beach, and, most importantly, it allowed the boys to take visitors to their room. Many of the hotels didn't allow such access.

When the boys got into their room, they dropped their bags, stripped down and put on swim trunks and galloped down to the beach. They were thunderstruck. They had never seen so many hardbodies. Ebrahimi exclaimed, "So many babes, so little time."

They began the afternoon rituals of posing while they played catch football, strutting about like peacocks and eyeing the babes. The sun burned brightly. David, who was pale skinned, began to redden.

"Hey, guys. I'm going back up to the room. See ya up there."

Bobo said, "Why don'tch go buy some beer?"

"We can get some later."

When David entered the room, he saw that the message light was flashing. He dialed the message center and heard the following: "This message is for David Issak. Please call your uncle Gotfried in Room 243."

David thought, *This must be for another David. But they said David Issak. But I don't have any uncle.*

Then he made the connection. *This must be Dr. Gotfried from the CIA. But why is he calling me here?*

David made the call. He wrote down a room number. "I'll be there."

He hung up the phone.

Chapter 14

GATHERING RESOURCES

John Smart knew that there would be trouble with dirt removal as soon as he opened up the sports section of the Washington Post to see if anything had happened in the pursuit of a baseball team for Washington. What captured his attention was an article in the lower left hand side of the Sports Page. It headlined, *Four-Day Bass Tournament at Occoquan Bay Starts Today.*

He turned towards Ahmad, who was making a cup of hot chocolate, and said, "We won't be seeing the Dirt Bagger boys today. In fact, we won't be seeing them for most of this week."

Ahmad asked, "Why not?"

Smart said, "Remember the first day they showed up. Do you remember the bumper sticker that was on the truck?"

"Yes. It was "Ranger 24.""

"Do you know what that means?"

"I thought that it was an elite military outfit. You know, like Special Forces or something."

"No, I'm afraid not. It means that these boys are bass fishermen. Ranger 24 means that one of them owns a 24-foot bass boat that probably cost him more than the house he lives in."

"So what does that mean?"

"When you hire builders or other helpers around here, you need to plan on them to be absent at least two times a year. One is during deer season. The other is during any major bass tournament. I'm just telling you. They won't be here this morning."

"But they didn't say anything before they left yesterday. And there is nothing in the contract that they signed that gives them the right to just not show up."

"It doesn't matter. They won't be here tomorrow. And we can't stop digging. We also can't just let the spoil pile up. The tunnel has got to be done on time."

Smart wondered why there was such a rush to complete the tunnel, but he didn't ask.

"Maybe we can hire someone else," Ahmad offered.

"You don't hear me. They'll all be at the bass tournament."

Ahmad asked, "So what are we gonna do?"

"We'll just hot wire the dump truck and the Bobcat and get rid of the dirt ourselves."

"We've got too much to do already." Then he added, "I can get a couple of my boys up from Florida. They can be here by tomorrow afternoon. They can help."

"The faster the better."

Ahmad called down to Miami. He let the phone ring twice and than hung it up. He repeated the call with two rings and hung up again. On the third call, he let it ring. After six rings, Hosein answered, "Hello."

Ahmad didn't use any names during the call. "We need the two of you up here now."

"I can come up. But the other one is not available for a week."

Ahmad remembered that the "other one" referred to Ebrahimi and he was in Cancun living his cover.

"Then you come up."

"Should I leave a message for the other?"

"No, nothing more than 'Wait for a call'."

"Where do I come?"

"Put the phone in the fax mode. I'll send directions in five minutes."

Ahmad hung up the phone and turned to Smart. He asked, "Do you have a good meeting place, preferably south of here?"

"How is he coming up?"

"By Greyhound bus, probably. The FBI is tied into the airplane reservation system, but not the bus system."

"I got a place south of here. It's a bus stop in Woodbridge,"

Ahmad asked, "Can you write out directions that I can fax to my boy?"

Smart answered, "Sure, let me get a pencil and some paper."

After five minutes had passed, Hosein heard the phone ring. He didn't answer it. The fax machine kicked in. After it fell to the floor, Hosein picked up the fax and read it, committing it to memory. He tore it into a few pieces and threw it in the wastebasket. Within two hours, he was on the bus, heading for Northern Virginia.

Chapter 15

RECRUITING EBRAHIMI

At 1:30 in the afternoon on the second day in Cancun, Bobo opened his eyes and moaned. He looked around the room. Both Ebrahimi and Isaak were gone. He reached over to the bed stand, picked up an open can of beer, chugged it, and belched. Throwing the bed covers back, he got up and stumbled in to the bathroom. He sighed a long sigh of relief as he took a pee. He put his left leg in to the right leg opening of his swim trunks, stumbled, and sat down on the bed. He took the trunks off and put his right leg into the left leg opening of the trunks. On the third try, he got it right. He stood up, pulled his trunks up, and stumbled out of the room to the elevator. As the elevator sped downward, he became dizzy and had to grab the arm of a matronly woman standing next to him. She smiled. He belched. She shrank back. The elevator door opened. She scurried out. He staggered out behind her.

Bobo staggered down the beach, looking for his two traveling companions. He tripped over a babe in a red bikini, kicking sand on her companion. Standing up, the young man said, "Hey, butt head, watch where you are ..." When he saw how large Bobo was, he sat back down on the sand, muttering "Butt head" in a very low voice. The red-bikinied babe smiled at Bobo.

Bobo staggered on until he heard someone shouting, "Bobo, over here."

He looked around but because his vision was blurry, he could not find the source of the voice. He staggered onward.

He felt someone tugging on his arm. He looked. It was Ebrahimi.

"Hey, man. Why-dya leave me?"

"I tried to wake you. But you wouldn't budge. Even poured water on your head."

"Where's David?"

"Don't know. He was gone when I got up. Did ya ever see so many babes in your whole life?"

"Aw, these babes ain't nothing. You should have seen the babes that the coaches at Southern Cal fixed me up with when they brought me out on a recruiting trip. Now, them was babes."

"Wow, awesome," Ebrahimi sighed.

"Come on over to the towels. Let's sit down."

David, in fact, was in deep conversation with a babe. Overnight, Alexandra Pack had flown down from Washington on an FBI jet. A special joint CIA/FBI task force had been formed two days previously. The task force wanted to know what Ahmad and his companions were up to. Their first operation had the goal of recruiting Ebrahimi. The way to get to the young Iranian was through his friend David. Alex had been designated to serve David's contact. She had been specifically instructed to stick to passing orders and messages back and forth. The important issues would be left to the men, who were seasoned operatives who knew what to do.

At 7:30 a.m. David quietly left the room where Bobo and Ebrahimi were both deeply involved in synchronized snoring and went to the room identified to him during the previous night's phone call. He knocked on the door. It was opened. Before him stood one of the most beautiful women he had ever seen, even though she had all her clothes on. He thought that she looked like a young Ashley Judd. And even an older Ashley Judd was a major babe in his estimate. She beckoned him in without speaking and closed the door.

She turned to him, smiled, and said, "I'm Alexandra Pack."

He responded, "I'm … ah, I'm … ah."

She said, "Yes, I know. You're David Isaak. I know all about you."

David said, "Why are we meeting … I mean why are you talking to me … I mean, why did you call me?" What he thought was, *Why would this major babe want to have anything to do with me?*

She smiled. His knees felt weak. She said, "Do you remember Dr. Sydney Gotlieb?"

When David ended his summer internship with the Agency, he had been briefed to not discuss anything that he saw or heard there. But she knew Gotlieb's name. He cautiously responded, "Maybe. Why?"

She said, "Oh, I almost forgot." She reached inside her pants pocket and pulled out a small leather Louis Vuitton credit card holder and opened it. She pulled out a card. It read, "Alexandra Pack. Central Intelligence Agency."

"We want you to help us on a special operation. I'm down here to be your liaison with the Agency. This is an important operation. We are working jointly with the FBI on it.

"No way," David said, "You don't need me for any of this operational stuff. I was just a lowly intern. I can't do anything."

"You set up a pretty good operation to get that young lady through Mexican customs."

David's face turned red. "You saw that?"

"Yes, we even videotaped it. Our extraction people are already reviewing it for ideas. It was well planned and executed."

"Anyway, that's not why we're down here. Do you know a young man named Ebrahimi?"

"Yes, he came down here with Bobo and me. But you already know that, don't you?"

"We have strong reason to believe that Ebrahimi is the member of a terrorist group."

"No way, not Eb!"

"Look at these photos. Do you recognize anyone?"

"No, should I? Eb said he had an uncle and a cousin in Miami, are they the ones in the photo?"

"These are the other members of the team." Pointing, she continued, "this is a man we know as Ahmad. And this is someone named Hosein."

"Come to think of it, Eb never had us over to his uncle's house. He did refer to a cousin named Ho, but I never met him."

"Here's a photo of Ebrahimi in terrorist training. That's him with the AK-47."

"Yeah, that's Eb alright. No bull, he's a terrorist." As soon as he uttered the words "bull," David felt embarrassed. After all, this was a classy lady.

The classy lady replied, "No bull, he's a friggin bonified terrorist."

"So what do you want to do? Arrest him?"

"No, that's the last thing that we want to do. We want to recruit him over to our side. According to our sources, Ahmad went overseas to Saudi Arabia. We're seeing a lot of funds being transferred from Pakistan and Sudan and we are sure that most of it is going to Ahmad's group. We need an inside man in this terrorist group so we can find out what they are up to."

"So you want me to turn on my best friend, my companion of several years, my confidant?"

Alex moved close to him. He could smell her magnificent fragrance. He could see her aquamarine eyes sparkle. She said, "Yes, we want you to turn on your friend."

David said, "Ok, when do we start?"

"Come on over to the bed. Sit down," she said as she patted the bed next to where she was now sitting.

She pulled out a bundle of papers and leafed through them until she found what she was looking for.

"First, let's take an inventory of Ebrahimi's characteristics to help us assess his weaknesses and vulnerabilities."

"Ok, what do I have to do?"

"I'll read of a pair of adjectives or attributes. You pick the one that applies to Ebrahimi.

"Ok."

"Introvert or extravert."

"Extravert."

"Analytical or intuitive."

"Analytical when he is sober. Intuitive when he is under the influence of beer."

"So I'll check both. It's situational."

"Yeah, it's certainly situational."

Alex worked her way though 98 pairings of attributes, collecting David's assessments of Ebrahimi.

She said, "Let's take a break. Would you like some coffee?"

"Yes, please."

After about five minutes during which Alex reviewed the list of attributes and David reviewed Alex, she said, "Now let's go to the second part of the assessment. I'll ask you questions about Ebrahimi and you'll answer as best you can. 'I don't know' is an ok answer."

"Ok, I'll try."

"Is Ebrahimi an alcoholic?"

"Ms. Pack, look out the window. It's only 9:00 in the morning and people are already drinking beer on the beach. Everyone here is an alcoholic."

"See what you mean. Let me rephrase the question, 'Can he handle his booze.'"

"No, not really. He's a wild man."

"How about his sexual propensities?"

"What do you mean? Does he like to get it on?"

"Well, is he into men, women, whatever?"

"Take men off the list. The rest applies."

"Does he exhibit erratic behavior?"

"Do you mean is he crazy? Tell you what, come with us to La Bomb tonight and you can see for yourself."

"What's La Bomb?"

David said, "It's the hottest nightclub in Cancun. You can assess him yourself."   What he thought was, *If I show up with this major babe, I'll be the talk of the University of Miami. And Jez, she works for the CIA. I never saw anyone like her in the Agency when I was there.*

Alexandra remembered her instructions - just be a conduit for messages and orders. Stay out of the operational end. But she saw the offer as a chance to gather first hand information about the target. And she wasn't going to pass it up.

Alex said, "I'll meet you at La Bomb. I'll be there at about 10:30. Pretend that you don't know me."

Brandi, Nikki, and Sherri ventured out of their hotel, heading for La Bomb at about 7:30 in the evening. The girls hit the strip for a while, stopping to dine at a small Mexican restaurant. At about 9:00, they looked through the doors of a place called Senior Frogs. The place was filled with people who were mostly wearing swimsuits. Sherri was hot to enter the place, but Brandi said that she would feel uncomfortable going in. There was just too much noise. "Look," she said, in horror, "The guys are pouring beer on that girl's t-shirt. Oh my gosh! You can see her … see her … nipples. Let's stay out of that place."

Sherri knew that she was going to have to work on Brandi. They passed by a small restaurant that had a long wooden bar running down the wall. Sherri said, "Let's go in here." Then she said, "Look at those cute little red drinks with the umbrellas. Let's get one." She winked at Nikki, who smiled with understanding.

As Brandi sipped her cute little red drink, she said, "Gee, these sure taste sweet. Don't they have a lot of calories?" Brandi kept a small notebook where she listed her daily caloric input, one item at a time.

Nikki said, "Nah, that's artificial sugar cane, you know, like Sweet-and-Low."

"No, really?"

"Yes, really," agreed Sherri.

Nikki said, "I bet that I can drink mine faster that you two can."

Sherri said, "You're on," and pretended to begin to chug-a-lug her cute little red drink.

Brandi, who was on the University of Maryland tennis team and was very competitive, said, "Me too." She set the umbrella aside and quickly finished off her cute little red drink.

Nikki said, "Oh shoot, Brandi, you beat us. Let's make it two out of three. She ordered another round.

Same three girls, same three cute little red drinks, same results, except this time after she put down her empty glass, Brandi issued a sweet little belch. "Oh, excuse me," she said. Then she added, "Let's go again. Last one buys."

After the third round, the three femme fatales exited the little bar and backtracked their path down the strip. As they were passing Senior Frogs for the second time, Brandi said, "This looks like a fun place. Let's go in. The girls found themselves wading in about a quarter inch of beer suds. Brandi slipped and was caught by two nice young men who felt her up as they lifted her off the floor.

"Nice jugs," one of them said. Brandi said, "Oh, you mean these?" lifting her t-shirt. Sherri smiled at Nikki and said, "Now, let's party."

Two hours later, the three girls left the bar and headed down the strip. Brandi was carrying a small trophy. As they came upon a place called La Bomb, Nikki said, "Weren't we supposed to do something here tonight?"

"What?" Asked Sherri.

"What?" Asked Brandi.

"Let's go in and maybe we'll remember."

The three girls snaked their way into the bar, which was filled with hundreds of people packed in. Everyone was dancing and drinking. Beer foam was all over the floor. Sherri issued a challenge to her two friends. "Bettcha I can collect more guys swim trunks that you can."

"Whatta ya mean, collect trunks?"

"Watch, I'll start."

She walked up to a guy with a crew cut and wearing a t-shirt that read Notre Dame Hockey. He was two-and-one-half sheets to the wind. She whispered something in his ear. He looked at her and then said, "Sure." He then pulled down his swim trunks and stepped out of them. He gave them to Sherri, saying, "Lemme have em before you leave. I don't wanna get arrested for showin off my thing. That's indecent exposure. Sherri looked down at him and said, "Looks pretty decent to me."

Sherri turned to her friends and said, "I got one. The score is one to zero to zero."

"Let the games begin," said Nikki, turning to three guys wearing Iowa caps, t-shirts and swim trunks. Soon they were only wearing Iowa caps. Nikki said, "Scores now one to three to zero."

For twenty minutes the girls hustled to rack up their scores. Then the band stopped playing, if that's what you could call what they were doing, and a nervous short Mexican man shouted in the microphone. "Please senoritas, please give the seniors back their pants. The cops is on the way. They's gonna bust you."

Sherri said, "Oh darn, this is fun. I got 12."

Nikki counted up her loot and said, I only got 10."

Brandi said, "I win , I win. I got 11 guy trunks and 3 bikini bottoms from girls. That's, uh, … 14."

Sherri protested, "Uh, uh. Girls' stuff don't count."

Brandi said, "I didn't ask, they just gave them to me."

The three girls heard the siren of a police car as it inched its way through the crowds towards La Bomb. They threw the swim trunks and bikini bottoms up in the air. There was a mad scramble for the apparel. In the mayhem, the girls oozed their way through the sweaty bodies and out the door.

Ebrahimi grabbed a pair of red trunks that were two sizes too small and wiggled his way into them. David Issak looked at him and said, "You can't wear those?"

"I gotta," Ebrahimi said, "The cops are coming."

"But those say Nebraska on them. What if someone from Miami sees you in them?"

"Oh, crap," he said, "I'd rather get arrested."

Another student standing behind Ebrahimi said, "Here, trade me." They swapped shorts, "Miami for Nebraska." Both were tying the drawstrings just as the cops walked into La Bomb.

David stood over in the corner quietly shouting at an attractive young lady wearing a Georgetown t-shirt. He said, "See what I mean? When Eb drinks more than three beers, he becomes a wild man."

"How many has he had?" Alex asked.

"At least seven, probably more."

Alex said, "I've seen enough for tonight. I'll go home and begin writing an assessment. I'll see you in the morning."

"Can I walk you back to the hotel?" David asked, hoping for a yes.

He got a no. "No you better stay with Ebrahimi. Keep him out of jail."

"Ok, how about breakfast."

"Sure," Alex answered, "See you in the small restaurant in the hotel at, say 7:30?"

"Goodnight," David said, aching for a good night kiss that was not to come.

Chapter 16

JASMINE

Workers at most of the hotels in Cancun, expected that things would be slow in the mornings during Spring Break. The Omni Hotel was no exception. The breakfast bar was almost void of guests, allowing the hotel help to snitch rolls, donuts, and éclairs. There were three young women, dressed in conservative clothes emblazed with Brigham Young University, sat in the corner of the bar talking to their boyfriend, Charles. But that was it.

Upstairs, on the seventh floor, room 724, to be exact. Three young nubile, but exhausted bodies lay asleep. Normally, Brandi would have been first up, rising at 0 dark thirty in the morning so she could shower and apply her suntan oil and bug spray before Sherri took over the bathroom. Sherri was a well-known repeat-offender bathroom hog. Nikki, on the other hand, was an au natural gal, who used little makeup and could be in and out of the bathroom in record time, say one hour.

But this morning Brandi lay comatose as both Sherri and Nikki did their magical things that girls do to make themselves noticeable to members of the other sex. At 11:35, Sherri became worried, and shook Brandi's shoulders. Brandi muttered, "The bikinis do too count," and fell back asleep. At 12:07, Nikki reshook Brandi and said, "Get up, it's beach time."

Brandi opened her eyes. "Oh," she said, "I'm dying."

"You're not dying," Sherri said, "You'll survive."

Brandi looked at the statue that she was holding, "What's this?" she asked.

"Don't you remember?" Nikki said.

"Yeah," Sherri added, "You took second place in a wet t-shirt contest last night."

Snapping fully awake, Brandi gasped, "I did what?"

"Don't you remember? Senior Frogs. Standing on bar with five other girls. Guys shaking beers. Beers spewing all over you. Wet t-shirts. Second place."

"Yeah, you'da got first place if you hadn't slipped and fell off the bar during the final face off."

"Oh My God. Did anyone see me?"

"Only about a hundred other people. They had a TV crew there too. Something about making a video *GGW*."

"Yeah, that means *Girls Gone Wild*."

"Oh My God."

"Hey, you're a star. Might even make MTV."

"Oh, my God."

Except for David Issak, who was up and at em at 7:00 in the morning, things were equally slow to start in room 1242 at the Hotel Casa Maya. Bobo and Ebrahimi were again engaged in synchronized snoring while David plotted with Alex down on the terrace that was adjacent to the hotel coffee bar.

Alex said, "I've wracked my brain and can't find a way to get to Ebrahimi. He has all the weaknesses, sex, booze, lack of character. But he doesn't care. So we can't hold anything over his head."

"You're right about that. If you had compromising pictures, he would just want copies to put up on the fraternity bulletin board."

"Is there anything that he really wants or cares for?'

"What do you mean?"

"Can we buy him off?"

"Right now he doesn't care about money. He's having too much time living la dolce vita."

"Ok, but is there anything that he wants but can't have?"

"No, I can't think of anything."

"Well think harder.   What does he like to talk about?"

"Well, girls, broads, babes, you know. You saw him last night."

"So, can we use that to entice him?"

"Hey, he gets all the girls he can handle."

"Is there any special one? One he talks about a lot. Maybe even obsesses on."

"Yes, in fact, there is one."

"Who's that?'

"You ever watch *Baywatch*?"

"Don't tell me he's hot for that blond that looks like a hooker."

"No, he is deeply in love with, desires to the max, is hot for, obsesses on – to use your words … Jasmine Breeze."

"Oh, she's the pretty one, the one that plays Caroline on the show."

"Yeah, Eb knows every line in every *Baywatch* episode that she has been in. Whenever we have reruns on the TV, he says her lines before she can get them out."

Alex thought for a minute. Then she said, "David, here's what we're going to do." She outlined her plan…

David returned to his room at ten o'clock, eleven fifteen, and twelve thirty, when he finally found his roomies awake. He said, "Get dressed.

Let's go down for lunch."

Bobo answered, "I need a beer."

"These are hot. Let's get cold ones down stairs."

Ebrahimi and David helped Bobo to the elevator and down through the lobby to the restaurant. They went through the restaurant and out onto its deck that overlook the ocean. They sat down at a table with an umbrella and waited for the waitress to come over. When she arrived, she started to say, "May I take …"

Bobo interrupted her and said, "Bring us beers, big ones, first. Then we'll order."

Just as the beers came, so did an attractive young woman with dark hair and wearing a t-shirt that had Georgetown printed across her perfect chest. She walked over to Bobo and said, "Aren't you Bobo Lambrowski, the famous quarterback?"

Bobo looked her up and down. "Yeah, that's me."

Ebrahimi looked her up and down and thought, *Bobo has all the luck.*

David asked her, "How do you know Bobo?"

She answered, "I'm taking politics at Georgetown. Someday I'll be a senator. Right now I'm studying polling techniques."

Bobo thought, *I've never banged a senator before. Least I don't think so.*

David asked, "So, what does that have to do with Bobo."

She answered, "Well, my current project is to compare how the polls rank Heisman candidates before the Trophy is awarded to the actual outcomes. I look at things like ranking in Sports Illustrated, how much money the university pays to advertise its favorite candidate and the like. Bobo is one of my subjects."

"So what are Bobos chances this year?"

"I don't think the Heisman's is his this year. But he is a strong candidate for next year."

"This project sounds hard."

"Not as hard as my last one."

"Oh, what was that?"

"I spent a semester in Hollywood and Hawaii. I worked on the set of *Baywatch*."

The minute she said the word "*Baywatch*," Ebrahimi sat up and began to stare at the young woman. "You were on the set of *Baywatch*?"

"Yes, for almost six months of shooting. I was looking at factors that stimulate the American male to watch the show. Turns out that the factors are cross-cultural. Men around the world watch the show for the same reasons."

"What's that?"

"They have such talented actors and actresses."

Ebrahimi said, almost shouted, "You didn't meet Jasmine Breeze, did ya?"

"Yes, we became friends. Jasmine showed me how to wear my hair. Do you like it?"

"Jez, you know Jasmine Breeze. I'm her biggest fan in the whole wide world. I've watched all the reruns."

David said, "Yes. Eb knows all the lines to all the shows."

"No, that's impossible."

"Na-ha. He knows them all, trust me.

"Alright, I was there when they filmed … uh … an episode named … uh … *Hijacked*.

Ebrahimi smiled. "That's when Caroline, who quits working as a lifeguard to go on a soap opera called *Shannon's Hope* then decides that she didn't like the acting life and wants to get her job back as a life guard. So she's carrying her bag and some asshole comes by and steals it. So she gets back with J.D. and then Taylor catches them kissin in the ladies room. So Taylor's pissed. She's that bitch that no one likes. So she tells J.D. that she busted him in the ladies room so he's gotta work switchboard. She give him a look before turning to go. When she turns her back, J.D. gives her the bird, not really, just a look. Anyway, after some other stuff happens, Mitch tells Caroline, 'Welcome back to the team.' Then some jerk hijacks her truck so she chases him and Mitch chases him and he pulls a gun and scares the crap out of both of them so he gets away. So later that night, Caroline climbs in the rack and starts reading a magazine. J.D. comes in and slides in beside her. He ties to put the moves on her but she says no and says she was bothered that someone robbed her. So the next day, Caroline sees the guy that robbed her and chases him, but he's the wrong guy."

"Yes, that's *Hijacked*. You really know your stuff. By the way, my name is Alexandra. I already know who Bobo is. And you guys are?"

"I'm Ebrahimi."

"And I'm David. We're all from the University of Miami."

"So you really know Jasmine?"

"Is she a babe up close like she's a babe on TV? Are those boobs real?"

David said, "Eb. She's from Georgetown, not Iowa. You shouldn't ask questions like that."

"Yes, Eb, is it? They're real."

"Do you think that you could get me a date with her?"

"Well, yes. You seem like a nice young man. I probably could. But it might cost you."

"Whatda you mean cost me?"

Well, remember, I'm from Washington. Inside the beltway, you gotta give a little to get a little."

"Anything. I'd do anything to get a date with Jasmine Breeze"

David noticed that Alex smiled when Ebrahimi said those words.

"Tell you what. I have to go back and work on a computer program that I am writing to do regression analysis on my data. What room are you guys in?"

"Ebrahimi said, "We're in 1242.""

"I'll leave a message. Maybe we can link up later," she said, as she got up.

When she walked away, Ebrahimi said, "Holy cow. I might get a date with Jasmine Breeze. Holy cow."

Chapter 17

MAKING THE PITCH

That evening, Alex called Sydney Gotlieb at his home in Front Royal, Virginia. When his wife answered, Alex asked for the Doctor. Mrs. Gotlieb asked, "Is this *Hounds R Us?*"

"No," Alex answered, "I work with the Doctor."

"Oh, sorry. One of his coonhounds is sick and we are trying to get some medicine for her. The doc's out back giving her an enema now. Let me see if he is done."

Alex could hear sorrowful baying in the background, then she heard a loud "yap."

She could hear footsteps – heavy hiking boots. Then she heard the Doctor's wife say, "Honey, I told you not to wipe your hands on my dishtowels. Use the rags I put in that bag for you."

Then Alex heard, "Hello. This is Gotlieb."

"Hi, Sydney. It's Alex."

"Oh, hello Alex. Why haven't you called?"

"We've been busy. Things are going fast."

"What do you mean, 'things are going fast?' You know what the Chief of Counter Terrorism said."

"Yes, yes, I know. I'm just here to be a conduit for information. Don't do anything real. But Doc, we've got a chance to make a pitch to Ebrahimi right now." Alex described her two meetings with David Issak, highlighting David's assessments of the target. She gave a long description of Ebrahimi's behavior at La Bomb. Gotlieb was impressed.

Then Alex popped the question, already knowing the answer. "Dr., do you have any contacts in Hollywood?"

Alex had heard of the long history of "back scratching" that had gone on over the years between the Agency and the motion picture business. She knew that the famous director, John Ford, had made films for the Office of Strategic Services, the forerunner of CIA. She heard that John Wayne had applied to join OSS in the early days, and was surprised to hear that the Duke had been turned down – not macho enough.

Alex had also read the adventures of the CIA team that went into Tehran to secretly exfiltrate Agency staff from Canadian Embassy staff homes. Hollywood had stepped forward to help build a whole legend of telephone and e-mail backstops, storyboards, and scripts to support the Tehran effort.

Alex also knew that the back scratching was a two-way effort. CIA provided Aris Papricka, the agency's top guerrilla warfare analyst, to provide advice on how small units could take on and destroy large armies by using hit and run tactics. Aris had a plaque on his office wall that read, "With gratitude to Aris Papricka for his support in bringing the movie *Lord of the Rings* to the big screen."

Alex knew that Dr. Gotlieb was instrumental in helping launch the career of the second greatest comedian to ever live – Robin Williams (Pee Wee Herman being the best, of course.) This was an accidental launching. Robin had been a simple little unimaginative man with no future, no past, and no expectations. He was recruited to take part in an experiment conducted at Ft. Detrick, MD. Ten dollars a day and free chow at the enlisted men's mess hall. Dr. Gotlieb had just joined the Agency's Scientific and Technology arm and was working on a project with the cover name, MKULTRA. The project was set up to determine the effects of hallucinogenic drugs such as LSD on people. Could these drugs, for example, make a spy reveal all of his secrets?

Mr. Williams was the last subject to participate in the experiment. Actually, he didn't even know that he was being infused with the drugs. In fact, none of the subjects were ever informed of what was happening to them. The key to the whole operation was the mess hall. Embedded in the morning's favorite offering, SOS (known as 'stuff on a shingle' in mixed company and something more racy amongst the men in the barracks) were healthy doses of the drug of the day.

Mr. William's behavior changed dramatically during the two weeks that he chowed down on the SOS. He began to draw multicolored pictures, then to sing songs. When he started to claim that he was from outer space (something about being Mork from Ork), the scientific team decided to cut down on his daily dosages. But it was too late; the change was complete. Although Mr. Williams will violently deny his participation in any experiment conducted by the Agency, the case is well documented under the code name MKULTRA. Alex had read the files. She knew that she could not discuss them with any unclassified individual. The public would have to wait for the story of Mr. Williams's metamorphoses until the year 2017, when the files will be declassified and turned over to the National Archives. Only then will the world know of CIA's greatest contribution to the World of Arts.

Alex's mind stopped wandering when she heard the doctor respond that, "Yes, I have some good contacts out in Hollywood. Why do you ask?"

Alex asked, "Doctor, have you ever watched the TV show *Baywatch*?"

"Of course. I'm a man aren't I? Normally I keep the *Outdoor Living Network* on so I can catch any dog breeding and training shows, but I don't miss an episode of *Baywatch*."

Alex told Sydney about Ebrahimi's obsession with for Jasmine Breeze.

"I fully understand. She's hot!" the Doctor said.

"What are the chances that we can set Ebrahimi up with her? You know, just for a date? Nothing more.   Then we got a hook to catch him with. Then all we'll need to do is slowly reel the line in."

"I'm with you. But none of this slowly reeling him in. We're getting reports. Something bad is about to happen. We don't know when or where, but we know it's soon. So it's set the hook and yank the fish in."

"You get the bait. I'll get the hook and line ready."

"Ok, Let me make some calls. I'll get back to you later this evening."

"I'll be waiting. Thanks, Doc."

"No, thank you. I'll try to make things ok at this end."

Alex hung up the phone and laid down for a catnap. She knew that it would be a long night.

Up in Front Royal, Sydney Gotlieb began to make a series of calls and collected a wealth of information about the young actress. Finally, he got a name and telephone - Al Brandstein. This was Jasmine Breeze's agent. He made the call.

"Hello."

"Good evening. This is Dr. Sydney Gotlieb. Aaron Spielberg gave me your number. He said to use his name."

"Ok, how can I help you?"

"It's your client, Jasmine Breeze."

"Oh crap, what kind of trouble is she in now?"

"No trouble, we just need her help?"

"And who is we?"

"I'm with the Central Intelligence Agency."

Brandstein was silent for a full twenty seconds. Gotlieb waited. Then Brandstein spoke, "What do you want Jasmine for?"

Without giving names, places, or organizations, Gotlieb outlined how the Agency, the President, and the entire country needed to recruit a member of a certain organization. He then said that after days of assessing what could be used to make this member of this certain organization turn against that certain organization and help us, us being America.

Brandstein said, "So you want to use Jasmine as bait?"

"Why, yes. In a nutshell, that's the plan."

"Would she be safe?"

"Absolutely, We're CIA. You can trust us."

"That's the problem. You are CIA and I don't trust you. It will cost you a lot to get her services."

"Won't she do it for God and Country?"

"Yes, but it will still cost you. She's in the middle of a shooting of a new TV show."

Gotlieb got tough. "By the time we got special funds through to pay for this, the target would be irrelevant. But there is something that we can do, and right now."

"And what's that?"

"You know that drug possession charge that got her three-years probation? We can make that go away. The charge, the record, the probation, all of it."

"You can do that?"

"Yes, this is a joint CIA and FBI operation. We can do anything."

"Let me call her."

"You got to do it now. Time is absolutely essential. She's gotta come to Washington. We'll only need her for a couple of days. We can make it over a weekend. The FBI jet can fly her out and back."

"I'll get back to you in half an hour."

Sydney hung up the phone and went out to check on his favorite female bitch, a sleek brown coonhound named Alice. He noted that she seemed to be feeling better since the enema. He scratched her ears. She crooned. After a while he heard the phone ring and started for the house. His wife called out, "Sydney, it's for you."

Sydney picked up the phone and said, "Hello."

"Doctor Gotlieb. This is Al Brandstein. Jasmine said that she is ready to stand up and be counted. But she wants two assurances. They are both deal breakers."

"What are they?"

"First, she needs to be sure that this deal doesn't include her being forced to have sexual contact."

"Tell her that there will be no, I repeat, no monkey business. All she has to do is go on a date with someone. We'll have someone else within twenty feet of her all the time."

"The date is with a man?"

"Of course, a young man. What's the second condition?"

Jasmine says that she wants to be put up both nights at the White House."

"What?" Sydney exclaimed.

"She wants to sleep in the White House."

"Why?"

"She says that is the only place she would feel safe. She thinks that she would be safe from perverts if she's in the President's mansion."

"Obviously, Jasmine Breeze was not a history major in college."

Gotlieb made an on-the-spot decision. "Tell her it's a deal."

"Remember, no White House, no date."

"Tell her it's a deal." Sydney knew that this would be a difficult obstacle. Usually White House overnights go to people who contribute $100K to the or more to the party in power. But he had some strings to pull.

He knew where the dirty laundry was. He picked up the phone and called the Director of Central Intelligence.

Just after two a.m., the telephone ringing awakened Alex. She answered, "This is Alex."

"Sydney here. I've got everything set up. Jasmine will be the bait. He can meet her here in D.C. two days from now. We'll fly him up by private jet and get him back in time for him to make his flight from Cancun to Miami."

"That's great news. Can you set the hook and reel him in by yourself?"

"Yes, for God's sake, keep the gumshoes away. They'll stick out like a sore thumb if they come down here."

"I'll do my best. Good luck fishing."

"Thanks Sydney. Goodbye."

Chapter 18

SINKING THE HOOK

At 7:30 in the morning, Alex sat down with David Issak on the patio next to the small restaurant in the hotel. Except for about ten comatose bodies, strewn around like fallen flowers, the beach was empty. Alex started the conversation. "We can give Ebrahimi what he wants."

David spoke in awe. "Do you mean, he's gonna get a date with Jasmine Breeze?"

"Yes, it's all set up. But not till we set a trap for him."

"Whatta you mean, a trap?"

Alex outlined the plan. David expressed some reluctance at setting up his friend and fraternity brother. Alex leaned closer to him, reached out and stuck her finger under his shirtsleeve, and twirled it a little. She said, "We've got to do this."

David looked into her eyes and sighed, "Yes, Ok, You're right. We gotta do this."

The plan began with a direct frontal attack. Hit him hard and hit him fast. At 10:32, David burst though the door of room 1242 and loudly announced, "Come on Eb. Get dressed. I've got some good news for you."

"Whaaat?" Ebrahimi sleepily said.

Bobo didn't stir. David heard no snoring. He hoped that Bobo was still alive, but there was no time to worry about that. He and Eb had things to do, places to go, people to see.

In three minutes, the two boys moved down the hall, into the elevator, and exited on the 7th floor. David banged on the door of room 710. Alex answered the door and said, "Come in guys. I was expecting you."

In rooms 708 and 712, video recorders were capturing images from six tiny cameras that covered every part of room 710. Twelve audio devices were picking up every sound in the room.

Ebrahimi looked like he was still in the twilight zone. David said, "Alex, you got any coffee?"

"Sure, there's some over by the sink. Help yourself."

Alex began to dangle the hook and bait. "So Eb, you still want a date with Jasmine?"

"Oh, jez, oh yeah, do I. I dreamed about her all night long. Dreamed that I was there to stop the jerk that stole her suitcase and that she rewarded me with a big kiss. Then, just as I began to feel her tits, David, you burst into the room and woke me up."

"Yes, but that's just in your dreams. What would you say if I told you that I talked to Jasmine last night and that she wants to meet you."

David and Alex both noticed the Ebrahimi had instantly developed a woody. *"Good,"* Alex thought. *Now his brain is being dominated by his prick.*

Ebrahimi responded, "Oh yeah. Oh yeah."

"Well, it will cost you."

"What do you want?"

"I'm starting a new project. It's the last one I need to graduate this semester. But I need some information fast."

"What kind of info do you need? I'll give you what ever you need."

Alex knew that the hook was in Ebrahimi's mouth. Now she needed to yank the line and set the hook good and deep. She reached into her purse and said, "This is a picture of Jasmine and me."

Ebrahimi and David both looked at an 8 by 12 color photo that had been composed back in Gotlieb's office. Both Jasmine and Alex were wearing bikinis. Ebrahimi stared at Jasmine, searching every part of her body and tracing her outline on the roof of his mouth with his tongue. David stared at Alex in the photo. His heart beat faster. "She's a goddess," he said to himself.

Alex knew that the hook was well set. She began to reel the line in. "My next project involves the Middle East. You know something about the Middle East don't you?"

Ebrahimi's attention was focused on the photo. His mouth ran without much constraint being imposed by his brain. "Yeah, I grew up in Iran."

"Oh, Iran. That's the land of Omar Khayyám isn't it?"

"Yes. It was called Persia back then."

"Ah, the land of lovers."

"So what is your project?"

"I'm doing a survey of the impact on the emerging theocracies on the governance of modern Islamic states."

"So whatta you want from me?"

"Tell me about the mullahs. What are they like?"

"Well, in the mosque, the mullahs all tell us how to behave."

"They do?"

"Yeah, but in private, they break all the rules." Ebrahimi found it easy to talk to this nice young woman from Georgetown. He was feeling that his words with this dreamy woman didn't really count. Besides, he was becoming fascinated by the way she spoke, what she wore, and how she moved. She didn't do anything provocative, but he still was beginning to get the hots for her. David saw how Eb looked at Alex and began to get a little jealous.

Alex asked, "Did you ever read the Rubáiyát?"

"Yes, but I'da got in trouble if I got caught. But Iranians will never stop reading poetry, no matter who is in control."

Alex deftly drew out of Ebrahimi how the Islamic revolution had been a fight against the separation of church and state and how it had become a new form of dictatorship. He expressed his frustration of the irreversible liberation of women in Iran, but then he countered these feelings by saying how he admired American women for their beauty and freedom. He said that he had grown up worshipping the Prophet's golden age but now he loved TV and movies and all the technogadgets.

Alex had masterfully helped Ebrahimi draw a self-portrait of change. And it was all recorded on videotape.

It was now David's turn to give a hand at reeling Eb in. His job was to broach Ebrahimi's defenses against the CIA. He began with an end run. "I saw some of the same problems when I was working in D.C."

"You worked in D.C.?" Eb asked.

"Yes. And I saw some of the guys who were married to successful women and were frustrated because their wives made more money than they did, sometimes a lot more money."

"So, what was the problem?"

"Well, the guys liked the money. But they also liked the idea of being boss of the home. Their dads ruled the household and they wanted to do the same thing."

"Where did you work when you were in D.C.

"I spent the summer working for the CIA. And I…"

Eb stopped staring at the picture of Jasmine and interrupted David, "No friggin way. You didn't work for the CIA."

"Yes I did. So what?"

"The CIA is all a bunch of killers, baby molesters and Infidels."

"Where did you ever get that from?"

"The mullahs told us."

"Am I a killer? How many babies did I molest this week? Don't I believe in a Supreme Being."

Ebrahimi turned towards Alex and said, "Yeah, and I suppose that you worked for the CIA too."

She answered, "Not worked, I work for them now."

Ebrahimi almost began to cry. "David, you bastard. You set me up."

"No, Eb. I'm just giving you a chance to be free. To live the life that you want to live. I know that you do. I see how you function in a free society."

Alex added, "Besides, in a more practical sense, I really have set up a date with Jasmine Breeze for you. We're ready to fly you up to D.C. this afternoon. You'll be there for two days and then we'll fly you back down so you can catch the flight back to Miami."

Ebrahimi looked at Alex, then at David. He thought, *I'm in deep camel dung now. I'm sure that they've taped whatever I said. Crap, if Ahmad ever heard what I said about the mullahs, he'd strung me up by the balls.*

He looked at the picture of Jasmine and thought, *Well, if you gotta go, might as well go with a smile on your face. Boy, this is really a carrot and stick operation.*

"All you need to do is tell us what your two companions, Ahmad and Hosein, are up to. Then you nee to help us get inside the network."

"And then what's gonna happen to me?"

"We'll take care of you. We've got a great witness protection program."

"Could I be Jasmine's bodyguard?"

"That's not totally out of the range of possibilities. First things first. If we fly you up to D.C. for the date are you willing to be debriefed, to tell us everything you can about your friends and what you were up to?"

David added, "They've promised that they would give me the job of watching over you. I'll watch your back. I'll make sure that they do what they promise."

Ebrahimi succumbed. "Ok, I'll do it."

Chapter 19

THE DEBRIEF

At 2:32 p,m, Ebrahimi and David returned to their room to find Bobo
still sound asleep. They packed a few items in backpacks. David wrote a
note to Bobo. "Will be gone for two or three days on an excursion to
Tegucigalpa. It's an old temple where they sacrificed virgins. Looking to
see if there are any virgins left around there to save. We know that you have
those interviews with the Sports Illustrated group so we didn't even bother
to wake you. If you get lonely call Brandi over at the Omni. She's really
hot for your bod."

The two boys met Alex in the lobby. They all entered a dark blue
Ford Expedition driven by a middle-aged man in a dark blue suit, a white
shirt and a school tie. He was wearing 15-pound wingtip shoes. The three
co-conspirators were whisked off to a remote part of the airport where they
boarded a Learjet with no markings. Four hours later the Learjet landed at
Andrews Air Force Base. They were entered a dark-blue Ford Expedition
for the trip to the FBI Headquarters. On entering the building, they were
met by Irving Wallace, the FBI point man on the joint task force. Ebrahimi
was taken to a small room with a large mirror on the wall. Alex and David
joined with Wallace, Gotlieb and two more FBI agents in an observation
room behind the mirror.

Ebrahimi sat down in a chair. He looked at the mirror on the wall. He smiled, waved and said, "Hi, Alex. Hi, David."

One of the FBI agents said, "Turn off the lights in the observation room, for Christ sakes." The lights were dimmed. Ebrahimi could now only see his reflection in the mirror. He frowned.

One of the FBI agents in the observation room said, "Now let's see what the raghead has to give us."

Agent Johnson was tasked to interview Ebrahimi. He looked at the mirror and said, "Turn off the microphone in the observation room. We can hear everything you say in here." The mike was turned off. Ebrahimi now looked upset.

Johnson, who had a master's degree in counseling, started the interview.

Johnson: "What is your name?"

Ebrahimi: "Hassan Ebrahimi."

Johnson: "Where were you born?"

Ebrahimi: "In Tehran, Iran."

Johnson: "How old are you?"

Ebrahimi: "20 years old."

Johnson: "What's the name of the terrorist group that you belong to?"

Ebrahimi: "Wait a minute. I'm not saying anymore until I have a contract in my hands."

Johnson: "Contract? What do you mean 'a contract?' What are we doing here? Planning to build a house? You're a friggin terrorist, buddy. Consider yourself lucky if all that happens to you is that we throw you in the slammer for life."

Ebrahimi: *silence.*

Alex saw that Ebrahimi was slipping away. She fully expected him to start reciting from the Koran. She jumped up and said, "You all are a bunch of friggin idiots. Don't you see? We're losing him."

She yanked the door to the observation room open and stomped over to the door of the interrogation room. She yanked this door open and stormed in. "Get the hell out of here," she ordered to the FBI agent. Johnson looked startled. He wasn't used to a woman using such language. He looked at David who was right behind Alex. Not knowing how to react, Johnson looked at the mirror.

Alex turned towards Ebrahimi and said, "Tell them that you will not talk to anyone except David or me.

In the observation room, Gotlieb whispered into Wallace's ear. Wallace shook his head in agreement and turned on the microphone. "Agent Johnson, it's ok. You can leave now. Ms. Pack and Mr. Isaak will carry on the interview. You may leave now."

Alex said, "These guys are a bunch of butt heads. Let David and me help you through this mess."

She then called for a paper and pen. "Make sure that it's an ink pen. We're going to write a contract."

In short order, a notepad and a black ink pen were brought into the interview room. Alex grabbed it and began to write. As she wrote she spoke:

"Contract between Hassan Ebrahimi and the President of the United States. "

She said, might as well have this go right to the top.

She then said, "Let's keep this simple." And she spoke as she wrote, "I agree to reveal all my activities against the United States and its allies. I will give all information that I can remember about people, funds, and activities."

She said, "That's what you're selling. Now for what they are paying."

She wrote, "In exchange, the United States will give me $1,000,000 US, a job for life, and safe harbor in a place of my choosing."

She asked, "Eb, how does that look?"

He said, "You forgot the date with Jasmine!"

She said, "Oh yes, you're right."

She wrote, "The United States will arrange a date involving me and Jasmine Breeze, star of the TV series, *Baywatch*."

"She asked, "Does that get it?"

He answered, "Yes, when do I get the date?"

She answered, "Maybe tonight."

He smiled and said, "No kiddin!"

She added signature blocks for Hassan Ebrahimi, the Director of Central Intelligence, and the Director of the Federal Bureau of Investigation. She pointed out to Ebrahimi where he was to sign. He signed. She then told Gotlieb that the interrogation would begin when the contract was returned with the DCI and D/FBI signatures. Both Wallace and Gotlieb made calls. They talked to each other. After nodding their heads in agreement, Wallace said to Alex, "It will take about one and a half hours to get the signatures."

Alex said, "Ok, we'll be right here waiting."

Agent Johnson was assigned the role of running around getting the signatures.

For one hour and thirty two minutes, Alex, David, and Ebrahimi discussed football. Although Alex was a Georgetown student, and Georgetown wasn't exactly a top ten football power, she was remarkably up to speed on college teams, players, and coaches. She explained, "I really did do a project on Heisman candidates. I know all about Bobo."

Ebrahimi said, "I wonder what Bobo is up to? I wonder if he misses us."

In fact, Bobo did not miss them. He was in a hot tub in the penthouse of the hotel with a lady senator from the great state of Missouri.

As soon as the contract was delivered, signed by what appeared to be authentic signatures, Alex began the interview. "So, Eb. Are you ready to talk?"

"Yes Alex."

"Let's see. We got your name, age, and place of birth."

"Why did you come to the US?"

"The Ayatollah sent us."

"You said us, who came with you?"

"Ahmad and Hosein."

"Why did the Ayatollah send you here?"

"We were supposed to kill Americans?"

"How were you going to do that?"

"We were part of what you call 9-11. We were gonna fly a big friggin' airplane into the Federal Reserve Building in D.C. and melt all the gold there."

"There is no gold in that Federal Reserve Building."

"No gold, none?"

"What happened?"

"We missed the flight."

"How did that happen?"

"Ahmad had the alarm clock. It didn't go off."

"Why not?"

"After everyone went to sleep, I unplugged it."

"Why?"

"Would you like to fly a big friggin airplane into a building? Besides, I like America and Americans."

"Where are Ahmad and Hosein now."

"They're back in Miami."

"Will you give us the address please? Just write it down."

Ebrahimi wrote on a piece of paper and handed it to Alex who handed it to David who handed it to Gotlieb who handed it to Wallace who handed it to Johnson. Wallace said, "Have Miami continue surveillance on the house."

Alex continued, "What are they up to now?"

"I don't know. But something big is up."

"Why do you say that?"

"Ahmad went off to Saudi Arabia to meet with some big mucky-muck. He should be back by now. But I was off in Cancun and didn't talk to him."

"Does he know that you went to Cancun?"

"Yes."

"Will he try to contact you there?"

"No, I didn't leave any telephone number and he doesn't know what hotel I'm in. That way he can't screw up my Spring Break."

"Do you have any idea, anything at all about what Ahmad is up to?"

"No. Well maybe. We did a brainstorming session. When someone threw out, 'if we can't get to them from the air, and from the ground, can we do it underground. Ahmad got real excited, like we gave him an idea or something, and ran out of the room."

"Do you know why he got excited?"

"No."

The interview continued for four hours. When Alex saw that the questions and answers were becoming repetitive and without contradiction, she halted the session.

David intervened. "Eb, you gotta get ready for your date. She arrives in D.C. in about one hour."

Ebrahimi looked nervous. "Is she really gonna be here? What do I say to her? Do I shake her hand, or kiss her? What do I call her?"

Alex said, "Just be your usual suave self. Things will be alright."

Ebrahimi confessed, "I can't do this alone. Would you two come out with us tonight? Like a double date."

Alex smiled and said, "Yes."

David was more emphatic, "Hell yes."

Chapter 20

THE DATE

The dark blue limousine pulled up to the entrance of the Dupont Circle Motel 6. The driver, a middle aged man dressed in a dark blue suit, white shirt and school tie, got out of the drivers side and went inside to the receptionist area. The lobby was vacant. He rang a small bell that sat on the desk. There was no response. He rang the bell again. A voice came through the door of men's room. "Alright, alright, hold your horses."

He waited for another minute. He heard a toilet flush then water running and finally what sounded like a blow dryer. A young man emerged from the men's room. "Welcome to Motel 6. You wanna room?"

"No, can you ring Ms. Pack and tell her that the car has arrived."

The receptionist looked in the register through the list of four names, checked the room number, and rang the room. "Car's here to get you guys."

"She said that they'll be right here."

Alex was wearing black slacks topped by a red and white blouse that was cut low in the front. Both David and Ebrahimi were wearing tan Dockers. Ebrahimi had on a muscleman t-shirt topped by an unbuttoned Hawaiian shirt. David had on a dark blue Polo short sleeve shirt. They went out to the limo. The driver opened the door. As Alex slid in, she said, "Hi, I'm Alex. You must be Jasmine."

Ebrahimi slipped on the curb and almost fell down. He straightened himself up, bent over and looked in. There she was. And she was beautiful. Alex said, "This is Ebrahimi. He's your date tonight."

Jasmine reached across Alex and held out a delicate but well tanned hand. "I'm pleased to meet you."

Ebrahimi just stared. He was speechless.

Alex then said, "And this is David. He's my date tonight."

David liked how she used the word "my." He wondered what it would be like to be hers forever, and ever.

Jasmine smiled. *She does have good teeth,* David thought.

Ebrahimi just continued to stare at Jasmine.

Alex said, "I've thought about where we should go tonight. Jasmine, we both know that if we show up at any popular place, you would be recognized and we all would be mobbed."

"Yes, that happens every time I go out to a public place."

"Our friends have managed to get us a nice little French restaurant just north of Georgetown, up near Washington's National Cathedral. Does everyone like French food?"

Jasmine said, "That sounds great. And we'll be safe from the mobs?"

"Yes, our friends have asked the restaurant to close down for a private party."

"Good, let's do it."

David said, "Sounds good to me."

Ebrahimi just stared at Jasmine. She said, "He doesn't say much, does he?"

The driver knew where to go. He got lost anyway and it took them an hour to find the restaurant. He drove up to the back of the place, got out, and knocked on the door. The door opened, and the owner motioned the two couples to hurry up and come in. Obviously, he knew how to handle celebrities.

They entered the small and almost empty restaurant. The owner was apologetic. See that old lady over there in the corner. That's Ms. Whittenbottom. She comes here every evening for dinner. Been doing it for the last five years. Seems that Mr. Whittenbottom had been a real cheapskate and would never let her go out for anything more expensive than a Big Mac and fries. He passed away. She is making up for his stinginess by spending all of his kids inheritance. She was his fifth wife and there are some fifteen grandkids.

The driver said, "We asked that the place be closed for this private party. Get her out of here."

"I tried. She won't budge."

"I'll take care of her."

"Be careful of her poodle. He's small but he's mean."

The driver went over to Ms. Whittenbottom and said, "You're gonna have to leave."

She looked up at him and gave him an eighty-five year old smile. She said, "Your ass I'm gonna leave."

The driver reached out and gently grasped her arm. The dog, whose name was Precious, struck. The driver screamed as Precious sunk her teeth deep into the soft flesh of his hand. Blood dripped all over the table cloth. With his left hand, the driver reached across to his right hip and began to draw out an automatic pistol.

Seeing this, Alex jumped up, went over, and gently tugged on the driver's hand. "It's alright. Let her stay. She has been grandfathered, or should I say grandmothered in. Please wait for us in the car. There should be a first aid kit in the back."

The driver sneered at the Precious. The dog tried to jump at his throat but fell short when her leash, which was caught under the leg of Mrs. Whittenbottom's chair, ran out. The dog squelched and fell on the floor. Mrs. Whittenbottom quickly picked her up and said, "Oh Precious. Are you all right? That mean old man." She dipped her spoon in her crème de brule and gave the dog a bite."

Alex returned to the table and sat down. "Now, let's look at the menu and see what we want. It's on our friends, so order whatever you like."

Dinner went smoothly. By the second glass of wine, Ebrahimi began to speak. By the second after dinner drink, he was his own suave self. "This is friggin good liquor. What is it?"

"That's Benedictine and Brandy. Be careful. It's pretty strong."

This time, when the couples entered the limo, Ebrahimi entered first. Then Jasmine sat next to him. Alex and David sat together. Alex said, "Now we can go to one of several places."

Jasmine interrupted her and said, "Let's go to where I'm staying tonight."

Neither Alex nor David knew of the special condition that Jasmine's agent had negotiated. Alex said, "And where's that?"

"Oh, it's a surprise. Just wait." She pushed the intercom button and instructed the driver to "Take me home. You know where."

In less than twenty minutes the limo pulled up to a guard stand at 1600 Pennsylvania Avenue. A uniformed guard came out of the stand. The driver rolled the window down. It's Ms. Breeze and her party. The guard checked a list and said, "Ms. Breeze is on the list. Here is her badge. But I don't know about any one else."

Jasmine said, "Wait here guys. I've got a call to make." She got out of the limo and walked over to the guard shack. She said to the guard, "May I use your phone?"

Jasmine talked to her agent who then talked to Gotlieb, who then talked to Wallace who then talked to the head of the President's security detail, who then talked to the head of Homeland Security who then said, "Let them all in."

Jasmine had already returned to the limo and she smiled and waved as the guard waved them though the White House gate.

Her companions just sat there speechless. Jasmine is staying at the White House! And they were going in to see it.

The limo pulled up to the back entrance next to the helicopter pad. The driver jumped out of the driver's side, ran around, and opened the passenger door. The two couples got out. Even Jasmine was impressed by the fact that they were about to enter the building, and she had even dated Prince Charles and spent the night in the Royal Palace in London. After all, this was the home of every President except George Washington.

David asked, "I wonder if the President and his wife are at home."

Jasmine answered, "No, they're up at Camp David. I've been promised the place to myself. Come on. Let's go check it out."

The White House Chief of Security had already argued against letting any of these four people into the facility. He just didn't understand. How could they let a movie star bimbo, two spooks and a friggin' in terrorist in this place that he had a sacred trust to protect. But the orders came all the way from the head of Homeland Security. And Homeland Security was very powerful. Almost as powerful as the IRS. So he just gave up and said that he would follow orders. Orders were to monitor every move that they make, and record everything on video and audio equipment. In addition, every room that is entered is carefully searched as soon as it is vacated. An FBI swat team would stand by in the Executive Office Building incase something goes awry.

The Chief of Security greeted the two couples. He gave them a quick orientation tour, pointing out all the rooms that tourists see: the RGB rooms, the Library, the East Room, and the Diplomatic Reception Room. Jasmine became impatient and said, "Where's the bedrooms?"

The Chief of Security said, "You've been assigned the Lincoln Bedroom."

"We need a second bedroom."

"I don't have any authorization for a second bedroom."

"Well, call someone. Or do you want me to do it?"

The Chief of Security used his walkie-talkie to make call using a series of code numbers. "Star is requesting a code 17 in addition to the assigned code 17. Need code 12 to ensure that code 67 is set up."

"Roger." After a pause, "Code 12 OK. Assign code 23 to satisfy code 17. Who's going in code 23?"

"Spook One and Spook Two. Also add BigT to previously assigned code 17."

"Roger."

The Chief of Security said, "You have the Queen Bedroom in addition to the Lincoln Bedroom," pointing out the rooms.

Jasmine said, "Thanks. How do we get anyone if we need anything?"

"Just pick up the phone. There's one in every room, including the bathrooms. You don't need to dial. The White House operator will answer as soon as you pick up the phone."

"Thanks," Jasmine said in a dismissive manner, "See ya."

After the Chief of Security left, Jasmine said, "Let's go to the bedrooms and get organized. Alex, you come with me and you guys have the Queen's room. Don't do anything naughty."

David was extremely disappointed.

As they entered the Lincoln Bedroom, Alex saw a stack of suitcases. They were already emptied and Jasmine's wardrobe filled the rooms closets. Jasmine said, "Alex, feel free to borrow anything that you want." She plopped down on the bed. Feeling around, she said, "This bed feels a little hard and lumpy. Maybe we should switch with the boys."

Alex was still looking around. "They're really giving you the five-star treatment. The bed's been turned back. There's a newspaper in the solarium next door. Here's a pass that let's us roam around. This is gonna be fun."

David and Ebrahimi both were quiet when they entered the Queen Bedroom. They both were thinking about Cancun and wondered what Bobo was up to. Eb said, "I'll bet he's some broad right now." He was wrong. Bobo was in the hotel hot tub with three broads, one blond and two brunettes. It was a challenge even for a Heisman candidate.

After a few minutes of browsing around the room, David said, "Let's go get the girls and take a tour of the White House."

"Good idea," Eb answered.

David knocked on the door. "Who is it?" Jasmine asked, as if she didn't know.

"It's us. Can we come in?"

"Sure, the door's unlocked."

David and Eb entered the room and saw Jasmine wearing a Raiders football jersey and Alex wearing a short, pink and white Lisa Kline dress.

Eb said, "David and I want to check this place out. Wanna come with us?"

"Sure," the girls simultaneously answered.

Alex said, "Let's find the Oval Office. That's a good place to start."

In the White House command center, a voice came over the loudspeaker, "Spook One, Spook Two, Star and BigT are heading for code 43."

"Roger," came responses from four different locations.

Alex asked Jasmine the question that was on everybody's mind, "How did you pull off getting to stay here at the White House?"

"My agent gets me anything I want. I told him that I wouldn't go anywhere I wasn't protected from perverts. You can't imagine how often guys and sometimes girls try to do stupid things like feel me up."

"I know what you mean. Men can be such pigs sometimes."

David said, "So you think that you are safe here in the White House. That there have never been perverts in this hallowed building."

"Sure, they were all presidents."

"Well, Clinton was a president. What about him?"

"Yes, but he was different than the other ones. Besides, he didn't have real sex. He just got a ..., well ... you know ..., a BJ."

David said, "More than one."

"How do you know?"

"Last year I was at an all night party in Georgetown. I got to meet both Lorena Bobbit and Monica Lewinski. It was like Celebrity Night."

Eb involuntarily crossed his legs, "You met Lorena Bobbit? I bet she's a cold hearted bitch."

"Actually, she's a very nice, quiet woman. Monica is the wild one."

"So, did you get the real story about her and the prez?"

"Yeah, We all kept passing her beers and she loosened up. We were sittin in a big circle and she was tellin us the story just like she was Uncle Remus or someone."

"What did she say?"

"Tell you what. Let me give you a sex tour of the White House."

As they approached the Oval Office, David looked at a map of the White House that he had found in the Queen Bedroom. "Here, I think that here is where we should start the tour. On November 15, I remember because it's my birthday, Monica said that she saw the Prez in George Stephanopoulos's office. He was alone inside, and he beckoned her into the room. She said that she told him that she had a crush on him."

As David moved the group through the President's private dining room, he said, "Apparently, he picked up her signals and they went though this room."

As they moved into another room, he said, "They ended up in this room. This is a study. On the other side of that door is the Oval Office."

"Monica claimed that at first they only kissed and she gave him her phone number. Apparently, the Prez's libido moves slowly but surely, like a glacier because within two hours he called her and met her in the little study. That's when she gave him his first B.J."

Eb said, "Awsome. History was made right here."

"The cool thing about it is that the Prez was talkin on the phone to Representatives Chapman and Tanner while she was doing her thing."

Eb said, "Boy, he must really have voice control. I'd be spazzin out."

Alex and Jasmine just looked at each other. "Men!"

"Well," David continued, "Two days later, Monica and the Prez had a pizza party here, topped by another B.J." This time he was talking to Sonny Callahan."

"Who's he?"

"Just another Representative in Congress."

"What about the cigar? What did she say about that?"

"Monica said that she had been promised a cigar by a White House steward but he never gave her one. The Prez fixed the oversight by giving her one of his on New Years eve. She paid him back with another B.J."

"A couple of months later Hillary was off to Ireland to kiss the Blarney stone while the Prez was in the White House kissin Monica. That's when he presented her with the famous cigar. The cigar, I mean. he claimed that he never had any real sex with her."

He concluded, "Anyhow, according to Monica, they did it ten times, B.J.s I mean. Most of the times it was right here in the study or in the hallway outside."

Jasmine was defensive. "So Clinton was different. He grew up in the sticks of Arkansas."

Alex responded, "Sorry Jasmine. Such behavior is fairly common among our Presidents."

"What do you mean?"

"Well, let's just review a little history. What do Harding, Roosevelt, Kennedy, Johnson, and Clinton have in common?"

"They're all democrats?"

"No, they all had mistresses."

Eb blurted out, "No kiddin, I wanna be President."

David said, "You can't. You're not a native American."

"You mean you gotta be a Navaho or something to be prez? I didn't know that."

"No, that's not what I meant. You gotta be born in America."

"Oh."

Alex continued, "But the funny thing is that when a cheating president is in the White House, things are better for the American people."

Jasmine asked, "What do you mean?"

Alex responded, "Well, I ran the figures to compare the goodie two shoes to the sex maniacs. By goodie two shoes I mean Truman, Ford, Carter, Reagan, and Bush No. 1. By sex maniacs I mean Roosevelt, Kennedy, Johnson and Clinton. Anyway when the sex maniacs were in the national debt went down, unemployment went down, average income went up and even trust in the Federal Government went up while the opposite happened when the goodie two shoes were in."

Jasmine said, "Politics, I hate politics. Anyway, it's getting a little late. I'm tired. Think that it's time to retire."

On the way up, she whispered something to Alex who shook her head to indicate yes. When they approached the bedrooms, Jasmine tugged on Eb's arm and said, "You're coming with me." Obviously she was used to having her way, she didn't ask, she ordered.

Alex and David went into the Queen bedroom. "Looks like the stories you were telling made Jasmine a little frisky. So where do you want to sleep? In the bed or on the floor? You pick. I'll take whatever you don't choose."

David, looking very disappointed, said, "I'll take the floor. Just give me a couple of pillows and the heavy comforter. I'll make a cold, lonely little nest down here."

Alex looked sadly at David, "Sorry David, we got to keep this on a professional basis."

"I understand," he said. But he wished that he didn't.

The next morning the two couples met in the little sunroom next to the Lincoln bedroom. Breakfast was already in place. Two newspapers, the Washington Post and the LA Times were laid out on a small table.

Alex asked, "How did you sleep last night?"

Eb smiled, "Great. I was worn out."

Jasmine smiled but didn't say anything.

David said, "Alex, I heard you stirring at about three o'clock."

"I know. You didn't see him."

"Him, who him?"

"Lincoln."

"What do you mean Lincoln?"

"He or his apparition appeared in front of the bed."

David said, "No way!" What he wanted to say was, "Of course I didn't see him. I was sleeping on the floor," but he wanted to maintain a manly image in front of Jasmine and Eb, so he kept his mouth shut.

"Dang," Jasmine said, "You saw Lincoln. Now there's a story to tell your grandkids."

"Sorry, Eb," Alex said, "But its time for us to head for the airport. The flight to Miami leaves in an hour. We're flying back commercial. Jasmine has our friends' aircraft at her disposal."

Jasmine said, "I'll ride out to the airport with you all."

"What are you doing tonight?"

"I'm scheduled to stay here in the White House one more night. But it wouldn't be the same without you guys. I guess I'll go back to L.A."

On the way to the airport, Jasmine and Eb held hands. At the departure gate, she gave him a warm hug and a long kiss. He promised call. She said that she would be waiting by the phone. They departed. As the door on the aircraft closed, Alex saw a huge crowd gathering around Jasmine. A large, fat boy was trying to feel her up. The driver hit him over the head with the butt of his automatic. The boy collapsed. The door closed. Alex, David, and Eb took their seats. The airplane took off.

Eb said, "Jasmine asked me to be her body guard. I accepted."

David said, "That's great."

Alex said, "We've got some other business to complete first."

Eb said, "I know. I know. I'm with you all."

Chapter 21

THE GRABBER

The three travelers were picked up at the Cancun Airport and taken to the Casa Maya. David and Ebrahimi went back to their room to see if they could find Bobo. They hoped that he didn't grill them about their whereabouts for the last few days. They found him lying on the couch, snoring. The TV was on loud. Two local newscasters, a crew cut Robert Redford look-alike and a perky blond dressed in pink. The blond was listing police activities over the last 24 hours.

"According to Sergeant Hermano, spokesman for the Cancun Police Department, last night was a quiet night. There were twenty-two arrests for drunken driving, fifteen for indecent exposure, two robberies and one gator bite. Leaders by Football Conference in the contest for most arrests during Spring Break are:

- Big 12 –211 students

- Big 10 – 125 students

- Southeast Conference – 154 students

- Pac 10 – 324 students

1. Independents – 12 students

Our hats are off to the Pac 10 for reclaiming the lead. First and second place trophies will be awarded tomorrow. MTV will cover the event.

Mike Tyson will be down to preside over the awards ceremony."

The faux Robert Redford reporter chimed in. "I always liked Mike. He got a bum rap over the assault charge."

The perky blond responded," For crying out loud, he raped that girl."

"Hey, he served his ten years. It's time to give him another chance."

"What about when he bit that guy's ear off? It that a sign of rehabilitation?"

David went over and turned the TV off. Eb shook Bobo, saying, "Wake up. Wake up."

It took a few minutes of shaking to get Bobo to respond. He opened one eye and said, "Get me a beer."

Eb went to the fridge, got out a Budweiser, popped the can, and handed it to Bobo. He said, "Didn't you miss us?"

"No. Hey, you been gone?"

"So how did the SI interview go?"

"Whatta you mean?"

"The Sports Illustrated interview. Remember, it was yesterday."

"Oh yeah, I guess I missed it."

"No shit!"

Bobo said, "Yeah, and they had some of the swim suit models there too. Too bad."

David thought, *Too bad. Too bad. Jez, there were at least five of those babes in bikinis set up for pictures and Bobo slept through the whole thing. Damn!*

Eb said, "Come on guys. Tonight's our last night. Remember, we leave tomorrow morning."

When they tried to recall the events of the last night in Cancun, none of the boys could remember anything more than a blur of booze, babes and boobs. They weren't even clear about how they got to the airport. As they went through immigration, they saw Brandi, Nikki, and Sherri arguing with the Mexican Immigration Official.

David thought, *Oh crap. We can't leave them hanging.*

He spotted two middle-aged men in Royal Caribbean hats and t-shirts. He recognized one of them to be Agent Johnson. David approached Johnson and said, "See those three girls. They are witnesses to one of Ebrahimi's meetings with Ahmad. They are having trouble with Mexican customs. Can you fix it for them?"

Johnson said, "I don't have anything about them. I can't help them."

Just then, Alex showed up at the immigration point. David gently grasped her arm and outlined the situation. She turned towards Johnson and said, "Just do it."

Johnson grumbled, walked over to the Immigration Official, flashed a badge, opened a paper and showed it to the Mexican, pulled out his cell phone and made a call. He handed his phone to the Official who listened and then said, "Si. Yo entiendo."

The Official waved the girls through. David yelled after them, "Good luck girls." They turned, smiled and waved. Brandi flashed her breasts at David. He thought, *Now there's a girl who has had a life-changing experience.*

After clearing US customs and picking up their bags, the three lads piled into Bobo's red Mustang and headed for Eb's house. As they entered the local neighborhood, David noticed a dark-blue Expedition parked in one of the Handicap slots in the McDonald's parking lot. As they approached Eb's house, they passed two dark-Blue Expeditions parked at the end of two of the streets that serviced the area.

As they pulled into Eb's driveway, he said, "Looks like no one is home. Wanna come in?"

Bobo said, "You got any beer?"

"No, not here. And don't bring any in the house. Ahmad gets really,

really mad when he catches me with beers."

"Damn, I'd move out if they did that to me," Bobo said.

When they entered the house, Eb noticed a note on a small table by the telephone. It read, "Wait for a call."

Just then, Alex entered the room from the back of the house. She said, "The house has been under surveillance for several days. There has not been any sign of anyone here."

Bobo said, "Surveillance, whatta you mean surveillance?"

"We've got people watching the place."

"Oh yeah, like the coach does when he sends people up to Notre Dame to get movies of their football plays."

"Yes Bobo, it's something like that. Except, it's the FBI this time."

"FBI? No kiddin."

"What's up Eb? You been caught screwing with minors?"

"No Bobo. You know me. It's nothing like that. I'm helping the FBI. So everything is all right."

"Ok. You sure you got no beer?"

Two FBI agents entered the room. They began to search the house for clues. After a few minutes Alex said, "I've found something." She pulled a crumpled piece of paper from the trashcan by a fax machine.

Unfolding it, she said, "Looks like a map or something."

She read it. "It's both a map and instructions. Say's to take the Greyhound bus from Miami to Ashland, Virginia. Say's to meet at the Taco Bell at two o'clock. There's a sketch of where to find the Taco Bell. Oh crap, it says to meet the day before yesterday. We're too late."

One of the agents said, "Let me look at the fax."

Alex said, "Be careful of fingerprints."

The agent said, "I knew that." After reading the note he said, "We need to run this through the 'Grabber.'"

David asked, "What's that going to do for us?"

"The Grabber has a 80 to 90% success rate at determining things like sex, background, age and the like based on an analysis of handwriting, type of ink used, and other factors. Grabber is really accurate and has given us good clues in many of our most important cases."

Not wanting to look stupid, David moved Alex aside and asked her, "Do you know what 'grabber' is?"

"Not a clue. I'll go in the other room and call Gotleib."

When she came back, Alex said to David, "Sydney doesn't have a clue. He says the best that we can do with our computer programs is 60 to 70% accuracy. He says that we should find out more about Gabber and try to get its software if we can. That's assuming that the FBI is telling the truth about Grabber's accuracy."

Alex turned to Johnson and asked, "Would it be all right if we courier the note up to FBI Headquarters. We'd like a look at Grabber."

Johnson made a call on his cell phone. After hanging up, he turned to Alex and said, "We're supposed to give you anything that you want. So be my guest. Just make sure that there are no flaws in the change of evidence incase we want to prosecute these guys instead of just shooting them."

It took Alex and David about an hour to drive to the J. Edgar Hoover Building in downtown D.C. When they arrived, Agent Wallace met them. Alex said, "We got something for the Grabber."

"We know. Johnson called me. We're trying to find and fix the Grabber now."

"What do you mean fix? Does the Grabber have a virus or something?"

"Yes, AD."

"What's that? Something like the computer Love Bug Virus?"

"No, no. AD means Alzheimer's disease."

"Alzheimer's. How does a computer program get Alzheimer's?"

"Grabber is not a computer program. Grabber is a man. In fact, now that Grace Hopper has passed on to the great computer center in the sky, Grabber is the oldest living government employee."

David chuckled, "So Grabber is an old fart."

"Speak of him with respect. He helped us break the Lindbergh kidnapping. He got us the key evidence to get the Rosenbergs. Ethyl wouldn't have fried if he wasn't there to be a key witness. We sealed the fate of the Falcon and the Snowman because of his analysis. And we nailed that son of a bitch, Hansen, because Grabber said look for a dirty, rotten pervert."

"Lindbergh? Jez, that was a long time ago. How old is the Grabber?"

"First off, the Grabber, as we call him, is Al Osborne. Back in the twenties, he wrote a book on handwriting analysis. Hoover himself read the book and hired Osborne on the spot. Let's see. He was about 22 when we hired him. That would make him about … let's see … a hundred and three, give or take a year."

"Holy cow. And he's still working?"

"Yes, but we need to really hold his hand."

"What do you mean?"

"Well, like for instance. We've lost him and teams are out looking for him."
"Lost him! Does that mean that we can't get his help?"

"Don't worry. It happens all the time. Osborne has Alzheimer's and, although we keep him under surveillance, he gets out now and then. We always find him."

Wallace's cell phone rang. He answered it. After hanging up, he said, "See, I told you so. They found Osborne in one of the stalls in the fourth floor ladies room. Said that he was looking for his wife Edith. She's been gone for forty some years and he still pines for her. Now that's love."

"But if he has Alzheimer's, how can he do the handwriting?   What use is he to us?"

"I could explain. But it's better if you just watch. They're bringing him to the Tech Services Branch. Let's go down there."

The threesome entered a room where someone was firing a machine gun at a dummy. Wallace said, "watch out for the shrapnel."

They entered a small room with a large light table, several microscopes and some chemical test equipment. In about three minutes, a decrepit looking man with deep-set eyes that were unfocused was led in by two aids, one on each of his arms. He was slumped over and the aids were almost carrying him in. He was dressed in a green gown that was open in the back. The two aids were dressed in white hospital uniforms. Each packed a 9mm automatic.

Wallace said, "This is Al Osborne, also known as the Grabber."

David attempted to shake Osborne's hand but the mummified old timer failed to recognize him or his offer at friendship.

Wallace said, "Watch this."

He turned to Osborne and said, "Mr. Hoover needs your assistance."

Instantly, Osborne stood up straight, shed himself of the two aids who were holding him up, and looked at Wallace with a clear and concentrated gaze. In a raspy but clear voice, he said, "What does Edgar want?"

Wallace simply said, "The boss wants to know about this document."

Osborne snatched the paper from Wallace's hand. He gave it a once over glance and then placed it under a microscope. He seemed to look at each and every one of the letters in the note, pausing on the vowels. He then cut a bit of paper with ink on it and placed it in a chemical bath. He repeated the cutting on another part of the paper. All along, he made notes. Alex was impressed by the concentration and attention to detail that Osborne was applying to his analytic efforts.

After he was done with the detailed work, Osborne stepped back and looked up at the soft lights that filled the room. He turned on a color wheel that spun an almost infinite combination of reds, blues, and greens.

He stared at the wheel for about ten minutes, then turned it off and began to write. Alex could see the heading of the section that he was writing. It read, "Conclusions."

After he finished writing, Osborne handed his report to Wallace. He said, "Tell the boss that I'll be seeing him soon."

Wallace looked startled. He said, "Osborne never said that before."

When Alex and David looked again at Osborne, they saw that he had returned to his almost catatonic state. Alzheimer's Disease had reasserted its control over the Grabber. Osborne slobbered and said, "I need a nappy."

His handlers led him away.

After a moment of awestruck silence, Alex said, "That was remarkable."

David agreed.

They all went over the report. Osborne had written the following:

Evidence: Writer's normal language includes "ch" character and sound, like in Chernobyl or Cherinko. Revealed by natural movement of hand through similar characters.

Conclusion: Writer grew up with Cyrillic alphabet. Probably Russian.

Evidence: Writer uses wide opening on bottom of characters such as 'y.'

Conclusion: Writer is highly extroverted, bordering on loudmouthed.

Evidence: Writer uses force slant of about 15 degrees in writing.

Conclusion: Writer has a hidden life of some sort that he is covering up.

Evidence: Writer uses style 15 lettering.

Conclusion: Writer is about 52 years old.

Evidence: Inconsistency if width of characters shows extreme propensity for unethical behavior.

Conclusion: Writer is likely to be either a lawyer, politician, or car salesman.

Evidence: Analysis of ink sample reveals it to be Carpathian Alure. Empirical evidence shows this to be favorite of German high-end automobile businesses.

Conclusion: Correlating factors of unethical behavior and German high-end business strongly suggest writer to be sales person for Mercedes, Porsche, or Audi. Perhaps Volkswagen in large urban area.

Summary: At the 89% reliability level, writer of sample is male, 52 years old, lived in Soviet Union throughout childhood through teens, possibly closet gay but not likely, more likely working undercover in US. Probably involved in the German car market. Although not based on evidence, strongly intuitively suspect that the writer is married with one female child.

Agent Wallace handed the report over to one of the Agents and said, "Run this by Profiler right now. Confine the hits to a one hundred mile radius around the D.C. area. I want to see the hits in five minutes."

David asked Wallace, "Is Profiler another old timer senior citizen?"

"No," Wallace answered, "Profiler is a computer program. It's linked up to federal, state and local databases across the country. We can even sneak into the e-Bay seller and buyer profiles in cases of national emergency."

In about five minutes, Wallace got a call on his cell phone. He answered it and after a few seconds said, "So there are 22 hits. Get teams on them right now. Be discrete."

He turned to the others and said, "Hopefully, we'll have some good leads by tomorrow morning."

Chapter 22

DIMITRIY IS CALLED TO VLADIVOSTOK

Colonel Slavinski stood in General Kutusin's private study outlining the details of the deal that he made with Ahmad. The general was critical. "You only got two and one half tons of opium? For one nuke? I need to send you back to negotiations school."

The general added, "Were there any complications?"

The colonel answered, "The only warheads that we have left are the ones from Semipalinsk, you know, the ones that we don't have any codes for."

"Can we sell him one without giving him the code?"

"No, we got caught doing that to Saddam Hussein. Now the word is out on the street. There's a new standard contract that stipulates that anyone who buys a nuclear weapon gets the code key to unlock it."

"Who can help us?"

"Do you remember that young fellow from the States named Dimitriy Nabakova?"

"From the States, why should I remember him."

"He was here on the day of your daughter's wedding. He had a request."

"Oh, yes. The young man who had the sick baby. The capitalists had taken away his health benefits and he needed money to get the baby treatment. I remember him. Nice young man. But how can he help us."

"Seems that he is one of the best code breakers in the world. If anyone can break the codes, he can."

"Where's he at now?"

"He's in Virginia working some kinda crap job."

"Make him an offer he can't refuse."

"How far should I go with this offer?"

"Does he own a horse?"

"No."

"Well, Colonel, you go to the States. You talk to him personally. He may be an honorable man and repay his debt. If he hesitates, go as far as you need. But leave his kid alone. We're not animals."

Four days later Dimitriy arrived at Sevastopol, Russia. Dimitriy was curious. What did the General want him to do? In a way, it didn't matter. Dimitriy would fulfill any request made of him by the General. The money that the General had given, not loaned, but given Dimitriy had saved his beloved daughter's life.

As the helicopter lifted off the runway, Dimitriy asked the Colonel, "Where are we going?"

The Colonel said, "You really don't need to know."

As they flew out, the city became countryside with small villages. Then the villages disappeared and all that Dimitriy could see was desolate hills with little signs of habitation. As the helicopter made a broad turn and began to land, Dimitriy could see the triple fences surrounding a large facility. As they got closer, he saw the weapons bunkers, some with doors open. The helicopter landed near a bunker that had several people standing around it.

Dimitriy and the Colonel climbed out of the helicopter and walked over to the bunker. A large, menacing looking Sergeant stood by the bunker door with an AK-47 held at an angle against his chest. The Colonel walked up to the Sergeant. The Sergeant saluted. The Colonel returned his salute. Dimitriy didn't know whether to salute or crap in his pants when he saw the sign that hang over the bunker door. It read, "Danger, Nuclear Material Inside."

"What in the hell are we doing here?" Dimitriy blurted out, "This is a nuclear weapons site."

The Colonel was blunt and straightforward. "There is a nuclear warhead inside. It has a coded safety device on it. We don't have the code. The General requests that you do two things. The first is to break the code and make the bomb useable. And after you do that, he wants you to set up a timing device. I'll give you the details when we get to that point."

Dimitriy was visibly shaken. "I can't mess with the safety device. It has an anti-tamper mechanism. If I mess with it one of two things will happen: the warhead will self destruct, or it will go off and we will be blown to hell."

"The General has confidence in you. He knows that you can do what he asks?"

"I can't do it. Take me home."

"You cannot refuse the General's request. Remember that your wife is back home alone with your sweet young daughter. She's at her aunt's house. Am I not right? That's in Los Angeles, I believe."

Dimitriy knew that he could not refuse to do what the Colonel said. With a shrug of resignation, Dimitriy said, "Where's the warhead. Let's have a look at it."

After three hours and twelve minutes Dimitriy stepped back from the warhead, smiled and said, "Dimitriy rules!"

"Did you break the code?"

"It's done."

"Now, the General wants you to set up a timing device."
"That's the easy part. Just let us program a little something into this baby."

After thirty-two minutes of rapid thinking and typing, Dimitriy once again stepped back from the warhead. "There," he said, "It's done. All you gotta do is put in the number of minutes that you want to elapse between the time you enter the start code and the time of detonation. Then you put in the start code itself using this small keypad."

"And what is the start code?" the Colonel asked.

"007," Dimitriy responded. Both he and the Colonel smiled.

By the time that Dimitriy was flying back to the States, the bomb was on its way to Cuba. Both were flying the unfriendly skies of Aeroflot. On landing at Dulles National Airport, it took Dimitiry forth-five minutes to clear customs. On landing at Havana, it took the crate holding the bomb five minutes to be downloaded from the aircraft, loaded onto a small cart, driven to a truck, loaded on the truck, and sent on its way towards the northern coast of Cuba.

Chapter 23

THE HONEYPOT

The next morning Charlie Willbran and Rocky Stonehead were once again parked in front of the Smart Residence. The bass tournament had not gone well. Rocky was pissed. "I done told you to grab the son of a bitch before he wiggled off the hook."

"You're the one who lost the net. I coulda brought him in easy with the net."

"He was a contest winner fer sure. At least twelve pounds."

"You're right. He was at least fourteen pounds."

"Damn straight. Like I said, musta been a fifteen pounder."

"We'da won with him being sixteen pounds."

"Didja watch Howard Stern last night? Had that babe from JAG on."

"Oh yeah. She's hot. She can be my lawyer anytime. I'd like to get her between the bars."

"Didja see Howard? Had his hands under the table again. Don'tja know Robin likes to watch him whackin off."

"Let's go and see how much we got left to do."

"Hey, didn't we leave the Bobcat around the back of the house.

What's it doing over here?"

"I don't know."

"Damn, that pile looks even bigger than the first day. We ain't never gonna get rid of all the dirt."

"Well, let's get it on."

Inside the house, John Smart and the two ex-GRU grunts were watching Jerry Springer on TV. Ahmad and Hosein were in a back room responding to a mental call to prayers. Stanislav asked Gorky, "Do you think this Springer guy would put on a show for ex-spies and how their wives abused them?"

Gorky answered, "Da, and we could be on the show. My Ludmilla is prettier than that fat slob."

"A garbage truck is prettier than that woman."

As the Springer Show broke to a commercial, the genetic mechanisms that men possess kicked in and Gorky began to flick through the channels. He spotted a bevy of bikinied babes and stopped flicking. "Oh baby, baby," He said, "Just look at those garbanzas!"

John Smart came in from the kitchen and looked. There were dozens of young girls dancing around, surrounded by young men who were drinking beer and staring. Smart saw an older woman dancing with a middle aged man. She smiled at the camera and lifted her t-shirt to reveal a pair of cantaloupe sized breasts. He recognized her. It was his wife. And she was dancing around with Dr. Jim. The good doctor moved forward and placed his face between the sumptuous cleavage. She smiled. Smart's face reddened.

Stanislav said, "Look at that older babe. Now there's a set of boobs."

Gorky said, "Oh baby, oh baby." He glanced at a silver framed photo that stood on top of the TV. He looked back at the television screen. He looked back at the photo. He said, "You know, she looks just like the woman in the photo."

He looked at Smart, who was staring at him. Smart's mouth formed the unspoken words, "Shut the hell up."

Gorky looked away. Stanislav changed the channel back to the Springer Show, where a pair of fat mommas were fighting each other like sumo wrestlers.

Ahmad emerged from the back room. He said to Smart, "Now that the two men are back to remove the spoil, I'm going down back to Miami. I've got some things that I need to get done back there. Hosein will stay here and assist you. I've given him orders to do whatever you ask."

That evening, Ahmad flew into Miami International, traveling under the cover name of Rick Genesis. He rented a Cavalier from Hertz and drove towards the hideout. As he passed by McDonalds, he saw the dark-blue Ford Expedition parked in the handicap space. He remembered that the vehicle was there when he left. This was too much of a coincidence. It could never take that long for McDonalds to correct an order.

Ahmad parked the Cavalier two streets behind the hideout. Crossing through the backyards of several houses, he approached his house from behind. Hiding in the dark of the trees, he spotted two dark-blue Ford Expeditions parked at the ends of the roads that fed into the house's front. Being careful not to knock over trashcans, he climbed the back fence of his yard. After first spending ten minutes hiding in the yard, he moved to the back door and carefully unlocked it. He entered the back hallway that led to the kitchen. He carefully slipped along the hallway wall towards the front room, where he heard a TV playing. Stooping low, he looked into the room and saw the back of Ebrahimi's head. He could see the TV screen where two girls were kissing and pawing a single man as if they were the bread of a sandwich and he were the meat in it. Ebrahimi's eyes were riveted on the TV screen.

Ahmad remained low as he slipped up behind the couch. In a single cat-like motion, he stood partly up, reached around and put his hands over Ebrahimi's mouth. He hissed, "Shhhh."

Ebrahimi struggled to get free. The best that he could do was partially turn his head and get eye contact with Ahmad. The older Iranian put his finger to his mouth, making the "keep quiet" sign. He then tugged on Ebrahimi's arm, indicating that he wanted the young man to follow him.

Ahmad led Ebrahimi out of the house and across the back yard. As he climbed the fence, Ebrahimi tried to kick the trash can over to signal the FBI agents who were sitting in the cars. Ahmad caught the can as it started to tumble and once again gave Ebrahimi the "keep quiet" sign. They crossed the backyards and made their way to the Cavalier. They got in and drove off.

Ahmad saw that Ebrahimi was frightened. He said, "Don't worry. We got away."

"Away from what?"

"There were FBI spies all around the house. I saw them when I was driving into the area. Looks like we've evaded them. I wonder how they found us?"

"Yeah, I wonder how they found us."

Ahmad said, "We've got work to do." He made a call on his cell phone, got a telephone number and made another call with it. Ebrahmi could only hear one side of the conversation. "Hello. ... This is Ahmad... Yes, Allah Akbar ... I need to use Jennifer for an operation. ... Yes, it has to be Jennifer. ... I don't care if you had a weekend planned, this is important ... It will take two days ... Yes, she'll be safe ... It's just a quick 'honey trap' that we need to spring... I'll pick her up at your place... She'll need a weekend bag ... bikinis, etc. Ok ... I'll make sure that the Ayatollah knows of your cooperation. ... Allah Akbar."

Ebrahimi was now excited. He had met Jennifer once at a meeting of the Young Students for the Revolution. She was a first class, absolute babe. Her real name was Hazra, but she was given the cover name of Jennifer because of her remarkable resemblance to Jennifer Love Hewitt, right down to the doe like eyes and a perfect body. Jennifer was reserved for "special operations" of high importance. She would do anything for the Ayatollah and the Revolution.

Two hours later, Ahmad and Ebrahimi sat in the Cavalier outside a small brick house. Ahmad gave two short beeps on the horn. Within two minutes she walked out the door carrying a small backpack. Jennifer was just as Ebrahimi remembered, tall, narrow-waisted , with long flowing brown hair that swept across her shoulders. She walked with an attitude. She was hot and she knew it.

She got in the car. No one spoke, but Ebrahimi breathed heavily. Ahmad drove to a Motel 6 near the Miami yacht harbor. When he went inside to register, Ebrahimi said to Jennifer, "I remember you from the YSR meetings in Tehran."

"Oh, you're from Tehran? Were you at the University there?"

"No, my father was a mullah who knew the Ayatollah. Because of his connections, I was picked to come to the States for school last year.

"Where are you going to school?"

"I'm at the University of Miami."

"They really have a football team."

"Oh, do you like American football?"

"Don't tell anyone, but yes, I do?"

"Maybe I'll get a chance to introduce to my friend, Bobo Lambrowski."

"Bobo, you know Bobo?"

"Yes, I do. In fact we just came back from Spring Break in Cancun."

She was surprised. "What? You got to go to Cancun. I'd love to go there sometime. Did the Ayatollah let you go there?"

He explained, "Well, not exactly. He did instruct me to live the role of a typical college student here in the U.S. I paid for my way to Cancun on money that I saved."

"And you," he asked, "You are not wearing the chador. That outfit you have on is not typical clothes of an Islamic woman. Did the Ayatollah also instruct you to live your cover?"

"I'm here to support operations. I'm what they call an access agent or a door opener." Looking sad, she continued, "They use me to lure other men. Then the men do things that they don't really want to do."

Ebrahimi began to look at Jennifer in a different light. No longer was she this cute little sex object. Well, no, that's not right. Although she continued to be this cute little sex object, she also revealed a different side. She was also a victim. The system picked her up and was now using her.

She was a pawn in the battle between the faithful and the infidel. Ebrahimi's heart went out to her. He would wait. Maybe he could help her.

Ahmad came back to the car and told the two youngsters to come with him to one of the rooms in the first floor of the motel. After they entered the room, Ahmad double-checked to be sure that no one was following them. He then sat the two down and explained the plan. After a two-hour briefing where they all rehearsed the plan, he ordered them to take a nap, to get some rest. At about 10:00 in the morning, the three conspirators headed for old Biscayne Bay Yacht Harbor. He parked the Cavalier in a position where all four of them could see the layout of the docks.

"Your target is Joshua Weintribe. That's his father's yacht, the big one on the end of B dock. See it? It's the one named *Movie Mogul*."

"Yes, I see it. How do you know that this Joshua is on board?"

"He lives on board. He's almost always here."

"And his father?"

"His father is some big shot in Hollywood. Produces movies or something like that. He lives in L.A. with his third wife. She doesn't get along with Joshua. When Joshua got kicked out of U.S.C. for drug dealing, she insisted that he not live with them. So his father told him that he could live on the boat in Miami."

"Is he still dealing drugs?"

"No, I don't think so. He lost his driver's license and won't get it back for a while. So he's staying on the straight and narrow. His only interests are booze, dancing and Latina women."

"So how do I get him to take me to Cuba?"

"You don't need to worry about making contact. He'll invite you on board as soon as he sees you. I've given you some clues, you know, dancing and Latinas. Play the role of being half Latina, half Iranian."

"That gets me on board. What do I do next?"

"Look, we didn't send you to acting school for nothing. You need to play to him. Use your feminine charms."

"Well, I'll try."

"Trying isn't good enough. The boat's got to be in Cuba three days from now. You know the location. I hope that you studied the map because I don't want you to take it with you. If you need reminders then use the boat's nautical charts."

Ebrahimi felt sorry for Jennifer. She was given an almost overwhelming challenge. But she didn't seem to be the least bit concerned. He thought, *What a trooper.* He said, "Break a leg."

Ahmad was angry. "What do you mean, 'break a leg?'"

Jennifer responded, "Ebrahimi was just wishing me luck. It's something that show business people say. It means 'good luck'"

She smiled at Ebrahimi.

Ahmad said, "There he is. He'll head for the coffee shop at the end of the road. It will take him about twenty minutes to drink his coffee and read the paper. It's a routine that he goes though every morning."

On of the smaller boats, aptly named *Party Animal*, was pulling away from the dock with a bunch of rambunctious twenty-some year olds who were already drinking beers although it was not yet noon. Jennifer slipped out of her t-shirt and adjusted her bikini top. She got out of the car and pulled on her bikini bottoms. She waited until *Party Animal* had pulled away from the dock and was on the way out of the harbor. Then she moved down to the pier and walked *Party Animal's* vacant slip, about half way down to where the *Movie Mogul* was tied up. She stopped in front of and looked confused.

Just then Joshua began walking up the pier with half a cup of coffee in one hand and the Miami Herald in the other. He couldn't help but notice how the young woman seemed distressed. A genetic sense of chivalry that exists in every young heterosexual man and is specifically targeted towards girls who a) look like Jennifer Love Hewitt, and b) are wearing a very small bikini, kicked in. He stopped and asked her, "What's the matter? You look distressed."

Jennifer sniffed and said, "My friends have left without me."

Joshua said, "You mean the yacht *Party Animal*?"

"Yes, we were going to cruise down to Key West. I was supposed to be down here by 9:30, but my mamma was ill and I had to make sure that she had her medicine before I left."

"Come on down to my boat. Let's see if we can raise them on the VHF."

"Oh, you have a boat? Gracias, you are so kind."

Joshua helped her on board the *Movie Mogul*. As he bent down to help her climb the stairs, he caught the full impact of her full breasts. He hoped she didn't catch the full impact his uncontrollable arousal. She did. She smiled to herself. She said, "It's so big."

Joshua was taken back. "What's so big?"

"Your boat. And it's so beautiful. Does she have a name?"

"Yes. It's *Movie Mogul*. My dad's in the movie business."

"And do you spend much time on the boat?"

"Yes, I live on it."

"You mean you have it all to yourself?"

"Yes, I can do anything I want to with it."

"You mean that you can even take it out?"

"Of course. I always keep her fully gassed up and ready to go."

"You know, my friends would be so impressed if they saw me on this boat. Do you think that we could go out, you know, just a few miles and catch up with them? You'd like my friends."

Joshua didn't have even a small chance to say "no." He looked in her doe-like eyes and said, "Of course. Can you handle dock lines?"

"My father was a fisherman in Cuba. I grew up on boats. But never one so big and beautiful as this one."

Joshua started the twin diesel engines and instructed Jennifer to loosen the bowlines and stay on the bow. He went back to the stern and disconnected the stern lines. As the engines reached operating temperature, he said, "Here we go." He sounded the horn and put the engine in gear.

As they headed out of the harbor, Jennifer returned to the helm where Joshua was busy watching both the depth finder and the radar. She said, "By the way, my name is Jennifer. And you are?"

"I'm Joshua. Welcome aboard. Which way did your friends go?"

"They were talking about going to a place called Hawk's Cay. It's about half way down the Keys."

"I know the place. A friend of mine, Georgie, his dad owns the place. Do you want me to raise them on the VHF?"

"Does this boat go very fast?"

"This boat goes real fast!"

"Then lets just catch up with them, Ok?"

"Sounds good to me. Hang on." He pushed the throttles all the way forward and the boat rose up out of the water and within 60 seconds was going 40 miles per hour.

In fairly short order, they were closing in on Key Largo. Joshua said, "Do you see your friends yet?"

"No, no sign of them."

"Maybe I should try to raise them on the radio now."

"I know what I'd rather do. It's such a beautiful day. Can you stop the engines and let's just drift a while."

"Why do you want to do that?" he asked.

Taking off the top of her bikini, Jennifer said, "I want to work on my tan."

Joshua said, "Sure, no problemo."

Jennifer said, "Oh, you speak Spanish?"

They drifted for about an hour, talking and drinking beers. Then Jennifer said, "Can I get a tour of this beautiful boat?"

Joshua said, "Sure, let's go down below."

Joshua explained, "This is a Pershing yacht. It's built in Italy."

"Oh, Italy. I always wanted to go to the Italian Rivera."

"Yes, my dad and I went to the French Rivera, just next to the Italian Rivera. He was showing something at the Cannes Film Festival. We went down to a boat show in Monaco. That's just down the road from Cannes. And he saw a version of this boat at the show, so he ordered a new one. They even delivered it right to Miami."

They entered a large cabin. "This is the main saloon," Joshua explained. Jennifer saw beautiful cherry wood lined walls, a large TV and a well-equipped sound system.

He moved just aft of the Saloon and said, "Here's the master suite." She looked in and saw a queen size berth that was angled to let anyone climb in from any of three sides. There were enough drawers and beautifully curved cherry cabinets to handle all of her possessions. But there was even, in addition, a huge walk-in closet with eight feet of hanging space and shoe racks.

Jennifer saw that Joshua would rather hang out here for a while. She stalled him off by saying, "Let's see the rest of the boat."

They went up on the foredeck. Joshua showed her how he could lift up a hatch revealing a small tender and a hoist to lift it over the side. He closed and latched the hatch.

She asked, "How big are the engines?"

Joshua seemed surprised. He wasn't use to girls asking about the engines. Usually they just wanted to know things about who decorated it, where were the closets and the like. He answered, "We've got two diesels. Each puts out almost 2,000-horse power. She can outrun almost anything."

Jennifer wondered, "Can she outrun the Coast Guard?"

"Can we go on down to Hawk's Cay? It's not much farther, is it?"

Joshua agreed. He had made the run down to Hawk's Cay several times. It would be fun to pull into the docks with such a beautiful girl sitting up in the trophy seat on the bow. Maybe his friend Georgie would be there and see them coming in. He called ahead to the dock master.

He picked up Marker 44 and swung the ship to a 255-degree heading. He followed the channel markers into the Marina. As they pulled into the docks, Joshua looked for the *Party Animal*. "I don't see your friends," he said to Jennifer, who was standing on the bow, her bosoms thrust forward like the figurehead of an ancient sailing ship. One of the powerboats that were motoring out struck the side of a sailboat. Neither captain was watching where he was going but was riveted on the young lady. Later, both settled for no fault on either's behalf.

Georgie was there to handle the dock lines. Georgie was impressed. Georgie was, in fact, flabbergasted. Joshua usually showed up with skinny, flat-chest girls with large horn-rimmed glasses and pale white skin that was covered with sunscreen. On one occasion, he arrived with a plump young lady who had thrown up over side all the way down from Miami. This was the first time Joshua ever showed up with a real live honest to goodness babe. And she had a perfect tan to boot.

As he tied up the boat, Georgie said, "Boy, Joshua, you really struck it rich this time."

"Hey, she's a really nice girl," Joshua said, smiling.

That night, Jennifer resisted Joshua's advances. "No really, we can't have sex. It's against my religion. I promised my mother that I would be a virgin when I married. I want to walk down the isle in white."

"But Jennifer, I've gotta do something. He invoked a plea from the 1950's. I've got blue balls. If I don't get release, I'll be in pain all night."

She countered with the Bill Clinton solution. "I'll help you. I'll help you in other ways and I can still walk down the isle in white."

When Joshua awoke the next morning he remembered the sweet ecstacy of last night. He saw psychedelic lights, felt deep emotions, shook spasms and felt depleted when Jennifer finished with him. This was better than any drug he had ever sampled. He turned over to face her, hoping for more. She was gone from the bed.

Joshua had a sinking feeling. "Has she left me? God, I hope not."

Slipping on a pair of swim trunks, he ran up to the boat's cockpit. Jennifer was standing in front of the navigator's table. She was plotting a course. She turned to Joshua and said, "How about spending the night in Key West?"

Joshua said, "I've only been to Key West once on this boat. And that was with my dad. I'm not sure ..."

Jennifer smiled and said, "Maybe we'll run into my friends there and I can introduce you to them. They'll really be impressed. And I can make sure that you are not lonely tonight in Key West."

Images flashed in front of Joshua's eyes. He said, "Let me gas up. We can be on the road in twenty or so minutes.

It actually took forty-five minutes to pull up to the pumps and top off the two 1,700 gallon tanks. Joshua put the diesel on his dad's account. He then pulled out towards Marker 44 and headed southwest towards Key West.

The next night proved to be an even better repeat performance by the great actress Jennifer. That night, Joshua dreamed of walking down the isle with the beautiful Jennifer dressed in white, with blazing red lips that formed a perfect 'O' shape. When he awoke he found her gone from the bed again. He went up to the cockpit and said, "Where to this time, Rio?"

She answered, "No, no, no. Have you ever been to Cuba?"

Joshua looked startled. "We can't go to Cuba. It's against the law."

"No," she responded, "It's not against the law to go to Cuba. It's just against the law to spend money there. And we wouldn't spend any money. We could visit my family. I'd love for you to meet them and for them to meet you."

He said, "No way. I will not take this boat to Cuba."

Lifting off her t-shirt, she walked over to his side and rubbed the front of his shorts. "No way. Are you sure?"

Within 35 minutes he had topped off the tanks and the *Movie Mogul* was headed in a southwest direction towards the western end of Cuba. The honey trap had been sprung.

Chapter 24

GETTING THE BOMB TO MIAMI

Jennifer plotted a course towards the west end of Cuba. She drew a line through a series of markers that would lead the *Movie Mogul* around the Pinar del Rio and into the Playa Maria La Gorde. Joshua had no idea where they were going, but Jennifer seemed to know what she was doing, so he followed her course.

Joshua was actually pretty excited. Some of his friends had made the run to Havana and had brought back some interesting stories, some cigars and in one case the clap. They all spoke of friendly people, good food and fun times.

As they entered a large bay, Jennifer pointed to a small village on the side of a hill, about ten miles away. Excitedly, she said, "There, that's my mamma and papa's home. That's where I grew up. I've been all over these waters."

Just then the boat struck something in the water. Jennifer looked over the side and saw mud churning up. She realized that she had better lay off bragging about knowing waters that she had, in fact, never seen in a country where, in fact, she had never been. Her actress skills could only take her so far.

She said, "Please slow down and watch the depth finders. The sandbars shift all the time here. Stay close to the channel markers."

Joshua slowed the boat down and swung the boat over to the deepest part of the channel. They approached a long, decrepit pier. Jennifer stood on the bow. She yelled back to Joshua, "Go really slow. Follow my movements."

She motioned for him to turn to the starboard, then forward, then to the port. Finally, she made a slicing motion across her neck with her hand, indicating that he should cut the engines. He could tell that she was used to handling small boats and put the diesels in neutral. The boat drifted up to the pilings and Jennifer jumped off, bowline in hand. Joshua put the boat in reverse, gently stopping its movement. Several people ran down the dock to help tie up the boat. Joshua shut the engines down.

Joshua saw Jennifer talking to one of the locals, a young woman with a child. He could not hear what they were saying.

Jennifer looked for her contact, a young woman with a baby. She spotted her coming down the pier towards the boat. She went over to intercept her. Jennifer said, "Is everything set up?"

The young woman said, "Yes, introduce me as Maria, your life-long friend. Two people are waiting at the village. The man will be wearing a red shirt and straw hat. The woman will be holding a small dog. They are ready to be 'Mama Isabela' and 'Papa Juan.' You have no sisters or brothers. I've got two bicycles ready for you. Take your time riding up to the village. The farm is just before the village, on the left. Don't let your friend come back to the boat for at least two hours, in case we have problems."

"What are you going to do at the boat?"

"Don't ask. We don't tell. No one will be harmed."

"What if I run into someone who I should know but don't"

"Don't worry, we have control over the entire area. You won't have any unexpected encounters."

Jennifer turned towards the boat and smiled. It was time to go back on stage for the next scene in this play.

Jennifer hopped back on the boat and joined Joshua in the cockpit where he was putting away equipment. She asked, "When's the last time you rode a bicycle?"

He said, "Bicycle? I used to do BMX races. I love bicycles."

"Well, we've got to ride for about eight miles. Are you up to it?"

"Eight miles, that's not even a warm up ride. Where are we going?"

My mama and papa have a farm up the hill towards the village. My friend, Maria, over there with the baby, says that they're home. Let's go surprise them."

"Let me lock up the boat first."

"Sure, whata you want me to do?"

"Nothing, I've got it under control."

As they began their ride up the hill, Joshua decided that he was going to show-off. He quickly rode up the hill about a hundred yards, then turned the bike around and started down hill. Holding on to the handlebars, he placed his foot on the bicycle stood up, just like Butch did in the first movie that his father had ever worked on. He came flying down the hill. Just as he reached Jennifer, a wild boar jumped out of the bushes and crossed Joshua's path. He turned the wheel to miss the pig. He crashed. Dust flew. He moaned.

Jennifer got off her bicycle and ran over to him. She lifted his head up and wiped the blood and dust away with the bottom of her t-shirt. "Poor baby, are you all right?"

He looked in her eyes and said, "I am now."

She kissed him on the forehead.

He got up and tried the bicycle. The wheel was bent. He stepped on it to straighten it out. It wobbled but worked. They continued up the hill, at a much slower pace.

As they approached the village, they heard someone yell, "Papa, come here. Look, it's Jennifer. She's come back."

An old man in a red shirt and straw hat emerged from behind a small barn. He joined up with the old woman who was holding a small dog. Jennifer stopped the bike, got off, and ran up to them. She said, "Mama, Papa."

She hugged the woman who hugged back.

She then hugged the man who put his hand on her behind and squeezed. She wiggled away and gave him a dirty look. She hoped that Joshua didn't notice the gesture.

"Mama, papa, this is Joshua. He brought me over here from Miami to visit. He's so kind."

Papa thought, *And horny too, I'll bet.*

After introductions and a little chit chat, Jennifer said, "Mama is going to make us lunch. I'll help her. You and Papa go look at the farm. Papa, give Joshua the tour."

Papa played his role to the hilt. He showed off the tobacco plants, talked about the amount of rain that they need and how the sun played a role in their texture and smell. He talked about the harvest and how the tobacco was changed into fine cigars by being rolled on the thighs of beautiful young virgins. This wasn't a bad dialog for a man who grew up in the slums of Havana, was recruited by the KGB in the 60's, and never spent a day in his life on a farm. Of course, there were very few virgins in the Pinar del Rio region, but spicing up the story made it more believable.

At the end of the tour, Papa gave Joshua a handful of cigars. He said, "Take these as a reminder of your visit to Cuba."

Mama had prepared a lunch, or at least the neighbor lady had made one up and delivered it the night before. In fact, mama never cooked a dinner in her life and got her meals from various restaurants in Havana. She was hired for the gig for her acting skills, not her cooking skills.

Joshua was completely snowed by Jennifer, so it was easy to fool him with idyllic stories of her childhood, how she grew up in a loving family, how they grew their own food and raised cattle, how her friends all played together and how she loved her life. This legend was a far cry from the facts. Jennifer grew up in the poverty of Tehran. Her father was snatched away by the Shah's secret police when she was seven. Her mother's family was able to barely provide substance level support. There were times where she had nothing to eat for days on end. Her father's disappearance ensured that she had no friends. No one could chance being close to her for fear of losing favor with the Shah. She found her first real home in the Students for the Revolution. All in all, Jennifer preferred the legend of the good life on a farm in Cuba. Something simple. No politics. No hatred.

But the game was being played out onboard the *Movie Mogul*. After the two bicycled out of sight of the harbor, three men approached the boat from the seaward side, tied up the small motor boat that they were in, and climbed aboard. They lifted up a small crate and carried it over to the center of the foredeck. They opened the hatch that contained the ship's hoist and tender. They placed the crate at the top of the opened locker and secured it with straps. They surveyed the results. Neat, clean locker, tender that had never been used, and a crate with letters that read, "ACME Inflatable Life Raft." They closed and secured the hatch. They climbed down into the motor boat and sped off. The entire operation took seven and one-half minutes.

The two love-birds made it back down the hill just as the sun was about to set. Joshua unlocked the boat and set up the electronic systems. "Shall we retire to the master suite?" he asked.

Jennifer answered, "Let's make a night-time crossing back to the Keys. It would be so romantic. The stars, the moon, soft music."

Joshua was ready to just get it on, but he acceded to her request. He started the engines to warm them up. Can you get the bowlines?"

She said, "I'm on it," and scampered up to the bow like a beautiful, graceful, sexy feline.

Joshua freed the stern lines and returned to the cockpit. "Ready?" he asked.

"All clear,' she answered, "Be sure to watch the depth finders."

As the yacht pulled away, Jennifer looked back at the island and thought, *How nice it would be to live the simple life.*

As they pulled away, the deep blue, green sea began to swallow the sun. The air cooled off and the colors began to mellow out. Jennifer climbed back to the cockpit and said, "This is the most perfect time of the day." She held Joshua's hand.

As the boat picked up speed, Joshua and Jennifer stood at the ship's wheel, arms around each other's waist. The last thought in each other's mind was sex. They were just clinging to each other for the moment of bliss.

Just outside the Cuban international water limits, a Coast Guard cutter, the *Richard Milhous Nixon*, was running a figure eight interdiction pattern. Known as the *Tricky Dick,* the boat is "Island" class patrol boat that displaces 155 tons fully loaded. The cutter is an old warhorse that had already outlived its programmed life and is now patched together with spare parts. This boat would have been scuttled years ago if it had been in the U.S. Navy's fleet. But the Coast Guard was an expert at scavenging old cutters and refurbished Navy ships. Although the ship had a 76-millimeter gun, no one currently on board has ever seen it shoot.

But a good craftsman never blames his tools. The *Tricky Dick* had a long history of exciting search and rescue missions and led the Group Key West in drug interdictions. Its territory covers the Straits of Florida from south of Key Largo down to the Old Bahama Channel and across the north coast of Cuban territorial seas.

The ship was into the third day of a five-day patrol. It's commanding officer, Lieutenant Sarah Barkley, supervised the sixteen men who round out the crew. Even though the boat was old, it had a sophisticated set of electronic equipment to include a global Positioning System, surface search radar with a computerized collision avoidance system, radio direction finders, fathometers and different types of radios. It was almost as well equipped as the *Movie Mogul*.

At 2335 hours the Lieutenant received an alert from the radar operator. "I've got a target about 30 klicks off Pinar del Rio. It's moving at about thirty knots."

"What does it look like?"

"Too fast to be a fishing boat. Too small to be a cruise ship. Must be one of those yachts."

"Do we have any reports of any yacht missing or on the watch list."

"No, Ma'am."

"Does it seem to be taking any evasive action?"

"No, Ma'am."

Barkley's exec, Lieutenant junior grade George Polowski had graduated from the Coast Guard Academy just two years ago and since then he rode a desk. The *Tricky Dick* was his first adventure at sea in any kind of authority position. He wanted action. "Let's go get her, Captain."

Sarah thought for a minute and then decided. "Plot an intercept course. Make sure that we are well clear of Cuban waters."

"Aye, aye, ma'am."

In about half an hour, the *Tricky Dick* intercepted the *Movie Mogul*. The cutter fell in behind the yacht. The cutter's lookout reported, "I can't see anyone at the wheel. She must be running on autopilot."

"Raise her on the VHF."

"*Movie Mogul*, this is the Coast Guard Cutter *Tricky* ... I mean *Richard Milhous Nixon*. Come in please."

The call was repeated several times but there was no response.

"Call her on the loudspeaker."

"*Movie Mogul*. This is the Coast Guard Cutter *Nixon*. Heave to and have your crew show itself on deck."

Down in the master suite, Jennifer and Joshua were busy making out. Jennifer looked up and saw a light flashing on and off through the porthole. Then she heard someone calling on a loudspeaker. "There's another boat out there," she said.

"Oh crap, what if it's pirates?" Joshua said.

Jennifer sat up and looked out of the porthole. "It looks like the Coast Guard?"

"Ours or the Cubans?"

"I think that it's the U.S. Coast Guard. I see stripes on the front of the boat."

Joshua heard someone saying, "Heave to or we'll fire."

He immediately jumped up, ran into the cockpit and shutdown the engines. The boat dipped back and settled into the waters. Jennifer came up beside him, tying her bikini top back on. She laughed when she looked at his neck. "What are they gonna say when they see all those hickeys on your neck?"

Joshua thought, *She is a girl that really has her stuff together.*

He didn't know that, beneath the façade she was scared to death. What if they find whatever the Cubans did to this boat? I'll be going to jail."

Sarah ordered the duty boarding party to go over to the *Movie Mogul*, check its documentation and search it. "Be thorough," she ordered.

The boarding party was led by Chief Petty Officer Pete Waterman and included two Boatswain's Mates. They lowered an inflatable boat with an outboard engine into the water, boarded it and sped over to the *Movie Mogul*. As they pulled along side, Jennifer leaned down to hand them a line. The two Boatswain's Mates just stared. CPO Waterman shouted at them, "Quit gawking and take the friggin line."

After securing the inflatable to the yacht, the three coasties boarded the ship. Waterman asked Jennifer, "Where's the Captain?"

She answered, "He's in the cockpit. There's just the two of us."

Waterman told his two companions to stay put. As long as Jennifer was standing there, they weren't going anywhere.

Waterman entered the cockpit, introduced himself and asked for the ship's papers, which Joshua had already placed on the navigation table in anticipation of the request.

Waterman inspected the papers. He then asked, "Where were you going to?

"We're heading for the Keys, probably Marathon. Depends on the weather."

"Where are you coming from?"

"We were down towards Jamacia."

"We saw you exiting Cuban waters. Were you in Cuba?"

"No, just around the other side. We rounded Pinar del Rio and were heading towards the Keys."

"We need to search your boat."

"Please, be my guest." Joshua hoped that they didn't find the contraband. How would he explain the Cuban cigars."

Waterman stuck his head out of the cockpit and said, "Picard, you take the decks. Sampson, you go below."

"Aye, aye," responded the Mates.

Sampson was impressed. This was a real yacht. Satin sheets, crystal glasses, full bar with the classy stuff like Chivas, three TVs, the works. Jennifer came down into the cabin and said, "Do you need me?"

Sampson looked at her. She was even more beautiful under the cabin lights. He thought, *Oh, boy, do I need you.* He said, "No thanks,ma'am. I'll be careful with these things."

He began to opening doors and hatches. Jennifer watched.

On deck, Picard started at the bow and opened the anchor line hatch. He was impressed. The locker included a washing system to clean the bowline as it was brought on board. He had heard about such systems but had never seen one. Picard moved to the center of the foredeck and began to open a large hatch.

Down in the cockpit, Waterman looked at the ship's log. Then he made a connection. You're name is Joshua Wientribe? Are you related to Jonathan Weintribe?"

"Yes, he's my father."

"The Weintribe that produces movies?"

"That's him."

"Well I'll be damn. I worked with your father on *Cocaine Busts*. I was his technical advisor on the movie."

Picard had opened the hatch and saw the small tender that was used to carry passengers ashore when there was no docking available. He also saw a small crate with the label, "ACME Inflatable Life Raft." He began to unlash the crate to open it.

Waterman shouted, "Sampson, Picard. Get down here."

Picard shut the hatch and latched it. He went down into the cockpit. "Yes, what's up?"

"Remember me telling you how I was in a movie?"

"Oh yeah," Sampson said, "We've heard the story a thousand times."

"Don't be a smart-ass. This is Jonathan Weintribe's son, you know the producer."

"Who, him or his father?"

"His father, bonehead."

Just then Waterman received a call over his handheld VHF. "The Lieutenant wants to know if everything is alright over there."

"Everything is A-OK," he responded.

"The Lieutenant says if you're done searching, get your butts over here. We are getting a distress call."

"Look Mr. Weintribe. Tell your father that Pete Waterman says hello. And if he needs more advice, just call me."

"Sure thing. I'll be sure and do that."

Jennifer helped their exit by untying the line that held the motorboat. Looking at Jennifer, Sampson forgot to sit down. When Picard put the outboard in gear, Sampson almost fell overboard, saving himself by grabbing a line that was slung along the edge of the small boat.

Jennifer said, "Those guys make me nervous."

"Oh, they're not bad guys. Just doin a job protecting America."

"Can we head back to Miami? I don't feel very good."

Joshua said, "I'm not sure that we have enough fuel to make it, but I'll try. We can always refuel in the Keys." He put the diesels in gear and pushed the throttles forward. The boat quickly got up to speed.

The *Movie Mogul* arrived in Miami just as dawn was breaking. Both Joshua and Jennifer looked beat. Joshua eased the boat onto the end of the dock. Jennifer hopped off and tied the lines off. She said, "I need a cup of coffee." Joshua said, "Me too." She said, "Let's go up to the coffee shop. It just opened."

Jennifer selected a table where she could look out along the dock. Joshua sat down with his back to the window. They both slowly sipped their coffees and looked at each other. "This was a wonderful three days," she said.

"It was like a dream to me," he responded. They reached out and held hands.

Through the window, Jennifer saw two men walk down the dock. They climbed on the *Movie Mogul*. They opened up the tender hatch. They removed a small crate from the hatch. One of them got off the yacht and the other handed him the crate. With a man on each end, they began to carry the crate down the dock.

Joshua said, "I forgot to hook up shore power. I'll go get it. I'll be right back." He got up and headed down the dock, passing two men who were carrying a crate.

When he returned, Jennifer was no longer at the table. Her coffee was half empty. He looked around. *Maybe she's in the ladies room,* he hopefully thought. Then he saw the note. He picked it up. It read, "This was the loveliest three days of my life. Thank you for taking me to see my parents. I'll remember you forever." She had signed the note with her name and a lip print shaped in a big red O.

Joshua sighed. "Was all this just a dream? Will I ever see her again? Will I ever meet anyone so wonderful again." He sadly sighed again and took a sip of his half-warm coffee.

Chapter 25

THE ASSESSMENT

The next street over, Jennifer joined Eb and Ahmad at the rental car. They had placed the crate in the trunk and found that they could not close the trunk lid. They tied the lid down with Eb's belt. The three of them got in the Cavalier and drove off. For five miles, no one spoke. Then Jennifer asked, "What's in the trunk?"

Ahmad said, "You don't need to know. Just wait. Within two weeks you will know just how wonderfully you served the Ayatollah and Allah."

Jennifer had a bad feeling that she really didn't want to be a part of all this, whatever it was. She looked at Ebrahimi. She saw in his eyes that he was thinking the same thing. Neither spoke. Ahmad drove them to the Motel 6, where they had rented a room for a week. They unloaded the crate and stored it at the foot of the bed.

Later that evening, while both Jennifer and Ahmad were watching CNN, Ebrahimi logged onto the Internet and brought up Hotmail. With one eye on his two companions he took a chance and prepared a message:

FYI THINGS R FUBAR. TPTB SHOWED UP OOTB

WITH :-8< BOTH ():) and }:>

TUK ME AWAY. NFW 2 GET OUT.

:-8< LEFT ON <-|) WITH YG 2 CUBA

RTN WITH :X CARGO

BSOM WHAT IT WAZ

IMHO YG KLULESS DUPE

X OUT <-|) LIKE HAL(NPWJF NPHVM)

X OUT MOTEL VI RM CXX

SWAG MAYBE TEOFWAWKI

HTH BBL EMSG NRN B4N

     He sent the message to both Bobo and David. Then he deleted the message and cleaned out the electronic trashcan. He went to bed.

     At 4:00 in the morning, Ahmad woke up both Jennifer and Ebrahimi and said, "We're going to move to a new location. Let's get the crate back in the trunk of the car and get out of here. Within five minutes they were on the road, heading north on I-95.

     At 9:05 in the morning, David logged onto Hotmail. He saw that there was a message from Eb. He opened but couldn't understand it.

     He called Sydney and said, "I've got some kind of encrypted message from Eb. I can't understand it. Can NSA help?"

     Sydney said, "Send it to me. I'll forward it to NSA."

     Ten minutes later, Sydney called David back and said, "NSA is working on it. Says it will take about ten hours to figure it out."

     David said, "That's a long time... I've got an idea. I'll call you back."

     He dialed a number. The phone rang and rang. No one answered. He called another number. "Hello, Campus Security. Would you go wake up Bobo Lambrowski? He's in his room. Tell him to answer the phone."

"Are you kidding? We're not supposed to bother the football players."

"This is a national emergency. If you want, I can send the FBI over there and have your ass for lunch. Now go and wake Bobo up. Do it now."

Ten minutes later, David redialed Bobo's number. "Hello, asshole, who ever you are. Why'd you wake me up?

"Bobo, this is David. Eb's in trouble. We gotta help him."

"Sure little buddy. Whatta I gotta do?"

"Turn on your computer and open the last e-mail you got from Eb."

"Ok, little buddy. I'm doing it now. Hey, here's some e-mail from Angelina Jolie. Sez there's a photo attached. Hey, she's necked."

"Bobo. We don't have time for that. This is an emergency."

"Ok. I got the message. What about it?"

"Do you know what it says?"

"Of course. Don't you?"

"Read it to me."

"Ok, little buddy. He sez:

For your information, things are fouled up beyond recognition. The powers that be showed up out of the blue with a major babe who is both angel and devil.' Then he sez, 'They took me away. There was no friggin'in way to get out. The major babe left on a boat with a young guy to Cuba.' Whoa, then he sez, 'They returned with a secret cargo.' He sez, 'Beats the crap out of me what it was.' In his humble opinion the young guy is a clueless dupe in the operation. He wants you to check out the boat... Now here I got a problem. I don't know what he means by LIKE HAL(NPWJF NPHVM)."

David turned to Alex, who had entered the room during his phone call. "Alex, does this make any sense to you." He showed her the phrase LIKE HAL.

"HAL, HAL, Let's see. Who was HAL?"

"Hal Holbrook, the actor?"

"Wasn't there a HAL in the movie 2001?"

"Yes, that's it. The computer on the spaceship. HAL. Now where did that name come from? Something to do with IBM."

"That's right. You increment each letter of HAL to the next letter in the alphabet and you get IBM."

"Bobo, I think that we got it. Increment each letter NPWJF NPHVM and you get OQXKG OQIWN."

"Oh sure. That really helps us."

"How about decrementing each letter. You then get MOVIE MOGUL. There, that's it. Call Gotleib. Tell him to find a boat named *Movie Mogul*. It's somewhere here in Florida, I'm sure."

"Bobo, what about the rest of the message" What does it say?"

"Sure little buddy, it says, 'Check out Motel 6, room 120.' Then it says ' It's a scientific wild ass guess that maybe it's the end of the world as we know it."

David asked, "What in the hell does he mean by that?"

Bobo responded, "I don't know. He ends up with 'Hope this helps. Be back later by e-mail message. No reason to respond. Bye for now."

"Bobo, you're a genius. How come you can read this message and we can't"

"I hadda take a computer course to be able to play football. Eb and me both took a course in Shorthand for E-Mail. It was easy. I gotta read symbols to understand my football plays in the play book. This message was a piece of cake."

David immediately called Sydney Gotlieb, who immediately made a call to Wallace, who immediately made a call to the FBI's Miami Bureau chief, who immediately made a call to the local FBI Swat Team member, who immediately ordered a condition red. At 10:05, the Swat Team broke down the door of room 102 of the Motel 6, awaking an intertwined elderly couple, Alice Sommerfield an 86-year-old widow, and Teddy Johannasen, a young 72-year-old man married to Sylvia Johannasen, who was visiting her son in Lake Louise, Canada. At first, Teddy thought that Sylvia was on to his secret love affair, but then when they started asking about a crate of some sort, he said, "Whatta you talking about? We don't have any crate."

The team leader suspected that something was wrong. He turned to his deputy, Agent Johnson, and asked, "What was that room number again?"

The response was, "Room 102… oh no, Room 120. Ah crap. We gotta hit room 120." Since he first began to read, Agent Johnson had struggled with dyslexia. Now the handicap has struck again.

"Damn! Let's move," ordered the Team Leader.

Within two minutes the Special Weapons and Attack Team busted down the door to room 120. The room was deserted. The agents efficiently tossed the room but did not find any clues. The Nuclear Emergency Search Team that accompanied them entered and swept the room. They found signs of radioactivity.

At the same time that room 120 was being searched, another SWAT team was approaching the yacht *Movie Mogul* where Joshua Weintribe lay dreaming of lips and breasts and happiness. The SWAT team leader spoke into his handheld radio, "Go, go, go."

A swift boat with twin 50-caliber guns approached from the channel. A team of four men and one woman, cloaked in black and carrying tools rushed on board the *Movie Mogul* from the dock. They pried open the door to the cockpit. Two men stayed in the cockpit while the other two men and a woman rushed downstairs. The two men moved into the VIP cabin. The woman rushed into the Owner's cabin. She saw a young man sound asleep with a smile on his face. She thought, *That must be some dream that he is having.* She paused for a second, and then loudly said, "Wake up, put your hands in the air."

Her two companions joined her. They grabbed his arms and dragged him out of bed.

She said, "Where are your friends?"

"What friends?"

"The girl.   The terrorists."

"What are you talking about?"

"You just came back from Cuba with a young woman."

"Cuba, I didn't go to Cuba."

"We know you did. What did you pick up there?"

"Nothing. Just cigars."

"Where's the girl?"

"What girl?"

"The one named Jennifer."

"I don't know where she is. She just left."

"Where did she go?"

"I don't know. I just met her."

"What's her name?"

"Jennifer."

"Jennifer what?"

"I don't know. I just met her a couple of days ago."

'You're trying to tell us that you went all the way to Cuba and back with a girl that you just met?"

"Yes, she wanted to visit her family. In the Pinar del Rio. Aren't you supposed to be telling me that I have the right to remain silent..."

"Listen, buster. This is a national security matter. Don't even think that you have any rights. We'll have you in front of a military tribunal and in the slammer in Guantanimo Bay in a matter of days. No lawyer, no judge, no appeal. Just life in prison."

"How so? What happened to my rights?"

"We're talking national security here. Hell, I could shoot you right through the eye right now and no one would say a word."

The NEST team commander came into the cockpit and said, "We've got a positive reading. Something radioactive was stored in the tender locker. It's gone now."

Back at CIA Headquarters, the DCI gave the orders to activate a joint task force with the task of handing the unfolding situation.   The DCI approved the following appointments to the task force:

Sydney Gotlieb – Head of OTS and the principle liaison with the FBI

Irvine Wallace – FBI Liaison to CIA

Carl St. John – Junior member of OTS with certain technical skills

Alexandra Pack – Case Officer with DDO

David Issah – Summer intern with close contact to member of terrorist group

Aris Paprika – Senior analyst from the Directorate of Intelligence

Aris was the Agency's top gun analyst. As a youngster in the business, he was sent to Cambridge, Massachusetts to study creativity under a private tutor. After that he moved over to MIT for training in analytic methodologies. Finally, he received the finest intelligence training at CIA University.

Aris spent his ten-year apprenticeship working on the hotspots of the world. He worked Afghanistan and even went to that country to provide training to the Mujahadeen in multiutility analysis using eigenvector solutions. His training was credited with bringing down seven Russian helicopters. The great Afghan warrior Masood himself had awarded Aris an AK-47 that he proudly displays in his office. Editors hesitate to make dramatic changes to Aris's work ever since he chased one down the hall while wielding the automatic rifle. Aris wept when he read the message that stated that Masood was assassinated. He wanted revenge against the Islamic terrorists responsible for killing his friend.

Aris was a master of connecting the dots. He was able to process 132 factors plus or minus 2 in his brain at any given time. Every morning he read over at least 200 reports from the field, from open sources, and from overhead imagery. By noon, he would prepare a simple statement that would invariably be the lead item in the President's Daily Bulletin.

Aris had received a call from the DCI himself, ordering him to go down to the Counter Terrorism Center and help them with a problem. Aris hated to work on task forces with inferior brains. He objected, saying, "I'm working on your response to Congress on why we screwed up the hit on Hussein."

"Forget Congress. We got real work to do. Get downstairs now."

Aris turned his work over to his protégé, Billy Gates and went down to the CTC. Alex briefed Aris on the situation, covering what the team knew and what was missing. Aris, a DI analyst by profession, normally did not let his mind stray to mundane things, but he caught himself looking up Alex's skirt every time she shifted in her seat. "That's some babe," he mused.

As Alex began to stray from facts and into speculation, Aris stopped her. "Let me form my own judgments. Just give me the facts as you know them."

First Aris mentally developed a time line for the events. Then he pictured a mental Link Analysis, complete with colored lines and multiple dimensions. He let them move around and connect and disconnect like synapses connecting paths throughout his brain. Finally he mentally added in the probabilities, using a mental Bayesian framework. He went to the board and wrote, "Terrorists will most likely set off a nuclear device somewhere in or near Washington, D.C. within the next three weeks." He said, "Most likely means there is a 90% chance of this happening."

Just then the gray phone rang. Alex picked it up and said, "CTC."

She hung up the phone and said, "NSA has decoded Eb's message and is sending it over by secure fax."

Chapter 26

THE INVISIBLE SPY

Over lunchtime, Sydney Gotlieb and Irving Wallace sat together and discussed the obstacles that faced them. Wallace said, "This could be the worst disaster ever inflicted on America. We can put all the resources we want to on the problem but unless we have an inside man, we can't do anything."

Gotlieb said, "We got an inside man. We got this kid Ebrahimi. We just don't know where he is at."

"Crap, we seem to always be one step behind him at every corner."

"Once he contacts us or we find him, how are we going to find out from him what's going on?"

"I don't know. What ever we do, we can't afford to tip off the others in the terrorist group."

"May be we can get something going on with the e-mail. Maybe we can get this guy Bobo to draft up an e-mail message and we could send it to Eb."

"What if the leader, what's his name ... Ahmad, intercepts the message. That could tip him off."

"Can we get David or maybe even Bobo back into the scene?"

"Ahmad's taken his group and headed north. We try an insertion with known faces, Ahmad will be very suspicious."

"What about those experiments that St. John has been screwing around with? Is there any hope for using them?"

"What are you suggesting? That we build an invisible man?"

"I don't mean a monkey. We need someone with operational savvy who can get into a room or somewhere. An invisible spy would be perfect."

"St. John is working his way up the mammal chain. He's had some successes with baboons up to three feet tall. I don't think he's ready for a human test."

"Well ready or not here we come. Otherwise something really bad happens here in D.C.

"Don't we need DCI approval? Maybe even the President?"

"I think that we need to follow the rule of plausible denial. In fact, let's carry it one step further. Let's keep the President out of this. Also maybe the DCI for starters."

Wallace asked, "How about my director?"

"Him too."

"If this goes bad, they'll have our ass."

"Our fall back position will be that we were testing a new device and something went wrong."

"How are we going to get volunteers?"

"Don't need to."

"What do you mean?"

"Look, I've had a lot of experience in these issues. My first job in the

Agency was to get subjects for our MKULTRA experiments. We didn't ask for volunteers, we just gave them the drugs and watched what they did."

He continued, "Besides, I got just the man to do the job. The DDO says that he's one of their best. They call him their 'Super Spy.'"

One thing about Sydney Gotlieb: he never got mad. But, although it might take him a long time, he always got even.

Gotlieb said, "Let's go down to the Lab."

They rode the elevator down to the second floor and went down the D corridor to the OTS Lab. Gotlieb punched a code in and opened the door. They went in and the door clicked shut behind them.

"Be careful,' someone cautioned, "We've got superslick on the floor."

Gotlieb turned towards Wallace and said, "Walk like you are ice skating. Otherwise you will fall down."

Wallace took a step and fell on his butt. "What happened?" he cried.

"They're testing some stuff that we use to discourage someone from following our case officers. We give our guys a rubber ball. When they want to get away from someone, they toss the ball behind them. It works kind of like an exploding water balloon, spraying this slick stuff around. The bad guys fall on their butts, just like you did. Here, let me help you up."

Gotlieb reached down and put his hand under Wallace's shoulder. He lost his balance and tumbled down on top of the FBI agent. They both tried to stand and fell back down, arms flailing. Finally, Wallace grabbed the side of a desk and pulled himself up. He then held out his hand and gave Gotlieb enough support to stand. They both made skating motions towards the door to the room in the back of the lab.

"That's some slick stuff," Wallace said. "Do our surveillance teams know about it?"

"No, we're still experimenting with the stuff. Haven't tried it on any surveillance detection runs yet."

Carl St. John looked up from the paper he was writing on and saw the two Super Graders coming in. He said, "I've got some good news."

"About the apparatus, I hope."

"Yes, I've made a modification that lets it work on larger objects."

"How large?"

"Well, anything that can get inside this cage," he said, pointing to an odd shaped object. It consisted of two dodecahedron shaped surfaces. From the front they looked like they were on a flat plane. From the side Gotlieb could see that they actually lay on a slightly curved plane. The two dodecahedrons were connected together along one of the edges. The apparatus was opened like a clamshell. There were ankle straps on the bottom edges and wrist straps on the upper edges.

St. John went over to the oddly shaped object. "I made it so that this could swing open and closed. The idea is to open the apparatus, put someone in it, then close it. When I fire up the frequency generators and aim them towards the center of the dodecahedrons, energy is concentrated inside the entire cage. Anything inside is affected."

"Does it work?"

"I put a life-sized manikin inside along with three mice. It made everything disappear. The mice are running around here somewhere."

"Will it work on a human being?"

"Don't see why not? You want to try it out on some cadavers?"

"No. Let me think."

Gotlieb and Wallace carried on a whispered conversation. Wallace obviously wasn't happy with what Gotleib was saying. The old OTS Chief loudly said, "We've got no choice. Don't you realize the threat that is facing America? Are you not a patriot?"

Wallace felt his loyalty, in fact his very manhood, threatened. He said, "Let's do it."

Gotlieb said, "Tonight. Be here at 10:00."

He turned to St. John and said, "Be here tonight. Have the apparatus warmed up and ready at 10:00 sharp."

St. John asked, "What are we gonna do?"

Gotleib said, "Don't ask questions.   Just be here."

Wallace quietly asked, "Who's going in the apparatus?"

"You'll meet him tonight."

He picked up the phone and dialed it. He said, "Alex. Come down to the lab. I need your help. Be careful when you come into the lab. They got superslick on the floor."

About five minutes later, Alex appeared in the back room of the OTS lab. She asked, "What's up, Sydney?"

He responded, "I need for you to get Mark Steel here in the lab at 10:15 tonight. I don't care how you do it."

"Why?"

"We're conducting an operational field test."

Alex remembered Mark Steel's episode at that party at Sydney's house. She blurted out, "You're not going to harm him, are you?"

"No. I promise you that we will not harm him."

Sydney instructed St. John to demonstrate how to open the clamshell. He then let her strap him in using the wrist and ankle straps. Then he showed her how to latch the clamshell shut. Finally he demonstrated how to activate the frequency generator.

Sydney interrupted the lesson. "Here's what I want you to do...."

At 7:00 p.m., Alex called Mark. At 8:15 she met him at O'Tooles. They drank several beers. At 9:00, Mark was nuzzling on her neck. He was feeling good. She had resisted his advances all through training and had remained the single unreachable goal. Now she seemed to have had a change of heart. His blood was pumping. He was ready to move in for the score.

In between tongue exchanges, Alex said, "I heard that OTS is testing a new form of Viagra. It uses electronic waves instead of chemicals."

"Hey, I don't need Viagra. I can get it up on demand."

"Yes, but the word is that this system lets you go at it all night long with multiple prolonged orgasms."

Mark was definitely turned on by Alex's description of the effects of the new device.

Alex said, "Wantta try it? I've got keys to the lab."

Carrying his jacket over the front of his pants to conceal his woody, Mark went out to the car with Alex. She drove them to the CIA compound. He nuzzled on her ear. As they approached the guard shack, he sat up straight and they both flashed their badges. The guard beckoned them through the gate.

She parked the car in the empty VIP parking lot at the front of the building and they went inside. They ran their badges through the badge machine and went down the hall. When they entered the OTS lab, the lights were turned off. She could hear a slight hum coming from the back room. Mark slipped and caught himself on the edge of a table. She said, "Oh, yes. Be careful. They were testing superslick this morning."

She led him into the back room and turned the lights on. He kissed her and ran his hands across her butt. She returned his kisses and unbuttoned his shirt. He pulled off his shirt and began to wiggle out of his pants. Standing in his underwear, Mark asked, "What's next?"

She pointed towards the opened clamshell. "I'm going to strap you in there."

He looked at the machine and back at Alex. He was really getting excited. This was really, really kinky.

She said, "I order you to take off your socks."

Mark really got into role. He said, "Mistress of pain, I obey your every command."

She said, "Drop your shorts."

He responded like a robot. "Mistress of pain, I obey your command."

She snapped, "Stand in the clamshell."

He entered the oddly shaped structure.

She said, "Hold your arms up."

He held his arms up. She strapped his wrists in the upper straps.

She said, "spread your legs." As she reached down, she stroked his manhood.

He spread his legs. She strapped his ankles in the lower straps.

She closed and latched the clamshell. She stood back. Mark looked like a model for the famous Da Vinci drawing, Vitruvian Man.

Mark said, "Mistress of pain. Now what."

Falling into the role that Mark had set up for her, she responded, "Shut up. I'll tell you when I'm ready."

Alex went over to the apparatus and held her hand on the activating lever. She hesitated, started to pull the lever, and then hesitated again. She said, "I can't do this. I don't know what is going to happen."

Gotlieb, followed by St. John and Wallace came into the back room. Gotlieb said, "It's too late to turn back now."

Mark's eyes widened. He said, "What the hell is going on?" As a sign of stress his private part withered.

St. John said, "Hi, Mark. Looks like your all tied up for the night."

Mark shouted, "Let me out of this contraption."

Gotlieb said, "Sorry lover boy." He pulled the activating lever to the maximum setting.

Although he was squirming, trying to get out of the straps that held him, Mark was not feeling any pain. He stopped struggling and watched the three observers. They were staring at him. Then Alex gasped, "Where did he go?"

Gotlieb said, "It worked. Oh my God, it worked."

Wallace said, "Mark, are you still there?"

"Of course I'm still here, you friggin idiot. Let me out of this piece of junk."

The three observers saw two wrist straps and two ankle straps wiggling back and forth. They appeared to be empty.

Mark said, "What are you staring at?"

He turned his head and looked at his hands. They weren't there. He could feel them. They were strapped in. But they weren't there. "Where are my hands?" He looked down. "Where are my feet?" And then he cried out, "Where is my pecker?"

When St. John unbuckled Mark's leg, he kicked the young man in the face. "There you bastard. What did you do to me?"

It took over an hour to get Mark to settle down enough to unstrap him the rest of the way. During that time, Alex protested that she didn't know what the apparatus would do, just that she was promised that it wouldn't hurt him. Also, Wallace told him about the huge threat that faced America. He described Aris's conclusions. He said that the Agency needed to put its best case officer inside the terrorist activities. Finally, St. John said that he didn't know how long it might take, but that he suspected that the effects would eventually wear off.

Mark began to consider the possibilities. He got up from the chair that he was setting on and walked around behind Alex. He noticed that the three observers were still looking and talking at the chair that he had been setting in. He reached across Alex's back, put his hand down her blouse and squeezed her breast.

Alex screamed. Then she said, "Mark, Stop that. Behave."

"That's not the way you acted at O'Tooles. Aren't you hot for me now?"

Alex didn't know how to answer. She felt sorry for Mark. But a pig is a pig and Mark was a real pig.

They decided that Mark should remain in the Headquarters Building for the evening. Alex went down to disaster preparedness and grabbed some blankets and pillows and returned. They set up a large brown leather sofa in Gotlieb's office as place for Mark to sleep. Carl stayed with him.

The next morning, when Sally Fairweather, Gotlieb's executive secretary, came into work, she noticed that her boss's door was locked. She took out a key from the back of her desk drawer and opened it. She saw Carl St. John sleeping in the boss's large leather chair. She turned towards the couch and saw a cup of coffee, suspended in air and tilted at an angle. She saw a stream of coffee flowing downward and settling in a puddle, also suspended in air. She screamed. The coffee cup moved to a table. St John woke up with a start.

"How did you do that," Sally grilled St. John. Is it an optical illusion?"

Remembering how the OTS fellows had placed a totally undetectable whoopee cushion on her chair, Sally said, " I know that you guys are always trying to play tricks on me."

She heard a laugh come from the deserted couch and saw the puddle of coffee jiggling.

"Don't do that any more."

The puddle of coffee move up and came towards her. She cringed back. Then she felt something brushing her cheek. It felt like a kiss. Then she felt something rubbing her butt. She said, "Now St. John, stop that. This isn't the office Christmas Party."

Sally felt uneasy. She couldn't figure out how St. John was pulling this trick off.

Her boss came into the room. "Sally, go back out into the front office. Close the door. Don't let anyone in unless I authorize it. And don't speak to anyone about what you've seen here."

Sally was now really curious about what was going on.

Within five minutes, Sally called over the intercom, "Alex Pack and Irving Wallace are here."

"Thank you, Sally. Send them in."

Gotlieb unlocked the door.

Alex was first to enter. "Is Mark still here?"

"Yes I am."

"How do you feel?"

"Fine. Although it's a little difficult to do things like picking up a coffee cup. It's like you don't know where your fingers are."

St. John said, "We have a small problem."

"What's that," Gotlieb asked.

"Well, I made a pot of coffee and Mark drank a cup. Seems that you could see the coffee flowing down his throat and into his stomach. It finally faded away. I think what happens is that when he goes through a physiological change, it takes a while for his system to adapt, to reach homeostasis."

"When does this happen?"

"We just noticed it with the coffee this morning. I don't know. I guess that he needs to be careful where he eats or drinks."

Chapter 27

FIELD TESTS

They discussed Mark's unusual characteristics throughout the morning. Lunchtime came. Mark said, "I'm going crazy. How about a test walk around the building?"

"Good idea. Let's see if anyone notices anything. But remember, you can't eat anything."

Gotlieb said, "And we're all going with you.

Gotlieb opened the door and told Sally, "We're all going for lunch. Be back in half an hour."

Gotlieb held the door open for a few seconds. Then Alex walked through the opening followed by Wallace, then St. John and finally Gotlieb himself.

They walked down the headquarters corridors. For a while, Mark walked behind the three as they walked abreast. This allowed him to get a feel for how to walk without seeing his arms and legs. Finally, he moved in front. Then he tried moving through small groups of people. The first time he tried to enter an elevator, he bumped into a young man. The man looked around. Alex stepped in, pushing the invisible Mark aside and said, "Excuse me. Sorry I bumped you." She flashed her best smile. He smiled back.

They went down to the basement and passed by a small convenience store. While the other three were standing outside arguing where to go next, Mark entered the stand. He was startled when he heard the man behind the counter say, "How can I help you?"

Mark looked around. No one else was in the room. The operator repeated, "How can I help you?"

Mark said, "Are you talking to me?"

The operator replied, "Who else. There's just you and me here."

Mark looked at the operator and remembered, the place was called the Blindman's Stand before politically correct language changed it to the Visually Impaired Person's Facility. He even remembered the man's name, Bob. He realized that Bob was relying on skills that he had developed to overcome his handicap, ultra sensitive senses of smell, hearing and temperature. "Hey Bob, I'm just looking around."

"Oh hey, Mark, take your time."

Mark said, "See ya later," and went back out to join his three walking companions. As they were walking though a dirty part of the building, St. John pointed out that although Mark was invisible, you could still see his footprints in the dust. Mark made a mental note to remember that.

They passed by the men's locker room, where a crowd of young men were exiting in running clothes and shoes, ready to do a few miles around the compound. Then they passed the woman's locker room. They continued down the hall.

Gotlieb said, "Mark, how are you feeling now?"

There was no response. He repeated, "Mark, is everything ok?"

Mark had broken off as they passed the women's locker room. He followed a young hardbody into the changing area. Before him stood a bevy of beautiful bodies, some fully dressed, some half dressed, and some undressed. He paused to smell the roses.

All the sudden, one of the women screamed and said, "Look!"

pointing towards Mark. She said, "It's a penis."

Twenty two pairs of eyes turned towards where he stood. "Oh, my god, it is a penis."

Mark looked down. Sure enough, there was his little Willie, standing at attention. He turned and ran out into the hall. His three fellow travelers watched as a penis flew like a laser-guided arrow down the hall and into the men's room.

Alex said, "Oh, oh. We've got a real problem. Looks like when he gets a boner, it counts as one of those physiological changes that Carl talked about. And Mark is always getting a boner."

Just then the men's room door opened and no one came out. Mark said, "I'm back. Looks like it takes a couple of minutes for my body to accept changes."

Gotlieb looked at Wallace and said, "This complicates things. We've got to do some careful planning."

For three days, the team conducted a "murder board" where every issue, every concern, every plan of action, every step was examined. They tried to examine all the knowns and all the unknowns that they knew about. They were, of course, unable to examine the unknown unknowns.

At the end of the three-day session, Gotlieb announced that there would be a serious field test. He had asked the Office of Security to do a survey and find out who in the Washington D.C. area had the best security system. This survey would include everyone, the President, the VP; all were fair game. Gotlieb figured that if Mark could penetrate D.C.'s best security system, he would be ready for the terrorist group.

Security delivered its report. The final choice won hands down. There was no better security than the system that protected Linda Lances. And the popular young singer was performing at the Nissan Pavilion that night. The plan would call for Mark to extemporize. He would have to find his own way in, go back stage past cameras, alarm systems, guards, locked doors, and past on big black fellow who has been known to break heads for fun.

The team built a collection requirements list to guide Mark through his efforts. The list included:

- What kind of makeup did she use? (provided by Alex)

- What kind of panties did she wear? (provided by St John

- What kind of shoes did she wear? (provided by Wallace)

- What kind of pets did she have? (provided by Gotlieb.)

He was also tasked to get general impressions of the young singer's habits and wardrobe.

Wallace arranged for transportation that evening. As twilight approached, a dark blue Ford Expedition arrived at the Nissan Pavilion and parked in a handicap space near the main entrance. The right back door opened. No one got out. The door closed.

Mark followed two fat ladies wearing spandex shorts and tank tops. They were as efficient as the Washington Redskins front line at clearing a path for him. As they peeled off to wedge themselves into their seats, Mark continued down the steps. He climbed on the stage and crossed it towards the backside entrance. He entered a corridor marked "Performers Only."

Several people jammed the hallway. He waited until a large black man came by and headed up the corridor. He fell in behind the hulk. They went towards a room marked "Private." The man knocked on the door and said, "Linda, I need to see you out here. There's a change in the lead band.:

Linda Lance opened the door. She had makeup on and had her hair in a hairnet. Mark avoided looking at the nipples that showed through her t-shirt. All he needed now was to get a physiological change. The black dude would rip it off.

As she exited her dressing room, Mark slid in, stopping the door only momentarily. The door snapped shut.

Mark began to respond to the collection requirements list, proof that he made it in the room and functioned well. He ticked off the requirements:

- Bonnie Bell Lip Smacker

- Sonia Dekar P-wash

- Mack Cosmetic Bag

- Versace Dresses

- Lisa Kline Hats and Dresses

- Victoria Secret underwear

- A Pink Movado diamond Watch

Just then the door opened. "It's all screwed up, but I'll make it happen," Linda said as she entered her dressing room. She went to her dressing table and sat down. She reached in a bag that was setting on the floor and pulled out a joint. She put it in her lips and reached down to retrieve a cigarette lighter. She lit the joint up and took a deep draw. She closed her eyes and sighed.

She then sat the joint down and pulled off her t-shirt. She stood up and examined her figure. She reached down and took another hit on the joint. She closed her eyes and smiled.

Mark went through and immediate physiological change. Willie woke up. He stood directly behind her so she could not see Willie standing at attention.

He reached out and gently rubbed her back.

Startled, she turned around but saw nothing. She turned back around and took another hit. She closed her eyes.

He resumed rubbing her back. She smiled and muttered, "This is some maryjane."

He reached around with both hands and began to gently massage her breasts. He moved his hands away as she took another hit. He resumed the massage. He then reached down and gently removed her panties. She stepped out of them.

About one hour later, Linda finally focused on the loud banging on her door. It was Big Rod, her bodyguard. "Come on, Linda. You're over due. The fans are getting noisy. Come on before a riot starts."

The next morning's Washington Post arts critic wrote, "Last night I had a chance to see Linda Lance perform live. She was stunning. I never saw so much sexual energy in a performance. Her entourage even said that they never saw her so animated. Whatever motivated her ought to be bottled."

Another report was sent at the same time. It listed Ms. Lance's wardrobe and accessories. Under the section of General Items, the report indicated that Ms. Lance was open to new and unusual experiences. Mark Steel signed the report.

Chapter 28

FINISHING THE TUNNEL

John Smart met with the three GRU goons and the rabidly Islamic young terrorist, Hosein, in the living room of his house adjacent to the CIA compound. "By my calculations, the tunnel is now under the center of the CIA compound. I set up some equipment and tested my calculations. We're right on target. We're under the ladies dressing room. Want to listen in on what the recorders are picking up?"

"Yes. Let's hear the babes talk."

The four conspirators went down to the wine cellar and entered the tunnel. They went into the listening room, where several reel-to-reel recorders were turning. He turned on some loudspeakers. They heard some showers running and some toilets flushing with a whoosh, gurgle, gulp.

John asked, "Can you figure out how I know we are under the ladies dressing room and not the men's room."

"Cuz they are taking so long in the showers. Crap, with my wife and daughter I never get in the bathroom."

"That's one factor. But also you don't hear any urinals flushing. You know. They go whoosh, gurgle without a gulp."

"Hey, you're right."

"We'll pick up a lot of conversations early in the morning, at lunch time and immediately after 5:00 p.m. That's when the girls all go out running and come back to shower."

"Do you got a camera up there?"

"No."

"Why the hell not?"

John ignored his question. He continued, "I'll fine tune the mikes, see if we can pick up some conversations." He tweaked the dials.

Three female voices came across the wires.

"Did you hear about the floating penis?"

"No, what are you talking about?"

"Right here, at lunch time. Five girls said that they saw a floating penis. Said it flew out the door , down the hallway, and disappeared."

"No way!"

"Was it, like big?"

"They said, one of the bigger ones that they ever saw."

"Was it black?"

"No. It was white."

"Then it probably wasn't too big."

"Hey, where do I get one?"

"Maybe it'll come back."

The conspirators looked at one another and said, 'What the hell are they talking about?"

John turned the receiver off and said, "Anyway, we're under the Headquarters Building."

"No *gavno*," Stanislav said. "We done it good? *Da*?"

"Yes, we've done good?"

"Break out the vodka," Gorky whooped, "Let's get drunk."

"Excuse me, I'm going to go pray to Allah. He made this happen."

"I didn't see him haulin any dirt," Stanislav hooted.

Hosein uttered, "Infidel!" as he walked into the back room and began to unroll his prayer rug.

Smart screwed the top off a bottle of Smirnov, filled four glasses and passed them around. "Nazdarovia."

"Nazda friggin' rovia," came the response.

After about the third or fourth "nazdarovia," no one was counting, Gorky looked at John Smart and slurred, "Thiz is a good friggin' tunnel ain't it?"

"Itz a great friggin' tunnel."

"So hows come its so good? Whered ya get the plans anyway?"

"Lemme tell the whole story. This ain't the first friggin' tunnel to be built for intelligence purposes. You all read in the Post about the CIA tunnel under our embassy."

"Na, I don't read the paper unless its got babes on the cover, you know like the Enquirer. Even then I just look at the pictures."

"Ha, he can't even read."

"No bullshit, I can read. Just ain't interested."

"So anyway. The CIA dug under our embassy and got caught at it. So their ass was in a crack."

"Yeah, uh hu, ours will be too if we get caught."

"We ainta gonna get caught."

"There were other tunnels. The best story is about the CIA's foul up in Berlin back in the 1950's."

"What happened then?"

"They dug a tunnel from West Berlin right under the wall to East Berlin. It was a work of art. Had air conditioning and everything."

"So how come we know about it?"

"That's the cool part of the story. My old friends at the KGB knew about it even before it was built."

"No kiddin, how did they know that?"

"Well, we had a spy in British Intelligence. Name was Georgie Blake. I met him in Moscow and he told me all about the CIA tunnel. We got lots of good ideas on how to build this one from Georgie."

"How did he find out about the tunnel?"

"That's the best part of the story. The CIA just gave him a big briefing on it. They told him, he told his case officer. His case officer told Moscow. And Moscow told the rest of the KGB."

"Didn't they tell us in the GRU?"

"No."

"Why not?"

"I don't know."

"You know, youse guys never gave us no respect. You're just a bunch of assholes."

"Hey, It wasn't me. I'd a told you, old buddy."

Gorky chugged another glass of vodka and said, "Am I really your buddy? That's nice."

"Anyhow, as I said I talked to Georgie…"

"Wait a minute, wasn't George Blake arrested and thrown in the slammer in England?"

"Yes, but he broke out and got to Moscow."

Gez, he musta been some kind of guy."

"Yeah, he was. Anyhow, we used CIA plans plus some ideas from the Chinese and North Koreans to build this tunnel. We got water pumps to keep it dry, air handlers to refresh oxygen, and even stuff above the tunnel liner to make sure that the ground on top isn't too hot or too cold."

"What do we care about the ground on top? Are you an ecology freak, you know, a tree-hugger?"

"No, I don't give a crap about the trees. But how would you like our tunnel to cause the snow to melt on top. That's be real cool. Point like an arrow to this here house."

Gorky took another slug of vodka and said, "Friggin A, you're right."

Stanislav asked, "What's that big red button I see next to the door?"

"That's part of our security system. We got a bunch of garden hoses filled with explosives, C-4 I think, that we stuffed above the tunnel liner. If I push the button, most of the tunnel collapses."

"Jez, don't push it if I'm in the tunnel."

"No, no. The plan is to get everyone out, seal off the doors in the wine cellar, they're steel and concrete you know, and pop the tunnel."

"Hey, don't get excited and do it while I'm in there."

"Don't worry, I'll look after all of you. This is a great day, isn't it? Good friends, good vodka, a good tunnel. Life is good. Nazda friggin rovia."

Small may have felt good about the tunnel, but he would have had bad feelings if he know that the FBI was closing in on identifying him. The final dot was about to be connected by FBI Agency Ralph Adams as he pulled into the parking lot of Langley Mercedes.

Agent Adams, wearing a dark blue suit, a white shirt, a school tie, and

12-pound wingtips, entered the salesroom. Margie, the New Car Sales Manager's secretary, met him with a smile and a greeting, "Welcome to Langley Mercedes. Are you interested in one of our wonderful driving machines?"

Before he could answer, she made a mental appraisal of this potential husband. He wore a neatly pressed, but inexpensive suit, probably an off-the-rack purchase. His shoes were well polished and his laces were evenly tied. These were signs of an anal-retentive personality. His hair was neatly cut and short.

When he spoke, she was able to add to her assessment. He said, "Who's in charge? I want to speak to him."

By the tone in his voice, she assessed him to have an authoritarian personality. This appraisal was verified by the content of what he said. However, he did not look her in the eye, so she mentally added "somewhat insecure" to her appraisal list.

These were not the attributes that she wanted in a man. Actually, they were almost opposite of what she wanted. Her ideal list included: laid back, flexible, and self-assured. However, she was quite aware that Prince Charmings very seldom fit the required profile for a less than perfect princess. Not that she was bad looking, she found that she could catch a one-night stand anytime she wanted over at O'Tooles. But she wanted more and what had emerged was the need for security. This need trumped all the others.

She appraised him on this dimension. He had that dogged look that all D.C. commuters cultivated over years of driving in morning and evening rush hour. That probably meant that he had steady employment. He had that unmotivated slouch that affects many government servants, so he probably worked for the government. He was wearing what looked like a college ring or a Marine Corp ring. He didn't look tough enough to be a Marine, so she figured him to be just a college graduate. Then she saw the clue. She was surprised that she missed it.

"You're with the FBI, aren't you?"

"What makes you say that?"

"Last year some of your colleagues came in to check us out for commies and terrorists. Seems that the Pope was coming to D.C. and he was gonna travel down Route 7 from Dulles Airport to the White House. He wanted to come this way to get maximum exposure to the faithful masses. I had a long talk with a nice young agent named 'George.' Do you know George?"

"We have lots of Georges in the Bureau."

"Well, he was wearing one of those ear pieces that you have on. Said that they all wear them. Showed me his gun too. You gotta gun?"

"Listen lady, I need to see the guy who is in charge."

"Oh, that's Mr. Smart. He's not here."

"How can I get a hold of him?"

"Well, he's been out for about a week. That's unusual."

"Unusual, what's unusual?"

"Well, he's been acting different since that foreign man came in and they went off for a ride. I knew that the man wasn't Mercedes material, but Mr. Smart spent a lot of time with him anyway."

"Can you describe the man?"

"Yes I can, in great detail. But you gotta take me to lunch first."

Lunch became a nooner. Agent Adams showed just how task oriented he could be. By 3:30 in the afternoon, he had:

- Found out that John Smart had been absent for several days under unusual circumstances.

- Got a description of both John Smart and a man named Igor, last name unknown.

- Got Smart's home, cell and business phone numbers.

- Got a photo of Smart and his family.

- Performed service above and beyond the call of duty, leaving Margie exhausted and smiling with a look of true love in her eyes.

Agent Adams reached over the side of the bed and pulled his trousers to his chest. He reached into a pocket and pulled out his cell phone. Before he dialed, he looked over at Margie and said, "Put my gun down. You're gonna hurt yourself."

She stroked the barrel and said, "Oh, it feels so strong, so alive."

"Put it down," he ordered. She put it back in its holster.

Agent Adams dialed a phone number. After a few seconds he spoke in the phone, "I think I found our man."

He described what he knew. Then after a few seconds, he answered, "I'm over at the Motel Six next to Langley Mercedes.... Ok ...That's at CIA Headquarters? I'll be right over. Should take about 15 minutes." He hung up the phone.

Back in the Counterterrorism Center, Wallace turned the team and said, "I think that we've got our Russian connection." He smiled.

Back at the Motel Six, the two lovebirds exchanged telephone numbers and expressions of everlasting love. Agent Adams got dressed and left the room. On the way by a trashcan, he pitched the slip with the telephone number.

Chapter 29

PENETRATING THE TUNNEL

A white pickup truck marked Fairfax County Property Assessor pulled up in front of the Smart residence. Alex Pack, dressed in blue jeans, workmen boots and a light blue shirt marked FCPA got out of the truck. The passenger door opened and no one got out. Alex said, "Stay behind me and behave."

Mark replied by pinching her bottom. He thought, *Damn she looks sexy in those workmen clothes.*

Alex walked up to the front of the house, climbed the five steps that led to the front door and rang the doorbell. The bells chimed the first few bars of *the William Tell Overture.*

In about 30 seconds John Smart opened the door. "No door to door salesmen allowed. It's against neighborhood rules."

Alex smiled and said, "I'm from the Fairfax County Property Assessor's Office. I'm here on official business."

Smart had a genetic aversion to officials that had been bred in by generations of relatives who suffered centuries of oppressive rule in Russia. "What's wrong?" he challenged.

"Well, its been reported that you are doing a lot of modification to your home. A search of our records indicates that you haven't filed for construction permits or notified the Property Assessment Office."

"We're only improving our rock garden out back. We're thinking about putting in a pool but haven't decided yet."

"That's a large pile of dirt and rock just for a rock garden. The neighbors have indicated that trucks have been hauling dirt away for ten hours a day for weeks. Just how big is this rock garden?"

"It's pretty big. I got the idea from People Magazine, you know, Madonna's back yard. Except mine will be bigger and better."

"Oh, well, anyway, I need to inspect the work."

"Just a minute. Let me turn the stove off. I'll be right out with you." Smart closed the door and went inside the living room. He told his fellow troglodytes, "Disappear upstairs."

Outside, Alex spoke to nobody, "I'll check the outside. I'll try to keep Smart occupied outside. You slip inside and see what you can find."

"Roger."

Smart opened the door and stepped out. He felt a rush of wind passing by him before he closed the door. He looked up to see if a storm was coming in. The sky was sunny and cloudless.

Alex and Smart walked around to the side of the house. She asked, "Have you made any modifications that increase the total square footage of the house itself?"

"No, all the work has been on the outside. Just yard work."

The pair walked around to the back of the house. Alex was startled by the size of the dirt pile. It was about forty feet long and ten feet high. "Wow," she said in amazement. "That's a lot of dirt."

"Well," Smart said defensively, "we are going to spread some of it around for top soil and haul some of it away."

Alex mentally calculated how much dirt was there. She increased the estimate by multiplying how many times the trucks came and went by the size of each truckload. Thank goodness the head of the neighborhood association, who lived down the block, kept careful book on such activities. After all, she was in a position of civic trust and she had to ensure that no one would step out of line. Rules are rules. She had the widow Jackson's wheelchair ramp taken away because it didn't conform to building rules. So what that the old lady broke her neck when she tried to back her wheelchair up the five stairs to her front porch and the chair ran down the hill and onto Route 123 where she got hit by a passing FedEx truck.

Alex's mental estimates were that some 600,000 cubic feet of dirt had been removed from somewhere. That's a lot of dirt and the back yard project didn't even begin to explain it.

Inside the house, Mark moved from room to room. He spotted three men lounging in an upstairs bedroom watching the Jerry Springer Show. He paused to watch Jerry back off the stage. That was a sure sign that the two fat girls were about to attack each other. He heard one scream at the other, "How could you –bleep - my husband. He's your brother."

The other bumptious behemoth yelled back, "We've been at it since he turned fourteen. Who do you think taught him all those good moves?" They ran at each other like two sumo wrestlers. Ozzie and Harriet it wasn't.

Mark went down stairs and into the basement. He found a beautiful carved pool table and a private viewing theater with individual leather seats. He sat down on one of the seats and leaned back. The chair reclined. He thought, *This is a real classy place.*

He opened the door to a small room off of the theater and looked inside. It was a wine cellar. He picked up a couple of bottles and noted that they were vintage samples from Northern California, Germany and France. He thought, this guy Smart has good taste.

Mark went back out to the poolroom. He couldn't resist. He picked up a pool stick. It was inlaid with ivory. He made a shot at the eight ball. The balls made a crack sound and the eight ball fell in the left corner pocket. He heard someone say, "What was that sound?"

Someone else said, "It came from down in the basement."

Mark put the cue stick down and went over to the corner of the room and stood behind a tall plant. He watched as two men came down stairs and walked through the basement, looking for the source of the sound. Not finding anything, one went upstairs and the other entered the wine cellar. Mark followed him. The man looked around the cellar and then reached out and turned two bottles, one on the upper left and the other on the upper right of the wine rack at the rear of the cellar. Mark watched in amazement as the rack split in the middle and slid into the wall. The man entered the room and pressed a button. The rack began to close. Mark rushed in and stood with his back against the wall of what looked like a long and well-constructed cave.

Outside Alex continued to walk with John Smart. She said, "Where are you thinking about putting the pool?"

"Over here to the left side of the yard. We are putting in a patio directly in back of the house. Then the rock garden."

"You won't need a permit for the patio. Nor for the garden. If you build anything more than a foot off the ground, you'll need to get it inspected. Get a permit before you start any pool."

Alex was concerned. She thought that Mark would be back by now. She began to stall. "What do you do for a living?"

"I'm at Langley Mercedes."

"Oh, do you own it/"

"No, I'm the new car sales manager."

"My friend owns a 500SL."

"Did he buy it from us?"

"I don't know."

"When he's ready to upgrade, have him give me a call. I can get him a deal."

Alex thought, *Salesmen. They're always hustling.*

As they walked back around to the front of the house a taxicab pulled up. An older woman and a younger one got out. Alex thought, they must be Smart's wife and daughter.

The younger woman ran up to Smart and hugged him. "Oh, daddy, it's good to see you." She gave her mother a dirty look. The older woman did not hug Smart. In fact, she seemed very aloof, also upset.

Smart said, "So, you're back from Cancun." Alex detected coolness in his voice and realized that there was a storm brewing.

The older woman said, "John, we have to talk."

The younger woman hugged Smart harder. She cried, "Oh, daddy!"

Smart's wife said, "You didn't even call to see how the operation went."

He responded, "I didn't have to. I saw your new tits on TV. So did millions of others."

She answered, "I know, MTV has forwarded to me over fifty letters, guys wanting my phone number."

"I also noticed that Dr. Jim seemed to enjoy his work. He has an interesting way of checking out how you were healing. Was that a tongue test he administered?"

"Dr. Jim is what we need to talk about."

"Don't tell me you two fell in love and he wants to run off with you."

Smart's daughter hugged him and cried, "Oh, daddy, I'm so sorry. I love you."

Smart's wife said "Yes, that's right. I love him. He said that I could be his ultimate Mona Lisa. He would make me perfect. My body and my face. He says that I'm the perfect canvas. He wants to mold me to his his ideal of a perfect woman. A work of art."

Smart said, "Let's hope he doesn't like Picasso."

His wife answered, "You know that this has been coming for a long time. You're so wrapped up in selling cars and making money."

"Like, the money doesn't mean anything to you. You got more diamonds that Liz Taylor. More shoes than Imelda Marcos. You're a spoiled brat."

Bursting into tears, she said, "But I don't have love. Dr. Jim showed me just what love can be."

Alex stood watching this family disintegrate. She thought, *Boy, is Mr. Smart having a bad day. And his whole week is going to be that way.*

About twenty feet below her, Mark was following the man down the lined tunnel. The invisible spy was collecting intelligence. Heavy door in the wine cellar. Looks like it's made of steel and concrete. Tunnel lined, lighted, and well ventilated. Seems to go straight. Can't tell the direction from underground. But goes away from the house in an almost perpendicular direction.

As they approached what appeared to be the end of the tunnel, Mark saw the man stoop down and begin to duck walk down a poorly constructed tunnel. It looked like an add-on. No lining, lights haphazardly strung up, portable fans that did a poor job of moving the air around. As he followed behind the man at a distance of about ten feet, he could detect gross smells, like someone had farted. His legs tired. Duckwalking never was easy. He tried to crawl on his hands and knees for a while but found that his Willie kept getting tangled up between his thighs. This was the first time in his life that he wished that he wasn't so hung. He stopped for a while to rest then hurried to catch up with the man.

Finally, the man reached a large chamber about six feet high. He stood up in the middle of it and began to inspect a series of wires and microphones. Mark climbed into the chamber and stood in the corner, watching.   He counted the number of microphones that he could see. He also saw that someone had attempted to splice telephone cables and had exposed a handful of fiber optic cables.

It seemed to Mark that the man would be in the tunnel for a while, so he decided to duck walk back to the main tunnel and go find Alex. As he climbed out he bumped his head and a bit of the tunnel top fell down. The man looked startled and confused. Then he saw a rat scurry out of the tunnel and into the chamber. He said, "Damn rats," and then resumed his inspection of wires.

Half way down the tunnel, Mark heard that someone had entered the side tunnel from the lined tunnel and was coming towards him. Knowing that there was not room to hide on the side to let this new man pass, Mark began to backtrack towards the chamber room. As he got close to the end of the tunnel he could see the first man leave the chamber room and start towards him. *Oh, oh,* he thought. *I'm stuck in the middle.*

It was like a squeeze play in baseball where he was caught between first and second base. He wasn't sure of what to do. If he tried to run over the second baseman and get to the tunnel he was sure that the second baseman would wrap his arms around him and he would be caught.

He decided. In a low voice with a faux accent, he said, "I'm coming down the tunnel."

It worked. The guy at first base said, "Me too. Back out."

The guy at second base replied, "Hey, butt head, you back out. I'm more than half way."

"No, you back out. I got things to do."

"Like, I don't"

Mr. First Base gave up, "Ok, ok, I'll go back to the chamber."

Mark moved back to the chamber at first base.

The second baseman came into the chamber.

Climbing into the empty tunnel, Mark made a crawl for it. Ignoring the pain, he scurried along like a rat. Reaching the lined tunnel, he practically ran to the wine cellar, went into the viewing room, scooted up the stairs and out the front door.

Mark found Alex standing to the side, watching Smart yelling, his daughter clinging to him crying, and his wife stomping to the garage. Mrs. Smart opened the garage door, jumped into a black Mercedes, started it and peeled out of the garage and down the driveway. She made a right turn on two wheels and sped down to Route 123. She made a right hand turn without stopping and sped off.

Smart's daughter said, "Come on inside, daddy, I'll make you a Rum and Coke."

"I don't want any of that Island stuff. Make it a scotch, straight up."

"Ok, daddy."

Mark walked up behind Alex and gently grabbed her arm. At first she was startled and then she remembered Mark. "Let's get out of here."

Alex returned to the white truck. She opened the driver's side door and got in. The passenger door opened by itself and no one got in.

Within and hour, Alex and Mark were in the CTC undergoing a debriefing.

After Mark described the lined tunnel, the hastily built extension and the listening devices, most of the team agreed that the tunnel's purpose was to gather intelligence.

Gotlieb asked, "Who they hell are they giving the intell to? The Ruskies are out of the game. What could they get from a tap on the Agency's phones."

"Maybe they're using it to get info for the Russian Mafia. We had word of Ahmad meeting with the General. Maybe he's the go-between connecting the tunnel to the Mafia."

"Why wouldn't they go to Smart directly?"

"I don't know."

"How about blackmail? Maybe they're trying to find out which Russians were spying for the CIA during the Cold War."

"Hell,, all the Ruskies that worked for us have written books about their spying activities and are rich. It's hard to blackmail someone who told his story to millions of readers."

"Maybe Smart is getting intell for the Iranians."

"That's a possibility. Makes sense. The Iranians would want to know what we know about them and what we know about what they know about us."

"I'll buy that."

"Sounds good to me."

"Then we have a consensus?"

"Sure."

Aris Paprika finally spoke up, "No we don't. I still think that its ground zero for a nuclear bomb."

"Oh Aris, you just don't want us to disconnect your dots. "

"Look, we heard that they discussed the problems with getting to a target in the air. That air coverage is so strong that the only thing that could get through would be a flying kite. We also know that they think that the roads approaching D.C. are well covered. They probably know about the radiation detectors we've deployed on all the approaches. So on the ground is out. So that leaves underground. They aren't going to get to anywhere through our pipes and conduits. So that leaves the tunnel. I believe that the chamber is ground zero."

"So, you said that they won't come by air or ground. How are they going to get the bomb here. Build a tunnel all the way from Florida?"

"I don't know yet. But they'll have a way to do it."

Alex said, "Aris might be right. We better beef up surveillance and find out if the bomb is heading here."

Aris said, "It's coming here."

"How do you know?"

"I don't know how I know. I just know."

Gotlieb said, "Well, this isn't a democracy. I'm deciding. We'll leave the tunnel as is. Wallace, can you set up surveillance teams on the house and its occupants. Also get taps on Smart's phones. We need video surveillance. Get photos of the three men that Mark saw in the bedroom and in the tunnel."

"Should we send Mark back into the tunnel?"

"Not right now. He almost got caught. If he was caught, it would blow the whole operation."

"How about sending him back into the house?"

"Let's hold off on that. It's an option for later on."

"The most important thing that we can do is to find Ebrahimi. Maybe he could confirm or deny our conclusions.

Chapter 30

THE FINAL VOYAGE OF THE BOMB

Ahmad and Ebrahimi were making good time in the rental car. Every time he saw a highway patrol car on the road, Eb got nervous, but it seemed as if no one was looking for a Chevelle. Ahmad stopped at a gas station on the South and North Carolina border and made a call to Hosein's cell phone. He gave the young terrorist directions on where to meet in the D.C. area. Hosein, in return, warned Ahmad about the high security level that Homeland Defense had set and that there was heavy aerial surveillance over the capital area.

Hosein warned, "It's so tight only a kite could get through." After a pause, he added, "They have some kind of radiation detection gear at major intersections all around the beltway."

As he continued driving, Ahmad tried to think of options for getting the bomb to the meeting site. Once there, they would probably be home free. His mind was drawing a blank when they approached Ashland, Virginia about 70 or so miles south of Washington on I-95.

It was early in the afternoon. Ebrahimi said, "Can we pull off for a while. There's a Taco Bell sign. I'd like something to eat."

Ahmad was feeling the bile in his stomach caused by stressing out because he couldn't think of how to get around the blocks that faced him in the D.C. area. He said, "Ok. I'll get off here."

Ebrahimi was munching down on his fourth hard-shelled taco. Ahmad was staring out the window, fretting over his dilemma. Then he shouted, "Allah Akbar, That's the solution." 30 pairs of eyes looked at him. He looked down at his lap and softly hissed, "Get rid of that taco. We're leaving right now."

Ebrahimin stuffed the remaining half of the taco in his mouth and, spitting out crumbs, said "I'm ready."

Ahmad rushed out to the Chevelle and started the engine. He put the car in gear and stepped on the accelerator. Ebrahimi said, "Holy shit, let me get all the way in the car."

Ahmad said, "I told you not to use blasphemy." He continued driving fast.

Ebrahimi finally got the door shut and looked up. They were following a old Ford Bronco with Virginia tags.

The Bronco was towing a small object that looked like a hang glider except it had an engine. "What the hell…heck is that? Ebrahimi asked.

Ahmad said, "That's my ticket to Washington. Hosein said that only a kite could get into D.C. through the air. Well, that's not much more than a kite."

"We're gonna fly that into Washington?"

"Not we, me. I'll need that second seat to carry the bomb."

"How are you gonna stop the Bronco?"

"I'm not going to stop him. He's from around here. I'll just follow him."

"How do you know that he's from around here?"

"Look at the bumper sticker."

Ebrahimi looked, it read, "Doswell, home of Kings Dominion."

Ahmad said, "Kings Dominion is just across I-95."

They followed the Bronco passed the entrance to Kings Dominion eastward. They continued past a large horse ranch that had a sign that read "Birthplace of Secretariat." They watched the Bronco turn into a driveway just past the ranch. Ahmad pulled into a short driveway just past where the Bronco had turned.

They saw a house, a small hangar and a short dirt runway. They watched as the Bronco's driver backed the ultralight into a small hangar, uncoupled the trailer, pulled forward, got out and closed the hangar's doors. They watched him get in the Bronco, pull out of the driveway and head back in the direction of Kings Dominion.

Ahmad started the Chevelle's engine and drove into the man's driveway. He pulled around behind the hangar and they entered through a side door. Inside were three ultralight aircraft. One was under a tarp. Ahmad inspected the two uncovered aircraft. Both might work. Ebrahimi was curious about the converted object and pulled the tarp off of it. At first it looked like a tandem two-seater ultralight. On closer inspection, Ahmad noted several interesting things about it. The front position was a seat for the pilot. The rear position had been altered to handle a small cargo load.

Ebrahimi said, "Look at the cool paint job. It's sky blue on the underside of the wings and looks like deer hunter's camouflage on the top side. That's pretty cool. Maybe he uses it for deer hunting."

Ahmad observed, "The engines have large mufflers on them. This airplane was built to fly quietly and be difficult to see from both below and above. I wonder why he has such a design?"

Ebrahimi continued to rummage through the hangar. Then he came upon something that his frat brother's would definitely like to find. It was a very large stash of marijuana. He connected the dots between the camouflaged airplane and the maryjane. "This guy is a drug smuggler. He carries his cargo in the ultralight."

Ahmad uttered, "Allah Akbar. It's built like a kite. And Hosein said, 'Only a kite can get through. Allah hears and he delivers.'"

"Who is gonna fly it?" Ebrahimi asked.

"I guess it's me?"

"Can you fly it?"

"I don't know. I know how to take off and fly a 747. Can't land one though. I should be able to handle this one. Can you find any manuals?"

They looked around. Ebrahimi found a bookshelf on the left wall. It included several books on ultralights. He found the one they needed, *Flying Ultralight Aircraft for Dummies.*

Ahmad said, "See if you can find anything that gives the specs on this airplane." He took the *Dummies* guide from Ebrahimi and began to leaf through it.

"Here's the user manual. Looks like this is called a Drifter XP-503. It's built in Canada."

Ahmad thought, *Those Canadians always do make it easy for us to move around America.* He said, "See if you can find the page that gives the specs."

Ebrahimi turned a few pages and then said, "Here they are. Wing Span: 30 feet. Engine: 503 Rotax. Empty Weight: 385 pounds. Gross Weight: 785 pounds."

"Hold it. Let's see. I weigh about 165 pounds. The box weighs about 230 pounds. That makes 390 pounds. Looks like we are just under weight limits. I should be able to get it off the ground. What about things like speed?"

"It says that the Cruise Speed is 60 m.p.h. The stall speed, what ever that is, is 35 m.p.h."

"Check the gas tank. Is it full?"

"No. It's empty."

"Find some gas. Hurry."

Ahmad read how to use the stick and rudder control. He hoped that the aircraft had a larger than standard engine in it.

After about an hour of prep, Ahmad said, "Let's load the box on and let me get out of here."

"Do you want me to drive up to Washington and meet you guys?"

"No, the car will be detected by the radiation detectors when you get up to the beltway."

"Radiation detectors. Why would the car be detected?"
"Because, Ebrahimi, there's a nuclear bomb in this crate."

Ebrahimi looked stunned. "A bomb. Where did it come from? Where are you going to use it?"

"You know the rules. Limit the details of an operation. Besides, you have not shown yourself to be a good follower of Allah. You have lived your cover role too well. I saw your behavior in Cancun on television, on the Infidel's channel, MTV. You will wait here in Ashland. When you see the light in the sky to the north that shows the great and glorious event that serves Allah, you will call the Ayatollah. You will say five words and hang up. Say 'It is as Allah willed.' Then you will find your way back to Iran and throw yourself at the feet of the Ayatollah. Only he can forgive you."

Ahmad went over and opened the hangar's doors. "Now, help me wheel this aircraft out onto the runway."

They situated the airplane so it was facing into the wind. Ahmad got in the cockpit and strapped himself in. Ebrahimi handed him a helmet that he found hanging on one of the other ultralights.

Holding the *Dummies* guide book on his knee, Ahmad turned a couple of switches, pulled a throttle back and said, "Spin the prop."

At first the engine didn't catch. Ahmad pumped the choke and throttle a couple of times. "Spin it again."

This time the engine sputtered and then caught. It rev'd way to fast and the airplane started to make a circle on the ground. Ahmad pushed the throttle in and the engine fell back to idle. He said, "Straighten the airplane up again."

Ebrahimi lifted the tail up and pulled the airplane back in alignment with the dirt strip. Looking like one of the Wright Brothers, Ahmad adjusted his helmet goggles and pulled back the throttle. The ultralight began to move down the runway. It began to bounce and rose up for a moment then settled back down. Ahmad put the stick forward and the airplane stayed on the ground. It sped up. The trees got closer. Ahmad looked at the airspeed indicator. I read 25 m.p.h. The trees looked bigger. The aircraft moved faster. The airspeed indicator read 30 m.p.h. The trees looked huge. The air speed read 35 m.p.h. Ahmad held it on the ground. Then he pulled the stick back. The ultralight took off, heading for the middle of the tree canopy. Ahmad yanked the stick back. The airplane rose rapidly just clearing the stand of trees, then began to go back down again. Ahmad finally got it into level flight. He looked down. The *Dummies* manual was gone. He reached inside his shirt and pulled out a map.

Back at the dirt airstrip, Ebrahimi stood looking up at the fading aircraft. He was appalled. A nuclear bomb. His friends were now in jeopardy. He broke into the house and picked up the phone. He called Bobo. The phone rang fifteen times before Bobo answered. "What the hell do you want?" he muttered.

"Bobo, I gotta get a hold of David, right now."

"Oh hey, Eb. Where are you? Hey guess what. Some government agency, NASA or SNA or NSA or something like that called me. Offered me a job. Said I had great intuition, what ever that is. So I sez, If my pro career doesn't pan out, I'll give them a call."

Ebrahimi interrupted, "Bobo, I don't have time for this. I need to talk to David now."

"Ok, little buddy. Here's his cell phone number."

Ebrahimi wrote the number down and hung up the phone. He dialed the number. David answered.

"It's Eb. Listen. They got a bomb, a nuclear bomb. Ahmad is on his way up there now."

David turned to the others in the CTC and said, "Listen up, it's Ebrahimi. Alex, Wallace, and Gotlieb rushed over to the young man's side. David picked up a magic marker and, moving to the white board, spoke into the phone. "Give me the details."

David wrote on the board. Ahmad in ultralight aircraft. Just took off from north of Kings Dominion. Headed North. Plane's spec's say it cruises at 60 m.p.h, can go 70 m.p.h. Has some kind of nuclear bomb in back seat. Painted in camouflage colors. Sky blue on bottom. Hunter's camouflage on top.

Gotlieb said, "Where is Ebrahimi now?"

"He said that he's just north of Kings Dominion."

"Tell him to go to the Burger King just outside the Park. Someone will be there to pick him up."

Alex turned to Wallace and said, "For Christ's sake, treat him nice this time. He's really on our side."

Wallace made a call. He turned to the group and said, "Someone will be there in fifteen minutes. And they'll treat him like royalty."

The CTC group was already moving into action. Calls were made to Langley Air Force Base. The wing commander immediately launched interceptor aircraft with orders to shoot the ultralight down on sight. Dulles air traffic control was directly notified and ordered to look for a small aircraft flying between 60 to 70 m.p.h. As soon as they locate it, they would immediately vector the Air Force planes in on it.

Alex observed, "It's just not enough. The airplane is like a kite. It goes so low and slow that the Air Force will never see it, particularly with its camouflage paint."

St. John added, "And if it's in the trees, it's below radar coverage."

Alex had a brain fart. "Let's issue an Amber Alert. We'll get everyone on the ground to find the aircraft."

"We'd set off a panic if we let them know some nut was flying around in a kite with a nuclear bomb."

"We won't say anything about the bomb. We'll say that someone kidnapped a little girl and is flying her around. Does anyone have a picture of a 3 or 4 year old girl in their wallet. Make it a little blond. Everyone will look to help a 4 year old blond girl."

Gotlieb pulled out his wallet and produced a string of pictures of his granddaughter, going all the way back to her birth some eighteen years ago. He said, "Pick one."

Alex took one taken just after her fourth birthday where she was dressed in a ballerina outfit. "This one will be perfect."

"We'll say, Be on lookout for Sally Fieldstone. 4 years old, blond. Taken by swarthy looking male. Carried away in an ultralight aircraft flying north from Kings Dominion."

"Fax this over to Homeland Defense, now. Include a picture. Get them to send it to the TV stations. Tell them we want it on the air in less than five minutes."

After surviving the near crash on take off, Ahmad seemed to be making good time. He was flying parallel to I-95. He was surprised how quiet the engines ran. He recognized the three Mattaponi Rivers and then the Rappahannock River.

As he approached the Quantico Marine Base, he wasn't sure how to get by it. He was worried about the FBI Academy that was located on the Base. They might have surface-to-air missiles or something like that. He flew in a circle trying to decide how which way to go. Finally, he decided to fly west for a while. He spotted the Lunga Reservoir on the west side of the Marine Base. He turned north and flew over it.

He was now entering the area of urban sprawl. He tried to stay along the river and creek beds where there was some tree cover. But every now and then he had to just bite the bullet and fly over houses.

Back at Homeland Defense, calls were pouring in. Sightings were reported all around the beltway. Two people in Maryland reported UFO landings. One report came from a camper in Prince William Park who had been watching TV in his oversized camper. He said that he saw a ultralight aircraft circle just east of Lunga Reservoir on the Marine Base and then head north. It was about three minutes ago, he added.

The Air Force pilots were frustrated. They couldn't see anything. Overcoming interservice rivalries, one pilot recommended that the Marines launch helicopters to help in the search effort. The politically insensitive pilot would probably be flying a desk in Elmendorf Alaska next year.

The helos were launched. Six spread out in an attack formation over the Lunga Reservoir and headed north at high speed, hoping to catch up with the ultralight.

Ahmad was now lost. The map had blown away and he didn't have a compass. He headed towards what he thought was east. He found I-95. Flying just above the tree topsss, he saw various highway signs. Then he spotted the Amber Alert. At that moment he knew that he was being pursued. As he passed over the Occoquan Reservoir, an alert woman named Ginny who was watering her tomatoes spotted him. She called to her husband, George. He snatched up an old M-1 rifle that hung over the fireplace, ran out on his deck, and aimed the rusty rifle at the fleeing ultralight aircraft. Although George had won the Marine Corp expert marksmanship medal, his vision was not as good as it was during the days of Vietnam. The shot hit a whooping crane. The bird fell into Ginny's arms. She cried out, "Oh, George. You killed the poor thing."

Ahmad continued on, flying low, under the tree canopies. Overhead a helicopter sped past him without stopping.

At Homeland Defense, a bicyclist called in on a cell phone and reported that a flying kite almost hit him as he was riding down a bike trail near Lorton Virginia. He reported this near miss happened about two minutes ago. Homeland Defense notified the Marines who ordered two of the helicopters to circle back and make another pass.

Ahmad was dismayed. The tree line opened up and before him he could see the Dulles Airport. He jinked to the right and popped back into the tree line.

One of the radar operators said, "I think that he was on my screen for a few seconds. Right here to the southeast of runway 2. He's gone now."

The Air Force was notified. Simultaneously, all commercial aircraft were ordered out of the area and told to divert to alternative airports. The jets made several passes to the east of Dulles but without avail. By this time an AWAC aircraft with look-down, shoot-down capabilities entered Washington airspace. It began to search. They could find a "noseeum" insect in a sandstorm.

But there was no longer anything to look for in the air. Ahmad was already on the ground. He had followed the Dulles Access Road to the beltway and then went down the Potomac to Turkey Run Park, where he crashed into the trees. Bruised but unbroken he climbed out of the wreckage and inspected the crate. It was cracked but the contents seemed ok. He prayed, "Allah Akbar."

Ahmad had a start. Was his cell phone ok? He pulled it out of his cargo pants pocket and turned it on. It lit up. He dialed Hosein's phone number. He asked, "Is everything ready?"

"Yes, I did what you asked. There was a complication."

"What's that?"

"The street is under surveillance. I don't know if it's just perimeter protection for the Infidels in the CIA or what, but I saw people watching the street that the house is on."

"Did you get away without being seen?"

"Yes, I went out the back door and down to Route 123. I hitched a ride to the car rental place and rented a car. I've got it here on the Island."

"Good, and you're sure that you weren't followed."

"I'm sure."

"I need to find you. Honk your horn twice. Then wait a few minutes and honk again."

Ahmad followed the honking sounds and came upon the parking lot. He saw Hosein standing next to a big red Hummer. "Hosein, they'll see us coming from a mile away."

"That's all they had left at the rental place."

"We can't go up to Smart's house in this. We need to find some other way to get there."

Ahmad had a brain fart. Remembering the e-mail that he had received from Hosein outlining the family problems that John Smart was having, he asked, "Do you know where Ms. Smart is shacked up with Dr. Jim?"

"Yes, I followed them and took pictures in case we needed blackmail material."

"Let's go there now."

They walked back to the crash site and carried the crate back to the Hummer. They then drove to Dr. Jim's residence.

Ahmad and Hosein rang the door bell. There was no answer. They rang again. Still no answer. Ahmad picked the lock and they went in. They heard noises upstairs. They followed the sound. Ahmad carefully opened the door to a bedroom. Ms. Smart was stretched out on the bed where Dr. Jim was examining her. He was drawing marks on her body. "Your nipples are perfect. So round and so perky. They're what attracted me to you. A little nip here and a little tuck there and then you're breasts will be even more perfect than I have already made them. It's called fine tuning."

Ahmad said, "What Allah made, you should not change?"

Dr. Jim was startled by the statements. He looked over at the door and said, "Who the hell are you?"

"Shut up," Ahmad said, yielding a Colt 45 automatic.

He turned to Hosein and said, "Tie them up. Face to face. Then the Infidels can do their thing forever.

After they were bound together, Ahmad ordered Hosein to disrobe and put on Ms. Smart's dress.

"But, I can't do that. It's … it's … it's an infidel thing to cross dress."

"We're doing this for the Ayatollah. You're going to look like Ms. Smart when you drive us to the house."

"Oh, Allah will understand?"

"Yes, he will."

Ahmad discovered a dressing room with a wide variety of cosmetics and wigs. Apparently, Dr.Jim did some consulting on makeovers in his home. Ahmad chose a wig that came close to Mrs. Smart's hair. He added it to Hosein's make over. All in all, Hosein didn't look too bad, except for the hair on his legs.

Ahmad said, "Let's transfer the crate to the Mercedes. They backed the Hummer up to her black Mercedes, made the exchange and closed the trunk.

"Let's go," Ahmad ordered and climbed into the back seat. Hosein drove the Mercedes back to the Smart house.

At observation point one, FBI agent Johnson reported, "Looks like Ms. Smart is back. She's pulling into the garage now." The response came back. "All vehicles. Hold your positions. It's Mrs. Smart."

A US Park helicopter spotted the crashed ultralight. Unable to land at the site, he called in the coordinates of the wreckage. The FBI was on the scene in five minutes. They reported back that there was no sign of people or the bomb. The NEST crew arrived and verified a radiation residue. This was the right bird. But where did Ahmad and the bomb go?

Chapter 31

CRUNCH TIME

The crisis management team in the CTC were concerned. Gotlieb noted, "We've lost them again. Call Homeland Security and recommend to them that they up the threat level to Red."

"You know what that will do. People will go crazy. Hell, the roads around here can't even handle traffic on the Friday of a three-day weekend. Depending where the bomb is at, we might even be exposing them to a higher risk."

"What can a nuclear bomb do?"

"Depends on how big it is and whether it's detonated in the air, on the surface, or underground."

Aris said, "I told you that ground zero will be in the chamber room of the tunnel."

"How do you know?"

"That's what my Bayesian Analysis calculations say. And they're almost always right."

"Well. Suppose that Aris was right. What would a 20KT nuke do if it were detonated 20 feet under the Headquarters Building?"

Alex drew a rough map of the area and drew rings around the CIA compound. She then outlined the probable damage. "The entire compound plus the Highway Administration would be totally destroyed. In fact, everything within about a mile radius would be leveled. 99% of the people in that radius would be killed. Within a five-mile radius, many buildings would be blown down. All windows and soft walls would be blown down. The blast and thermal effects would kill over 50% of the people. 30% more would be hit by prompt radiation, resulting in death within hours to days. The underground explosion would cause much more fallout. Our wind patterns would cause the fallout to travel eastward over D.C. Northern Virginia and Maryland. Soon it would reach Annapolis and then the Eastern Shore of Maryland. People would be exposed to radiation levels that could lead to death within weeks to months."

Gotlieb said, "Tell Security to vacate the Agency compound now just in case Aris is right. Have them all leave out the back gate. Head them west."

"Has anything happened at the Smart house?"

"Mrs. Smart returned to the house about twenty minutes ago. Other than that, no one has been on the street."

"I thought that Mrs. Smart had moved in with Dr. Jim. What's she doing back at her old house?"

"I don't know."

"Get someone over to Dr. Jim's house. Find out what he knows."

"We'll never make it over and back in this traffic."

"Take the helicopter."

A team of FBI agents was dispatched to Dr. Jim's house. The helicopter carrying them landed in a playground two blocks down from the dwelling. The team surrounded the house and entered it. Two agents went through the first floor while two rushed up the stairs. At the top of the stairs, they heard noises. They opened up the door to a bedroom and found two people tied together and leaning up against the far wall. A rope was wrapped around them. They were doing the dirty deed. The agents could see rope burns on their arms and legs where the friction of the rope had rubbed as they bumped bellies.

One of the agents said, "Put your hands up and move up against the wall."

His partner said, "For Christ sake, they can't put their hands up. And they are already up against the wall."

The first agent, a hunter who raised his own coon hounds said, "Maybe we should pour water on them to get them to separate."

"Shut up and untie them."

As the agent untied the two lovebirds, he noticed how round and perky the woman's breasts were. He thought, *I should get the doc's card. Maybe he can do something for my wife.*

"We thought that you were at your husband's house."

"It's my house, at least it's going to be when I get through with him. You saw some stupid man who broke in here, tied us up and put on my dress. He stole a wig from Dr. Jim and left with another man. We heard them drive away. You thought he looked like me? Why, he even had hair on his legs. I don't have any hair on my legs."

The FBI agents were looking at hair but it wasn't the hair on her legs. The senior agent said, "Perhaps you should cover up."

Dr. Jim was defensive. "The female body is a work of art, to be looked at, to be admired."

"Yeah doc. You ought to cover up to. I'd be embarrassed to show such a little peewee."

Mrs. Smart defended her lover. "It's not the size of the wand. It's how you wave it."

Dr. Jim petulantly said to his lover. "You think it's too small. You never said anything like that to me before."

She gave him the Goldilocks defense. "It's not too large. It's not too small. It's just right."

"Well, it's gonna be fried if we don't contact to headquarters."

The senior agent called Wallace on his cell phone. "We've got Ms. Smart here. She saids that someone is impersonating her. Says two people left in a car. Her Mercedes is gone. There's a red Hummer sitting in the driveway. Its back door is open."

"Send the helicopter back to pick up the NEST team. They need to check out the Hummer."

"Roger."

Within twenty minutes the helicopter had picked up NEST and returned to Dr. Jim's residence. They ran some tests and called back to Gotlieb. "We've got a positive reading. The bomb was here but it's gone now."

"Ok, come on back."

"The helicopter went back to base to refuel. We'll return as soon as it gets back here."

"That's bad news. The bomb is probably in the house now."

In fact, the bomb was not in the house. Ahmad and Hosein had carried it down the old tunnel and were now under the Child Care Center. They were lifting it up to put it into the new, smaller tunnel.

"We need to take them down now."

"First let's send in Mark. He can find out what is going on."

"Get the SWAT team ready to back him up."

Within five minutes, Mark had shed himself of the OTS makeup and his clothes. He walked out of the command van and down the street. He entered the Smart residency and immediately went down stairs. The three GRU grunts were riveted to the TV watching CNN. The tunnel door was closed. He went back upstairs and checked the garage. The bomb was not in the Mercedes, nor in the garage. He went upstairs. No one else was in the building. He went upstairs to one of the back bedrooms, picked up the phone and called the CTC. "I checked the house. The three goons are in the basement watching TV. No sign of Ahmad, Hosein, or Smart. They must be in the tunnel."

"Stay in the bedroom. SWAT is coming in to secure the house."

Gotlieb made a call to the SWAT Team Leader. "Take down the house. Do not go upstairs. I say again, do not go upstairs."

"Roger."

It took SWAT five minutes to secure the house. The three GRU agents were handcuffed and sat in front of the TV. One of them asked the FBI agent who was watching them to put on the *Jerry Springer Show*. He didn't want to miss today's topic which was "Who Makes Better Lovers, Cousins or Uncles and Aunts?" The agent was curious about the answer. He turned the TV to the channel. On the set, Jerry Springer was backing away. The audience knew that something was about to happen. Then a skinny, bucktoothed woman jumped like a monkey onto the back of a huge lady. She dug her claws in and shouted, "You stay away from my Charlie." Elephant lady turned spun around, trying to free herself of the monkey lady on her back. She kept turning and picking up speed until she was like a whirling dervish. Then monkey lady came flying off her back directly towards the live TV camera. All three of the GRU men and the FBI agent ducked as if she would come through the camera.

Within ten minutes, the CTC crisis response team was in the house. They were discussing the next move. Aris said, "They have the bomb in the tunnel. We've got to take action now."

"We could send Mark in."

"I need to go in with him."

"Why?"

"It would take at least half an hour to get NEST back. We don't have time. I've received first level NEST training. We practiced disarming bombs. I can be in place if we gotta do something fast."

"Take a handheld radio with you."

"I'll take one but it probably won't work in the tunnel. Get someone back to the girls' locker room. You can communicate with me from there. In fact, find out if Louie the loser, I mean Louis Applebee, is working today. He's a contractor with the computer people in OIT. If he's here get him down to the locker room. He's *the* expert in breaking codes."

As Alex and Mark were entering the wine cellar, at the opposite end of the tunnels, Ahmad and Hosein were lifting the crate into the chamber. John Smart was watching video from the small fiber optical camera he had inserted in the girl's showers above the chamber. He didn't notice that the two terrorists had entered the tunnel.

Ahmad said, "Hello, John, the time has come."

"The time for what?"

"To serve Allah."

"What's in the crate? More listening devices? Do you have a better video camera? This one is pretty low resolution."

"No, we've got something better."

Hosein broke the sides of the crate away revealing the device.

"Bojay moi, that's a bomb. An atomic bomb."

"It's a nuclear device, to be precise. A 20 kiloton nuclear bomb."

"What the hell is it doing here?"

"We are about to obliterate the infidel's intelligence agency."

It took Smart two seconds to react. He flew from where he was sitting at the monitor to the entrance to the chamber. He dove head first into the tunnel and began scurrying like a rat down the tunnel. Hosein picked up the Colt 45 automatic and aimed down the tunnel.

Ahmad said, "Let him go. He won't make it far enough away when we celebrate Allah."

At the chamber underneath the Day Care Center, Mark was entering the new tunnel. He climbed in. Alex followed. They moved about twenty feet when Mark said, "Back out, someone's coming."

Alex backed out and moved to the far side of the chamber, partly hiding behind the listening apparatus. Mark stood against the side wall. In about two minutes, John Smart came scurrring out of the new unnel and down the old one. He did not notice Alex.

Alex said, "Something's going on. Let's get down the tunnel. Let me go first so I don't accidentally shoot you." She climbed into the tunnel. Mark followed her.

As they approached the end of the tunnel, Alex looked into the chamber under the girl's locker room. She saw the two terrorists hovering over a device. Stepping into the chamber, she said, "Put up your hands and step to the side."

Hosein made a lunge for the Colt 45 automatic that was lying on a small table. Before he could reach it, she shot him, double-tapped, right in the forehead. He fell to the floor motionless.

She turned the automatic on Ahmad, who stood frozen in place. She said, "Mark, check out the bomb."

Ahmad wondered whom she was talking to.

John Smart entered the wine room and closed the steel and concrete doors. He pushed the red button. He heard a rumble as the old tunnel collapsed from the detonation of the C-4 explosive that was placed in its liner. Smiling, he walked out of the wine room and into the waiting arms of six SWAT members. They flung him down on the ground and placed six guns at his back and head.

In the chamber room under the girl's changing room, Alex heard a rumble followed by a blast of air that came out of the tunnel, knocking her down. When she got up, she saw that Ahmad was typing a code into the keypad of the bomb's control panel. She shot him in the chest. After one shot, the automatic jammed. She quickly cleared it, and as she aimed to fire again, Ahmad pushed the enter key. She fired again. Ahmad sank to the floor.

As he lay on the floor, his life slipping away, Ahmad saw a bright light. Then he saw a dark obelisk. It looked like the Kabbah. He saw a figure walking towards him, dressed in white. It was Hajira. She did not speak but he heard her thoughts:

Ahmad, Allah has sent me to tell you that you have failed. You became one of his followers but you did not hear the message. Allah wanted you to overcome the infidel but not through violence. He wanted you to follow the path of truthfulness, forgiveness and enlightenment. Instead you chose the violent route. You were ready to kill little children. You were ready to destroy families. You were ready to kill even the faithful who follow Allah. He does not want you by his side. You will have … nothing. The light faded into nothingness.

9:23 - Mark looked at the control panel and said, "There's a timer. It reads 9:23. It's counting down in seconds. We've gotta work fast."

"Can we stop the timer?"

"Cut the red wire. No. Stop. Cut the black wire. No. Wait. Cut the red wire." Nothing happened to the timer.

"Cut the black wire?" Nothing happened to the timer.

8:02 – "Can we take the timer apart?"

They loosened a plate with four screws and opened it. There was a tangle of wires and two small vials of what looked like mercury. Alex said, "Those gray things, they're mercury switches. When Ahmad pressed enter they were activated. If we tilt this apparatus to the left or right, the bomb will go off. And don't touch those wires. If they short out, the bomb will go off."

6:20 – "Can we remove the core from the bomb?"

Alex lay down on the ground and looked up at the bottom of the bomb. "No, it's welded on the bottom. Can't get out from the bottom."

Mark added, "And there are welds on the top too."

4:15 – "Alex, Mark, can you hear me?"

Alex and Mark looked at the speakers and the video from the girl's locker room. They saw Louie the Loser. Behind him they saw two hardbody blonds wrapped in towels. Alex spoke in the handheld radio, "We can hear and see you. Can you hear us?"

Speaking into his handheld radio, Louie said, "I got you on this end. Describe the control panel to me now."

Alex said, "It's a small standard keyboard, you know a QWERTY without a numbers pad."

3:20 – Louie said, "Let's see if we can find a back door to the system. Give it the three finger salute."

Alex pressed the Control Alt Delete, keys all at the same time. She said, "The system is rebooting. But the timer is still ticking."

Louie said, "Press F5 and F8. One of those should put the system in the SAFE mode."

Alex pressed the keys several times. "It's giving me a choice. I'm selecting SAFE."

"Good. Now go into DOS. And search for a .exe file that is titled something like ABORT or TURNOFF or something like that."

"Here it is. It's DISARM. There are some REM comments."
"What do they say?"

"The first one says "REM: Ivan the Terrible was here"

"Holy cow. Dimitriy set up this system."

"Dimitriy, who is Dimitriy?"

"He's a friend of mine."

0:32 – Mark said, "We've got about thirty seconds."

"What does the next REM say:"

"It says enter password."

"Crap, what's the password? Quick, enter Ivan Rules"

Alex entered the words.

0:10 – Nothing happened. "What now?"

"Press enter, Now."

She pressed enter. The system stopped at 0:02. The system began to whirl. Then music came over the small speaker in the bomb's control panel. It played the tune I'm proud to be an American, but the words were in Russian.

Louie pulled out his cell phone and pressed a number. He said, "Ivan the Terrible. What the hell have you done now."

Dimitriy said, "The bomb could never go off. I buggered up the program. Don't let it out or me and my family are dead."

"We'll protect you," Louie promised. The two blondes hugged Louie.

Inside the chamber, Mark hugged Alex. He squeezed her bottom. She said, "It's ok this time, but forget it tomorrow."

They could hear the jackhammers breaking through the floor of the girls' locker room.

EPILOGUE

The Agency's Office of Medical Services conducts studies to
determine factors that predict performance in the field. The hypothesis that
a good agent is "born and not made" is constantly examined. When the post
mortem was conducted on the project known as *Groundhog Removed*,
Alex's name came up. A study was conducted to determine what made her
perform so well under pressure.

Two psychologists were assigned the job of examining Alex's history,
including how her parents and grandparents were, where she grew up, and
where she went to school. When they attempted to develop Alex's family
tree, they could not find anything out about her grandparents. Finally, after
searching through secret files and examining correspondence of anyone who
might have a clue to her lineage, they were able to unfold the entire tree.
The story they uncovered gave great weight to the "born, not made"
hypothesis. This is the story, patched together from diaries and journals.

The brown Cadillac wound its way up through the tall pines and up
the narrow road that lead from the town of Berchtesgaden towards
Obersalzberg. Passing through the small village, the car continued up the
mountain towards Hitler's other German capital, the Eagle's Nest. The
driver clumsily maneuvered the large automobile around the curves. The
woman sitting by his side, nuzzled up against his shoulder, said, "You're not
used to driving. I am your driver. Why don't you let me get behind the
wheel, dear."

"No, Kay," the general answered, "For years, I wanted to be the
driver."

"Carl Jung always said that you like to be in control. He said that all
good generals are that way," the petite young woman said.

"Don't give me all that psychobabble. Just sit back and relax. I'm enjoying myself." The general swerved to the right, then to the left, clipping a tree, then a stump. Two rabbits jumped up and ran deeper into the woods.

It was late afternoon and the road was encompassed in dark shadow. The general could hardly see his way. The passenger said, in a frightened voice, "Please, Ike, let me drive. We are already late because you refused to ask for directions when we got lost."

"I can't stop and talk to anyone. I'd be recognized."

The passenger, Kay Summersby, had been General Eisenhower's driver for a number of years. She knew all the techniques of defensive driving. She had survived Nazi aircraft attacks against her car. But she was not prepared for the sheer terror of being a passenger in a car driven by the general himself. She just closed her eyes, tightly grabbed his arm, causing him to swerve to the right, and prayed.

As they approached the base of the Eagle's Nest, the general spotted a roadblock guarded by two Army privates. Misjudging the car's speed, he caused it to slide into the barrier that spanned the road. The privates jumped back and the barrier cracked. The front half of the barrier lay on the ground like a broken arm. The general rolled the window down and shouted, "Open the barrier, soldier."

Private Sledgehammer, a native of Chicago, Illinois, had been a traffic cop in the windy city prior to being drafted in 1942. He knew how to handle situations like this. He looked inside the car and saw an old man in a brown sweater with tan pants. A young, attractive woman was sitting by his side, looking up with doe-like eyes. He saw no badges of rank. Although the man looked vaguely familiar, Sledgehammer was unable to put a name with the face.

The driver said, "I told you, open the barrier, private."

Sledgehammer walked slowly around the car. He saw a place on the front bumper where a flag could be placed, but there was no flag there.

Inside the car, Kay nibbled on the general's ear and whispered, "Let me take care of this."

She slid over to the passenger door and got out. Sledgehammer said, "Get back into the car, lady."

Kay ignored his command. "Hey big guy, let me save your career," she said to the private.

He looked skeptical. First off, he didn't know what career she was talking about. He would soon be leaving the Army and going home to Chicago to resume his duties of intimidating negros and commies when they don't come to a complete stop at a stop sign. "You didn't stop, your wheels were still rolling" was his favorite line, when they protested. Nobodies' wheels ever stopped rolling at a stop sign unless there was a deuce and a half truck in the intersection. Second, he was curious. He thought, *Who the hell are these people?* But he was curious; the driver did look familiar.

"Ok," he said, "whatta you want."

"Don't you recognize who that is in the car?" Kay said to Sledgehammer.

Private Smiley, the second part of this two-man roadblock had been leaning against a tree during this whole encounter. A graduate of Harvard University, he didn't like guard duty. It was too boring. But even he became curious, when the passenger got out of the car. She was a babe of the first degree. He looked again at the driver and gasped, "Jesus Christ."

Smiley grabbed Sledgehammer by the arm.

"Leggo," Sledgehammer said, pulling his arm away.

Smiley grabbed his shoulder. Sledgehammer turned and looked him in the eye. "What is it?"

Smiley said, "The driver. That's General Eisenhower."

"Go on," Sledgehammer said, "El Supreme-O wouldn't be driving his own car."

Kay said, "Yes he would. That is General Eisenhower. Let's talk."

Sledgehammer was flabbergasted. Smiley almost wet his pants.

"Look, the General is travelling incognito. We have an important military meeting to attend up at the Eagle's Nest. Has another car arrived?"

"Yes, Ma'am. We signed them in about an hour ago."

"So you are signing people in."

"Yes Ma'am. Orders are to get the names of everyone going though this checkpoint."

"Tell you what. How would you two like to be on an early ship back to the States?"

"Yes Ma'am."

"Then sign us in as Mary and Lou Grant, civilians."

"Can't do that, ma'am."

"I can make it the first troop ship. Leaves in three days."

"Ok, it's a deal."

Kay batted her eyes, smiled sweetly and said, "But if I hear that any of this leaks out, both of you will be sent to the Pacific Theater and fight Japs there. In the jungle. In the heat. They got kamikaze planes. They got flame-throwers. All that bad stuff."

The deal was struck. The barrier was lifted. The car rolled through the barrier, clipping the rest of the gate off and causing the privates to jump to into a ditch that lay along side the road.

Three minutes later, the car careened up to the front of a small stone building that housed the entrance to an elevator shaft. The general got out, ran around to the passenger side of the car, and opened the door. "Come, my dear, let me help you out."

Just then the elevator door opened and two couples came out to greet the newly arriving guests. Kay cried out, "Allen, it's good to see you again.

The general added, "And there is Mrs. Bancroft. I haven't seen you since, let's see, since July, was it 1943, or 44. You're looking as beautiful as ever."

"It was 1944, remember, in Bern." Turning to reveal a stunning woman standing behind her, Mary Bancroft added, "And let me introduce Mrs. Amy Pack."

The general stepped forward, took Amy's hand and gently kissed it. "It is indeed a pleasure to meet such a charming lady."

He then shook the hand of Allen Dulles, the Office of Strategic Services Chief from Bern, Switzerland. Allen whispered in Ike's ear, "Do you know who that woman is?"

"Mrs. Pack. Well, no. I can't say that I've ever met her."

"But you have heard about her. This is the famous spy, Cynthia."

"Cynthia, you mean the one who paved the way for us to get the Enigma machine and break the Ultra code."

"Yes, that's her."

Ike looked at Mrs. Pack with a different eye. He couldn't wait to tell Kay who she was.

They entered a brass-lined elevator that took them up over 400 feet through the heart of the Kehlstein Mountain. On the way up, Allen turned to Kay and said, "Have you met Ilya yet?"

"No, I haven't had the pleasure."

"Kay Summersby, this is Ilya Tolstoy."

Ilya bowed slightly, bumping his butt on the rear wall of the elevator.

Kay said, "Tolstoy, now that's an interesting name. Are you any relation to the Russian novelist?"

"Yes," Ilya answered, "Leo was my grandfather."

The door to the elevator opened and the three couples entered directly into the famous Eagle's Nest.

Kay and Amy walked over to the window. Cynthia stayed over by the men and compulsively began to assess their weaknesses by observing their nonverbal behaviors and listening carefully to what they were saying. She hated herself for having this weakness. While it paid off in her agent recruitment activities, it made wives and significant others instantly jealous of her.

Amy said, "Just look at the view. It's beautiful."

Kay agreed, "Yes, isn't it. Those mountains are lovely."

Cynthia thought, *I wonder if the general is any good in bed.*

Allen Dulles was making similar assessments of Cynthia. He thought, *I know how good she is in bed. I've read all the cables on her.*

Allen told the group, "Dinner will be brought up from Obersalzberg in about an hour. I've made arrangement for some very fine wine made from the best grapes on the Rhine River. We have harder stuff in the cabinet over there," he said, pointing to the left of the windows that opened up to reveal the majestic scenery of the German Alps.

"Do you have any vodka?" Ilya asked.

"Yes, Marshall Zukov himself sent me a supply just yesterday to celebrate the victory."

The victory referred to the German surrender that was signed just two days ago. This was, in military parlance, Victory in Europe, or VE, Day +2. In fact, the gathering of the three couples was set up to celebrate the victory. It also represented a bittersweet farewell party. These warriors had reached the same sad point that had been reached by other warriors in other conflicts over the centuries: Soon the men would be leaving their loved ones and returning home to their wives and families.

A bell rang in the elevator shaft, some 400 feet below. The elevator rumbled. It's door opened. Two men dressed in lederhosen with long stockings and white shirts started to push carts from the elevator into the dinning room of the Eagle's Nest.

Allen thanked them. "I'll take care of things from here on," and sent them back down on the elevator. He was protecting the identities of his guests.

Allen announced, "Dinner has arrived. Ilya, can you help me move these carts into the dining room?"

The couples moved to the dining room, filled plates buffet style and sat down at a long table with General Eisenhower at the head of the table and Kay seated at his right.

Allen raised his wineglass and said, "To General Eisenhower, savior of the world." They chugged down their glasses of wine, or in Ilya's case, vodka.

The general looked embarrassed. He raised his glass and said "To all of you who contributed in your own unique way to this victory." Having refilled their glasses, they once again chugged them down.

They refilled their glasses. Kay raised hers and said, "To all the fallen heroes." This brought a tear to the general's eyes. Noticing this, Kay hugged the general. They all chugged the glasses down.

About this time, Ilya was getting a little frisky. With a slight slur in his voice, he said, "Ya know, I'm the one who won the war."

Looking a little bleary-eyed himself, Allen asked, "How's that?"

"Well, I did travel across those Himalayan Mountains all the way from India. These mountains around here look like hills compared to them there monsters."

"So?" Allen challenged.

Ilya said, "Don't you know the big picture. I opened up the Burma Road. This saved the Chinks' ass. The Japs had them on the ropes and we needed to get them supplies, not that they would use them very well anyway. If China fell, then Russia would go, and then Overlord would not have worked, cuz them Krauts would then bring them bad boys on the eastern front over and kick our asses off the beaches of Normandy."

Kay noticed that when Ilya got lit, he lost his Russian accent and began to sound like a West Virginia redneck. She wondered if he was a real count or not. Dulles swore he was.

Allen countered Ilya's claim with his own. "Well, you know, I'm the one who recruited Fritz Kolbe. He did give us all the secrets we needed."

"Recruited, smicuited, he fell right into your lap. You weren't even his first choice, cept the Brits were too stupid to make him an offer," Ilya countered.

Allen's voice rose, "Well, I could have ended the war months ago, if Washington would have backed me on the assassination plan against Hitler.

They were too weak-kneed."

Ilya countered, "Well yea, FDR himself sent me to Tibet."

Allen fired back, "So! I was his personal rep in Bern. I sent mail to FDR every week. Big deal.

Kay began to fume. She knew that the general would not speak for himself. So she decided to jump into the fray. "I guess you are forgetting everything that Ike did for the war. He had to handle that little snob, Montgomery. Monty never followed orders, almost lost it all for us at Arnheim. Ike had to save his ass."

"Now, Kay," the general said, "Just let it go."

"No, I won't let it go. I cried for you when you were so upset about sending the boys into Normandy. And these jerks have no idea of what chances you took when you gave the go ahead in spite of the weather. And..."

"No, Kay," the general repeated, "Just let it go."

Kay, sulking, fell silent.

Through all these arguments, Cynthia did not say a word. But she knew down deep, below her heart, lower than her belly button, who won the war. She mentally prepared her resume, one that would never be published. Amy Pack, known as WWII's Mata Hari. As an intelligence agent, she:

- Conducted secret operations in Spanish Civil War

- Joined his Britannic Majesty's Secret Intelligence Service as war was approaching.

- Slept with Polish officer leading to the procurement of the coveted Enigma machine that allowed the breaking of the German Ultra code.

- Slept with Italian Naval Attaché in Washington. Pried the Italian naval codes from him.

- Slept with Vichy French Press Attaché in Washington. Got embassy cables and reports on other employees in the French embassy from him.

- Slept with a US Senator. Got him to swing on his vote from
  Isolationism to Interventionism. Led to US entering the war on the
  side of Britain.

Mentally reviewing this resume, Cynthia thought, *These studs can
argue all they want, but it's the woman behind, no, I mean on top of the man,
that counts. Truth be known, I won the war.*

She thought, *Who should I sleep with tonight?* She looked around the
room.

The general looked drowsy. "Besides," Cynthia thought, *Kay is very
protective of him. There would be a catfight if I went after him.* She had an
additional thought: *After the war, Ike will just fade away, like all the other
old soldiers.*

She looked at Allen Dulles. "He's a burned out old spy. He won't be
going anywhere after the war either. Why waste my time."

She looked at Ilya Tolstoy. *Well, I guess you got to dance with the guy
you came with,* she thought.

She said, "Ilya, baby. You were in Tibet during your trek from India
to China, right?"

"Uh huh, even met the Dali Lama himself." he responded.

"Do you know anything about Tantra Yoga; you know, that sex stuff
from Tibet that's the rage in Hollywood?"

"Hey, the Dali was only seven years old."

Cynthia asked, "I know, but didn't you talk to his spiritual advisors?"

"Well, I do remember something the high priests talking about
differences in man's and woman's yoga."

"Oh, what's that?"

"Well let me think. A man meditates by going up in his body."

She asked, "So what does a woman do?"

"Women need to go down into female creative. I don't know what that means, but that's what they said."

Cynthia fully understood. As she helped him up from the couch, she said, "Come on to the bedroom. Let me show you how I can go down."

The general said, "You know Kay, we need to retire to the other room. I have some correspondence that I want to go over with you. Are you ready?"

"Yes, dear," she answered, "Allen, can I take this bottle of wine with me?"

Allen responded, "Please, take what ever you want. And Mary, are you ready to retire?"

"No Allen, come sit with me on the balcony. Let's look at the stars."

It hit Allen; this would be their last night together. Tomorrow he returned to the states.

That night, as Ilya and Cynthia morphed into the fourth position of the Kuma Sutra, Alexandria Pack's grandmother was conceived. The mother gave birth in a closed off wing of Walter Reed Hospital near Washington D.C. Information on the pregnancy and birth were closely held in military and intelligence circles. Who the father was remained a secret for sixty years. After a couple of rounds of biblical begatting, Alexandria II was conceived.

www.ingramcontent.com/pod-product-compliance
Lightning Source LLC
Chambersburg PA
CBHW030529030726
47495CB00004B/923